Wreck of the Huron

Cuban Secrets

ERIC DOUGLAS

WRECK OF THE HURON
CUBAN SECRETS

BY ERIC DOUGLAS

This is a BooksbyEric 2012 original.

DEDICATION

As with all of my writing projects, I would be nowhere if it weren't for the people in my life who support me. Thank you Beverly, Mom, Dad, Ashlin, Jamison and so many others. Thank you for believing in me, even when you didn't know exactly where I was headed. Thank you, God, for giving me the imagination to write.

CONTENTS

ACKNOWLEDGMENTS

So many people have assisted with this book, I'm afraid to name them for fear of leaving someone out.. Regardless, thank you Beverly, Bonnie, Jeff, Pam, Suzanne, Rae, Bill, Steve and Teresa for your encouragement, your comments and your inspiration.

CHAPTER 1

The air was chaos. Hurricane winds pushed the rain sideways and roared past like a freight train with no stops in sight. Boards from old houses, palm fronds and sand blew around as Mike and Sarah ran through the night looking for shelter — both from the weather and from the men chasing them.

It was almost pitch dark, but the night sky was punctuated by flashes of light as lightning shot over their heads. Sixty feet away, a power transformer exploded and the darkness deepened.

"In there. I think we'll be safe!" Mike shouted, pointing to the remains of a small house.

"Anything has to be better than this," Sarah yelled back as she ran onto the broken-down porch of the small bungalow. She grabbed the door handle and pulled the old door open in one motion. The wind caught it and nearly wrenched it from her hand as they jumped inside. With effort, they got the door closed

Inside they surveyed their surroundings and realized the house had been abandoned for a long time. The furnishings were toppled and strewn about. The windows were broken. Rain leaked through holes in the roof. But it was still better to be out of the wind and rain for a moment. At least they could talk without screaming.

"Do you think they followed us out into the storm?" Sarah asked after she caught her breath, leaning against the wall.

"Don't know. Probably best if we don't wait to find out," Mike said.

"I'm not too thrilled about going back out into a hurricane right now," Sarah said, looking through the broken window as the remnants of an aging curtain flapped in the wind, her sodden clothes glued to her body. "My arm is killing me."

Mike was still up and was moving around, checking out the house. "I wish I could do more to help you with that arm. I know it must be pretty tough to keep it in a sling when you're running for your life. When we get out of this I'll find a way to make them pay for that. "

"It's not your fault, Mike. They knew they would never get you to tell them anything. Easier to hurt me and get to you. Always the way it goes with you tough guys," Sarah rationalized. "Hurts like hell, though. And you'll have to stand in line behind me to get some payback for it."

The men chasing them had used Sarah as leverage to get to Mike, slowly twisting and finally breaking her arm. He had fashioned a makeshift sling for her when they escaped, but it wasn't enough to keep it steady…definitely not while running. He knew it had to be killing her, but she refused to complain.

Mike explored the two-room shack, moving into the kitchen to see if there was anything they could use as a weapon or to communicate with their friends on the research ship. They weren't going to be able to last forever without help. When the storm passed, they would still be on the run.

"Hold on, it looks like this house has a storm cellar. If it's solid, it'll keep us safer than up here," Mike said as he pulled on the small door built a few steps down from the kitchen. The angled door seemed to point straight into the ground.

"How does it look?" Sarah asked. She stood and began to follow, then hesitated at the top of the steps. Mike eased his way down the narrow steps with their one slowly-dying flashlight. The room was built into the earth below the house with wooden walls to keep the sandy soil from collapsing. The ceiling was so low that Mike couldn't come close to standing up. The air was musty and stale, but dry.

"Looks solid," he called from below. "I definitely think this is going to be safer than staying up there. We'll be out of the wind and away from prying eyes," He waited for a response that didn't come. "Come on down." He shone the light on the steps while Sarah began climbing down, gingerly holding onto the wall with one hand while she cradled her injured arm against her body.

Sarah was on the third step when her instincts told her it was time to move. She leaped forward into the small, dark room. A fierce wind from the storm slammed the angled storm cellar door shut behind her.

"Did I suggest diving in?" Mike asked with a laugh as he lay sprawled on the floor where Sarah had tackled him.

"You made it sound so appealing I just couldn't wait to join you. You know how I am," she said with a chuckle as she rolled away, and then hissed from the pain in her broken arm. She moved to sit up, but Mike held his arms around her for a minute.

"Do you really think this is the time and the place for that?" Sarah asked, looking at Mike through the dim light and dust.

"Probably not, but it felt pretty good," Mike said, relaxing his hold and helping her to sit up. He watched Sarah move in the half-light for a minute before he half-stood up to examine their surroundings — his 6'2" frame filling up the room.

3

Sarah began moving around the cramped, musty cellar, looking through shelves and behind boxes with only the dim light from Mike's light to see. Mike moved up the steps toward the door. He turned the knob but nothing happened. He pushed against it and then shoved upward with his shoulder, bracing on the steps below. Nothing.

"We're not getting out this way any time soon. Part of the house must have fallen against it," Mike said.

"Then we aren't getting out at all. That's the only way out. No back doors," Sarah said. "I did find some candles, though. Got any matches?"

"No such luck."

"It's going to be a dark, wet night until this storm passes," Sarah said. "Maybe we'll see another opening in the light of the day. I see lightning flashes through cracks in the ceiling from time to time. We'll find a way to get out when we can see something."

She slumped down to the floor with her back to a wooden wall. Mike moved toward her and placed his arm around her shoulders. She leaned into him and they sat still for a few minutes, listening to the wind and rain howling and crashing above them.

"Are we going to make it through this?" Sarah asked during a lull in the clamor.

"Of course we are," Mike said, doing his best to lighten the mood. "If we don't, you can tell me I was wrong."

"Very funny."

"Who knows? Maybe those guys chased us out into the storm and they'll get killed," Mike said, trying to sound reasonable. "It could save us the trouble."

"That would be nice, wouldn't it?" Sarah said, looking up with a sparkle coming back in her eye. "Although it would be a little disappointing - I wouldn't get my revenge."

They sat quietly for a moment, muscles slowly beginning to relax, breathing returning to normal. Mike couldn't believe everything that had gotten them to this point.

Without warning, light flooded into room. The storm had stopped and the sun was shining. Mike heard Sarah shout that they should run, but she sounded like she was down a tube and falling farther and farther away. All he could make out through the storm was a ringing sound.

Much to his surprise, Mike was in a bed with the sunlight streaming into the room. He didn't know where he was. Nothing looked familiar. Where is Sarah? What's going on? His heart was racing and his body was sweating with panic.

Suddenly, he realized where he was. It's not real, he began to tell himself. You were dreaming. You're home now. Relax and breathe. Things slowly began to look familiar. He was in his bedroom in his house. He hated when his dreams intruded into the day. He didn't sleep walk, but occasionally woke up and was still dreaming. Like today.

Mike had to stop and think for a moment to realize where he was. He had been on the road, on assignment, for two weeks and his body was still on a time zone 12 hours away. The ringing had stopped. It began again. The phone. His voicemail inbox must be full. He picked up the cell phone from his bedside table where he had plugged it in.

"Hey, Mike, what are you up to?" It took Mike a second to realize who was on the line. He was still trying to shake the feeling of the hurricane, Sarah and their escape. Was that a dream or a premonition? It felt so real. He glanced out the window and the sun was shining. He was in his house on Roanoke Island in the Outer Banks of North Carolina, not on some nameless Caribbean island being tormented by a hurricane. And then there was Sarah. That wasn't even a topic he wanted to think about. He hadn't seen her in more than a year, but she still popped up in his dreams from time to time. Mike ran a hand through his wavy dark hair, speckled with gray, trying to wake himself up.

"Sleeping," Mike grumbled into the phone as he sat up on the edge of his bed. "Mac, you know I just got home."

"True, I do realize that," Mac Williams said with a grin audible over the phone line. "But it's nearly the crack of noon and there's something you'll want to see. I thought it worth getting your lazy butt out of bed."

"Okay, so, what is it?" Mike said, trying to rub the sleep out of his eyes. "Don't mean to be rude, but you've got about 10 seconds to impress me before I fall asleep again."

"It'll take five. Remember that big storm that rolled up the coast?" Mac asked.

"Sure. My flights were all screwed up because of it. You have three seconds," Mike replied.

"Fresh debris is washing up on the beach because of it. And it can only come from one wreck. The Huron," Mac finished. All he got in return was silence.

After a moment, Mac asked, "Mike, did you fall asleep?"

He heard a distant snort in reply. It sounded like the noise was coming from down a well. Mike had placed him on speaker phone.

"I'm up. Trying to find some shorts and a t-shirt. And my toothbrush. I'll be there in about 15 minutes. No clue where my dive gear is right now. Can I borrow some?" Mike said, over the sound of running water.

"Thought you might react that way. I have a full set of gear waiting on you along with your camera housing. I just got it back from having it serviced. Bring your camera. We're on the way to the beach right now. Meet you there," Mac explained. All he heard in reply was grunting over the sound of brushing teeth. Mac hung up the phone.

Mike Scott's job as an international news photographer took him all over the world, but between assignments he called Roanoke Island home. It was a quiet little place, at least when the tourists were gone, but still full of interest, history and even some occasional intrigue. The first European settlement in the Americas disappeared from the island mysteriously in the late 1500s and things had remained interesting ever since.

CHAPTER 2

Rubbing his face while shoving his feet into sandals, Mike stumbled out the door of his beach house and jumped into his green Jeep CJ-7. It was old, (Mike preferred to think of it as 'classic') but he liked the older Jeep body styles to the new models and he enjoyed tinkering with the off road vehicle. As an inhabitant of the Outer Banks, it was also important that it was well-suited to driving on the beaches near his home.

He had just gotten home from assignment in Asia the night before and had been back on the East Coast for less than 24 hours. After spending the day in New York dropping off files at the magazine's office, he flew to Raleigh-Durham International Airport and then drove the three hours to his beach house. Now, Mike paused long enough to pull the doors off the old Jeep before leaving his house so he could feel the warm spring wind in his face. The sun was high overhead, and the sky was bright and clear, making for a perfect day to go to the beach after a long winter.

Mike leveraged his 6'2" frame into the seat. He pulled a worn-out dive hat off of the rearview mirror and placed it on his head to contain his unruly hair as he tossed a camera bag onto the passenger side floor. Crossing the Virginia Dare Trail Bridge that led from Roanoke Island to

Hatteras Island, Mike scanned the waterline to see if he could spot anything unusual on the beach. In spite of his curiosity, there was nothing for him to see above the water. Mike reminded himself that the Huron had been underwater for a long time and he would have to have just a little more patience.

The USS Huron sank off the coast of North Carolina on November 24, 1877. There are more than 1,000 shipwrecks off the North Carolina coast; many are from that same era. What made the Huron unusual were the circumstances surrounding the wreck and its location. Huron sailed from Hampton Roads, Virginia the day before she sank, headed for Cuba to perform environmental surveys. The ship encountered a heavy storm blowing from the southeast.

The Huron wrecked just 200 yards from the beach but most of the crew decided to remain with the ship until morning, hoping help would arrive. It never did. The coastal lifesaving service had shuttered its doors for the winter and the supply houses with rescue equipment were locked up tight. They weren't set to reopen until the following spring. Of 134 officers and crew on board, 98 lost their lives that night. That wreck and another one two months later prompted the federal government to fund the United States Lifesaving Service, forerunner of the U.S. Coast Guard, to operate year-round. Previously, the lifesaving stations had closed in the winter.

Mike pulled his Jeep into the beach parking lot between Mileposts 11 and 12, near where the Huron went down. The late spring day was warm and sunny, but not quite summer yet so the parking lot wasn't crowded. Mike saw Mac's truck already there.

"About time you got here. We were just about to go on without you."

Mike chuckled when he heard the female voice. It was Andrea "Andie" Williams, Mac's 24-year-old daughter.

"You sure you even remember how to dive anymore?" Mike asked.

"You've been away at school for a while."

"Don't worry about me. I think I'll remember. How about you? You're the one who's been traveling so much lately," Andie replied with a laugh as she walked up to Mike and gave him a hug. At six feet tall, Andie almost looked Mike in the eye. Her long blond hair was tied back in a pony tail and she wasn't wearing an ounce of makeup. Regardless, Mike was struck — as always — by her beauty. Beyond her physical appearance, though, Mike was actually more impressed with the brains inside her head. She had just finished up a master's degree in marine archeology and regularly spent time searching for shipwrecks off the coast with her father.

"Something tells me it'll come back, Andie," Mike said, smiling as he released the hug. "Where are your dad and Red? I know they're around here somewhere."

"They're setting up gear on the beach," Andie gestured with her chin toward the sand dunes. "Let's go. We're just waiting on you."

Andie turned and walked away between the dunes without another word. Mike laughed to himself for a second. "It's good to be home," he said to no one, then grabbed his camera bag and followed the young blonde. The beach was mostly deserted, although a few people were out walking their dogs. The air was warming up, but the water was still a little too cool for tourists.

"Howdy, boys," Mike said as he crossed the sand dunes and caught sight of Mac Williams and Red Oates. The two older men had four sets of dive gear ready. They had gear set up on tarps under a portable, four-legged picnic shade. Salty-haired and weathered, but still strong with quick, bright eyes, Mac Williams had grown up on the Outer Banks and operated the local dive shop for years. He raised Andie around the shop and taught her to love and respect the ocean. Mac and Red had been friends for years, since before Andie's mother died. Now the three of them formed an inseparable family unit.

"Hey Mike, good to see you," Mac said as he walked over to shake his friend's hand. "You ready to go take a look?"

"Sure, Mac, but what are we going to look at?" Mike replied.

"That big storm that rolled up the coast really churned things up. That happens from time to time around here, especially on this wreck, but we've actually had some stuff uncovered and washed ashore — a couple of boards and whatnot. It can only be debris from the Huron," Mac explained. "Today is the first time the visibility has cleared up enough to make it worth getting in the water to take a look, but we figured you'd want to come along. You never know what the storm might have uncovered. For all we know it could have turned the whole wreck over. Remember the storm that righted the Spiegel Grove?"

In 2005 Hurricane Dennis hit the Florida Keys and rolled the 510-foot-long Spiegel Grove from its side to its keel.

"Sure, I remember," Mike said. "And, you know I'm interested. I love this little wreck. I wish I knew what time zone I was in, but I'm glad you called."

"Who knows? Maybe we'll figure out what really caused her to sink," Red Oates chimed in. A former naval engineer and part-time conspiracy theorist, Red had never accepted the official explanation of why the Huron sank.

"Wouldn't that be cool," Andie answered. "But if we don't get in the water soon, we'll never know. Let's move, men!"

"The lady speaks and we all jump, right?" Mike commented with a chuckle. "Where's my gear?"

"Over here, Mike. It's all set up, but you'll want to check it out," Mac said, walking over to the dive equipment. "As soon as you're set up, we'll swim out on the surface. The marker buoy on the surface is right in the middle of the wreck. We'll drop down and see what we can see. Mike, you and Andie can team up this time. Red and I will dive together."

Mike set up his camera in the housing quickly and reviewed his dive gear. Divers use several pieces of equipment to survive underwater. Most of the time they use air in their tanks, delivered through a multi-stage regulator that takes the air from the high pressure tank to a usable pressure at the mouthpiece. A special jacket that can be filled with air allows the diver to float effortlessly underwater and holds all of the equipment together. To stay warm in the water, divers wear wetsuits. Wetsuits, however, cause the diver to float, so to sink, they have to wear extra lead weights. An expert diver, though, can check it all out in just a minute or two and confirm it is all working properly.

It took Mike a couple more minutes to prepare his camera for the dive. He was using a standard digital single lens reflex camera, or a DSLR, with interchangeable lenses. But to take it diving, he had to place it in a specially-made underwater housing. The housing protected the camera from the water and the pressure, while allowing Mike to still use all of the camera controls. He was also able to see the photographs as he made them through the viewing port that allowed him to see the LCD screen on the back of the camera.

When he was ready, the foursome made their way into the water, chatting and joking among themselves. While the little family unit was tight and Mike travelled a good bit, they always immediately accepted him back into the group when he was home.

In spite of the warm air temperatures, the foursome donned heavy wetsuits to protect themselves. In the summer, the Gulf Stream moves in close to the North Carolina shore, warming the water into the low 80s, but in the spring, it was still relatively cool. In full scuba gear, they walked across the sand slowly, more than 50 pounds of portable life support on their backs.

"All right, children, act like you've done this before," Mac chided as they stood at the water's edge. "Take it slow and easy through the surf zone. I don't want anyone getting tumbled and losing a mask."

"Yes, Dad," Mike replied before Andie got a chance to say it, eliciting a laugh from the whole group. While all four of them were dive instructors, Mac always took the lead when they made dives together. The others expected no less and never took offense. The irony of it was there was barely a surf zone at all — only ripples washing ashore — so the chances of anyone getting "tumbled" were nonexistent.

Walking out into the water, they carried their fins in their hands until they could float and let the dive gear support its own weight. From there, they swam the remaining 200 yards out to the red ball floating on the surface that marked the wreck.

"All right, seriously this time. Red and I will dive together," Mac continued as the four divers did a quick check of their own equipment and got their bearings. "Mike, you and Andie will work together as a team, too. This may be a simple little pleasure dive with nothing to report, but look for anything on the wreck or on the bottom that seems different from the last time we were out here."

"You never know what could have changed," Red said. "I'm really looking forward to seeing what we can see."

"Come on, Andie. These old men are going to talk us to death speculating when the wreck is right below our feet," Mike joked. "I wish I could see it from here, though."

"I'm right there with ya," Andie agreed, nodding her head.

"Let's get underwater and see if you learned anything in school. I'm following you. Now that you're a marine archeologist, this is your baby."

"I'll see you on the bottom, Mike," Andie said with a grin and a saucy toss of her head. She placed the regulator in her mouth and signaled she was ready to descend. Mike did the same, and the water quickly closed over their heads. Mac and Red were right behind them.

The wreck was only 25 feet below, yet they couldn't see anything but sandy, green water until they were 10 feet down. Mike relaxed as he listened to the sound of his breathing. He checked on Andie as they descended and then turned his attention to the remains of the wreck below them.

As the top of the wreck emerged from the gloom, Mike met Andie's eyes and he could see the excitement there. She must already be able to see something that he couldn't. Mike moved his camera into position. He took a couple of photographs to capture the greenish cast of the water and the shadowy structure.

As he dropped another three feet in the water, Mike detected the differences on the wreck that Andie must have seen. The storm had pushed it around all right and sections that had been buried by sand were now uncovered. Mike began slowly photographing the scene in front of him so they could preserve the placement of the wreckage if they found anything. The storm had moved enough sand around to uncover sections Mike had never seen before. He also knew that the ocean waves and currents would eventually fill those sections back in and hide them from view again. This was their best chance to really see what the wreck looked like after some natural house cleaning.

The wreck had collapsed over the years, turning the site into more of a debris field than a recognizable shipwreck. Mike circled one of the few remaining upright sections to see Mac and Red looking at something. Mike photographed the men and then moved to one side to photograph what they were looking at. They were amidships, closer to the stern and Mike instantly realized they must have found a ship's strong box. The case was two feet wide by three feet long and nearly two feet deep. On ships of that era, sailors kept very little of value and none could afford an expensive box like this one. There could only be one or two boxes of this type on board. It had to belong to the Captain or the Chief Purser.

In spite of being submerged for more than 130 years, the sea chest was in good shape. Being buried in sand had kept it mostly clean and free of growth. Mike moved in close and photographed the case from all angles. One advantage to underwater photography is that it's possible to move in three dimensions. Mike could move from the side and then swim over top of the case, photographing the entire time, almost without ever taking his eye away from the camera's viewfinder.

After he was satisfied that he had captured the chest where it sat, he signaled to the other three divers and they moved in to clean away the remaining sand piled around the case. Underwater they were unable to speak to each other, but they all instinctively knew what the others were thinking. They were going to recover this chest.

Mike could see his friends' excited faces and gestures. In spite of that excitement, they were seasoned professionals and he was impressed by how they all moved methodically. They were careful to move only sand away. None of them wanted to throw away an artifact while excavating the sea chest.

Within just a few minutes, they had the box uncovered. At that point, they all stopped. They had found something important, but they also knew they couldn't just bring it to the surface on a whim. Although the Huron wasn't considered to be a terribly significant shipwreck — compared to Blackbeard's Queen Anne's Revenge a few hours down the coast — it was protected by the state of North Carolina, so they were forbidden to remove anything from the wreck without permission.

In addition, if they were to find anything inside the case that might be historically important, they would need professional help to conserve it.

Red took a small lift bag out of his dive gear jacket pocket and tied a line around the strong box. He inflated the bag and let out enough line so it would float just below the surface. He wanted to make sure they could easily find the box when they came back in case something happened and stirred up the sand again.

At that, the divers agreed to ascend with a simple "thumbs up" gesture repeated by all four of them. They hadn't found anything else significant in the overturned wreckage, but in truth they had stopped looking when they came to the strong box. Reaching the surface, they all began talking at once.

"Is that what I think it is?"

"What do you think is in it?"

"Can we bring it to the surface?"

"This is so cool!"

"What do we do next?"

"Hold on, guys," Andie finally broke in. "I know just who to call about this. My adviser from school is over at the aquarium doing some research. He is looking over some artifacts that were brought up from a World War II shipwreck and using the aquarium's water purification system to keep everything safe. He should be able to do the same with this strong box."

CHAPTER 3

It took a few hours to get everything organized, but they were amazed at how quickly everyone responded to the news they had found something on the shipwreck. Mike emailed a few photographs along with their reports to the authorities in charge of preserving the shipwreck and that got everyone's attention.

Later that afternoon, Mac, Red, Andie and Mike gathered again on the beach in dive gear. The North Carolina Department of Cultural Resources gave them permission to remove the trunk from the wreck. This time, though, instead of just four divers acting alone, they had attracted a crowd of onlookers and assistants. Andie's college adviser had set up on the beach, recruiting students from the marine archeology program at nearby East Carolina University to come over and help out.

"Mike, I want you to meet Dr. DeSutton. He was my master's program adviser at ECU. Dad, Red, you remember Dr. DeSutton, right?" Andie said.

"Hello Mr. Williams, Red," DeSutton said, deferentially to Andie's father. "Hi, Mike. I'm Dr. Peter DeSutton. Nice to meet you. I've heard a lot about you."

Mike met the man's gaze and was surprised to realize the researcher was about his own age, 40ish, with salt and pepper hair and bright blue eyes that didn't miss much.

"My pleasure, Dr. DeSutton. I've heard about you from Andie as well. Nice to put a face to the name," Mike replied, glancing at Andie and seeing her look quickly away. "Andie has spoken very highly of you."

"I'm really looking forward to hearing more about what you've found. I've been interested in this wreck for many years. As a marine archeologist, I've often wondered about what caused the Huron to go down, but it wasn't on the top of my priority list," DeSutton explained. "But as it turns out, I've recently just learned that one of my forebears was lost when it went down," DeSutton said.

"That's really interesting," Mike said, surprised. "I wasn't aware of that. Which crew member was it? I've read the ship's manifest and the Navy's inquiry into the sinking."

"His name was Frame. He had just transferred onto the Huron as a helmsman," DeSutton explained. "It was his first cruise on the Huron and unfortunately it was to be his last."

"That's a really fascinating bit of history, Doctor," Mike said, nodding his head. "I had no idea you had that sort of connection to it."

Andie interrupted the conversation by saying "Dr. DeSutton is involved with a lot of different projects involving shipwrecks on this coast."

For years Andie had a crush on Mike. He knew it was more admiration for what he did than any real attraction. And Mike thought of Andie as more of a niece rather than a potential date. Meeting DeSutton, Mike realized that Andie might also have some feelings for her adviser. Working together in a close and collegial way tends to form those bonds and Andie had a bit of a "thing" for older men. In a flash, Mike knew she must be feeling some internal conflict and tried to ease the tension by keeping the conversation on the project in front of them.

"I look forward to discussing this more later," Mike said. "but for the moment, what are your plans here? We're all pretty good at recovering artifacts, but I think this is the first time we've recovered anything like this."

"Sure, Mike. I understand. We really don't know what's inside the trunk you found, but if it is full of documents, we want to keep it submerged and wet until we can get it in a controlled environment," DeSutton explained. "If we were at sea, we would lift the case out of the water and put it back in a tank on the boat. Since we're here on the beach, we don't have to expose it to air at all. We can keep the strong box completely covered in sea water all the way to the lab. In the grander scheme of things, it probably won't make a bit of difference because the case wouldn't have time to dry out and allow the salt to cause any damage, but if we can do it, why not? If nothing else it will impress on these undergrad volunteers the need for environmental control."

"What do you want us to do?" Red asked.

"I'll have swimmers in the water with a large container tied to floats. When you lift the trunk off the bottom, bring it up to the surface and then float it over into the container. We'll slide it inside the container and the swimmers will push it to the shore. We'll get it out of the water and up the beach," DeSutton explained. "Your job will be done at that point."

"Hold on. We found this trunk so we want to see what's inside," Mac bristled.

"Sorry, sorry, Mr. Williams. I didn't mean you were out of the picture, just that we would handle the heavy lifting part. Of course, I expect you all to be around and involved when we look inside and see what you found," DeSutton answered.

"You okay with that Dad?" Andie asked, looking a little worried.

"Sure, honey, I understand. Sorry if I got a little defensive," Mac replied.

Mike decided to keep the conversation moving forward. They were already in their wetsuits and the late afternoon sun was making things a little uncomfortable. "How do you guys want to handle this?" he asked.

"Red, Andie and I have more experience lifting objects from the bottom than you do, so why don't you document the lift? Red and I will rig the trunk, and Andie will act as the safety diver for all of us," Mac said.

"That works for me. Sounds like a good plan," Mike agreed.

"Okay, so what're we waiting on? Let's get wet," Red said as he turned away and headed for their dive gear at the water's edge.

"Well, there you go," Mike laughed. "Red's ready. Guess we better move."

The three divers followed Red to their dive gear and repeated the process of entering the water and swimming out on the surface. This time, though, there was less chatter. They were all focused on the task at hand, thinking about what might be in the box.

"All right. Let's get to work, guys. Simple and easy. No messing around," Mac said as they gathered by the marker buoy on the surface, a few feet away from the floating lift bag Red had left behind.

They all agreed with a simple nod of their heads, gave each other an okay signal with one hand and began venting air from the dive jackets with the other. Mike was again carrying his camera in its underwater housing. This time, however, he had the digital camera set to video mode. He wanted to capture the action of the trunk being rigged and lifted. The other three divers were carrying the lift bags and additional tanks to lift the box.

Lift bags are sealed canvas bags with one open end like a grocery store shopping bag turned upside down. They have a harness system attached to the bag and a venting system on the top. As a diver fills the bag by venting air from a regulator into the open bottom water is displaced, creating lift to bring heavy objects to the surface. It works like filling a balloon with helium. Helium is lighter than air and the balloon floats. In water, the air is lighter than water so the lift bag floats, bringing its load to the surface, too.

Under normal applications, it would be a very simple process to lift an object from the ocean bottom. The divers would attach the bags to the object, inflate the bags and swim it to the surface.

The problem was going to be attaching the lift bags to the trunk. It was a square box with no handles. There was no easy way to attach the ropes to the box to lift it. Red and Mac would have to fashion a basket out of the ropes and gently float the case to the surface, but they had to do it underwater. If they made a basket or net on the surface, there would be no way to slide it under the heavy, water-laden case. They were going to have to tie it in place, while digging the sand out from under the corners and edges.

If the case rose too quickly or unevenly, it could slip out of the harness and sink back to the bottom, potentially damaging the chest or its contents. Obviously, they wanted to make sure that didn't happen.

The four divers went straight to the trunk following the line Red had rigged earlier, rather than swimming around to get their bearings. While the dive was shallow, they didn't want to waste bottom time or their air supply in case they had problems with the trunk. The foursome also knew the students would be swimming out on the surface with the larger container for the trunk and they didn't want to make them wait any longer than necessary. The water temperature was still in the low 60s and the students would get cold very quickly, even with wetsuits.

Mac, Andie and Red kneeled around the box. Mike floated just above them and began recording the process by panning to the side and over the top, moving closer and further back to capture the work from all angles.

Once they got started, Mac and Red worked quickly creating a rope harness to fit under the corners of the heavy trunk. They attached four bags to the trunk, one on each corner. The divers could easily fill the bright yellow bags by flowing air from a regulator into the open bottom. Each lift bag was also outfitted with a dump valve in the top that would allow them to vent air quickly and lower the case back to the bottom in case there was a problem. Andie pulled back and kept an eye on Mac and Red while they worked. She held the extra air cylinders they would use to fill the lift bags.

When everything was all set and Mac and Red were confident the harness would hold the trunk, they signaled Andie to move in with the cylinders. They could have used their own air supply to fill the lift bags but, in the interest of safety, they chose to use separate air sources. In case something went wrong they wanted to make sure they had plenty of air to breathe.

Mac and Red didn't want to fill the bags too quickly. If the lift bags were suddenly filled to capacity, or one was filled faster than another, it could cause the trunk to rise out of control, hitting the surface and slipping out of the harness to crash back to the bottom. Mac and Red were patient adding small bursts of air to the lift bags in turn.

When the bags were half full — the point that Red had calculated should be enough to lift the trunk — Mac stopped to see if they had made any progress. Nothing. From this depth, the air in the lift bags would nearly double in volume as the compressed air rose to the surface. They didn't want to get the bags too full before they started to rise.

Mac reached forward and pulled, trying to slide the trunk off of its foundation. Red and Andie joined in, realizing what Mac was doing. The three of them were able to break the trunk loose from the suction caused by the sand on the bottom. It took some movement and tugging, but then the case was free. Suddenly the trunk was floating and moving slowly toward the surface.

Mac and Red guided the trunk while Andie stayed below. Mike was filming the scene as the strong box rose toward the sun and the air for the first time in more than 135 years. Free from the sandy bottom, Mike got his first good look at the case. He could make out hinges on one side and an encrusted latch on the other. Beyond that, the entire case was fairly nondescript. He noted what appeared to be leather reinforcement straps on the corners and the sides on the rectangular case.

As they approached the surface, Mike could see the swimmers' legs above them. He captured the scene of the waiting student volunteers, as the trunk rose slowly toward the dive fins waving back and forth. Suddenly, he saw a serious problem. The case was rising right into the swimmers.

Andie was below him, rising slowly, but looking back down at the wreck for a moment. Red and Mac were focused on the trunk and had no way to communicate with the swimmers on the surface. And the swimmers weren't looking down to realize they needed to move out of the way.

The first waving fin hit the rising lift bag. The swimmer didn't seem to notice — until the second kick. The young man reacted to the presence of something unknown beneath him by panicking. He couldn't see the lift bag through the cloudy water, and momentarily forgot what he was doing. He began screaming that a shark had grabbed his foot. Frantically, he began kicking and struggling to get out of the water. In the process, the panicked student jostled the heavy trunk and released the dump valve on the top of the lift bag.

Red had no idea what was going on above him on the surface but he saw the trunk shaking and rocking in the harness. He grabbed the ropes to try and keep them from slipping off of the case. Mac was on the other side and couldn't get to the ailing lift bag that was venting air and sinking back toward the bottom under the weight of the case. The trunk started to shift to one side. Any further and it would fall back to the ocean floor — and on top of Andie who was unaware of the danger just above her head.

Mike dropped his camera and surged forward. He pulled out his backup regulator and flooded more air into the faltering lift bag while he fought to seal the opened dump valve. Time slowed down for Mac, Red and Mike while they fought to regain control of the heavy box.

Mike's fingers struggled to grab the dump valve and reset it. He couldn't let the trunk crash back to the bottom and he couldn't take his eyes off the airbag to see whether Andie was still in danger or not. Flowing air into the bottom of the bag to replace that which leaked out of the top, Mike knew the situation couldn't last long. With a final effort, Mike surged upward, pulling himself to the top of the bag. He quickly realized a line had gotten fouled in the dump valve when the swimmer kicked it. He cleared the errant rope and air stopped flowing out of the bag. Mac moved into position below him and vented more air into the lift bag to fill it back to the same level as the other three. It took a moment for the case and the lift bags to settle underwater and the three divers all kept their hands on the equipment in front of them.

As quickly as the crisis began, it was under control. The lift bag was floating again and Mac and Red had the trunk swaying calmly as waves passed over their heads. The three of them looked from one to the other and grinned, shaking their heads and pointing to the surface. Andie rose into view at that point, holding Mike's camera and continuing to film the action as if nothing had happened. They all began to laugh through their regulators, bleeding off the excitement of the situation. Just another day in the ocean — never predictable.

They brought the sea chest within a few feet of the surface and moved it into the floating box the college students were holding steady in the water. It all floated easily until the group got the box to the beach. Then it took the strength of the college students to ease the water-laden strong box across the sand and into a waiting truck. Still, they managed it and were able to keep the box wet and safe from exposure to air.

CHAPTER 4

It was a foggy, dark night in November of 1877 when the two men walked down a back street, in search of the saloon for their meeting. They did their best, in spite of the nice, clean coats and expensive boots they wore, to make sure they weren't noticed. They kept to the shadows and watched out for others who might be following them until they found their destination and stepped through the door. On this end of town, near the docks, no one wanted to be noticed. Everyone kept to themselves and avoided eye contact so it wasn't as hard to do as it sounded. Still, between the clothing and their demeanor, it was obvious the men were not accustomed to the back streets and dirty wharf alleys.

The country was still recovering from the "War between the States" although it had ended more than 12 years before. The recovery was especially slow in places like this one – Norfolk, Virginia – where the locals had sided with the South. Since the U.S. capital wasn't too far away, it wasn't uncommon for men to be drinking side by side in tired blue uniforms and old gray coats. Those men did their best not to notice each other, too.

As soon as their eyes adjusted to the dim light inside, the two men immediately began to look around, searching the crowd for the man they were told to meet. But all the sailors and longshoremen looked the same to them: rough, unkempt and dirty. Finally, they spotted their mark. The man was wearing a red scarf around his neck. Not totally out of the ordinary, but the single splash of color in the dark and dingy room was a sure signal. The man with the red scarf spoke as they approached.

"It's about time you two got here. I was getting tired of waiting," he said.

"We made our best time," the first one replied with a haughty sniff. "But remember, you work for us, not the other way around. You can wait all night for all I care."

"I know full well who works for who. You're an errand boy who is here because the Admiral didn't want to be seen in this part of town. And I work for him, not you. So if you want to go back and tell the man the plan fell apart because of you, be my guest," Red Scarf replied, his voice barely rising above a growl. He may have appeared to be nothing more than a scallywag on the docks, but he was no pushover and no stranger to dealing with important men.

The second visitor broke the tension. "Stand down, men. We fight for the same side –let's not lose sight of that. We're simply here to pay your fee and confirm that all has been arranged. You've been transferred to the ship. It sails in the morning and you will report there at 0700 hours," Number Two continued. "We don't care what you do or how you do it, but that ship is not to make its rendezvous. Our mutual commander doesn't know the exact plan, but he does know the ship will receive further instructions at Fort Jefferson. You have to stop the ship before it reaches the abandoned fort. Is that understood?"

"Aye and what about the crew?" Red Scarf asked.

"The crew is none of our concern. Do what needs to be done," the first man replied. "You simply must stop the ship from making Fort Jefferson. Nothing, including the crew, can be allowed to interfere with our plans."

"That's an awful lot of good men you're sending to the deep without so much as a thought," Red Scarf said, squinting at the two men. "There better be a good reason for it."

"That's enough. Your orders are simple. You don't need to know the rest of our plans. You're not to know the reason behind any of this. Is that clear?" Number Two asked.

"I'll do my job," was the only answer Red Scarf gave them. "Now leave my money and go away. I've want of another drink before I ship out in the morning."

Without another word, the two visitors stood, dropped a wallet on the table, and walked out.

CHAPTER 5

The wind was blowing a steady five knots. The sky was overcast and a light mist filled the air, reducing visibility inside the Hampton Roads harbor of Norfolk, Virginia. The men of the USS Huron were working too hard to notice the slowly declining weather as they prepared to leave harbor. They had come down from New York three days ago after receiving a new propeller, and now they were taking on supplies and arms for their next voyage.

It was Friday, November 23, 1877. The Huron, although only two years old, was already obsolete in the terms of modern navies. She and her two sister ships were the last three ships built with iron plating over timber rather than a steel hull.

A steam-driven ship, with five boilers and a massive 12 foot propeller, the Huron also had three masts to supplement her speed and help push her bulk through the water. She carried a complete set of armament as well, although she was one of the last ships placed into service to use an older style of smooth-bore cannon rather than rifled barrels. Newer, more modern ships were coming on line as the government worked to rebuild the once-formidable Navy.

Still, for the 134 officers and crew that filled out her 175 feet, the Huron was a fine ship and the pride of Norfolk. The ship was new enough that several members of the crew had been on her since she first set sail and visited foreign ports in Mexico, Venezuela and Columbia. The ship had also traveled all along the Eastern seaboard, stopping in Key West, Florida; Mobile, Alabama; Charleston, South Carolina; Norfolk, Virginia; Boston, Massachusetts; New York City; and Washington, D.C. While most of the crew hadn't even learned where this latest trip would take them, they assumed it would be somewhere interesting as the commander always seemed to draw choice assignments.

Commander George P. Ryan has been the master of the USS Huron since she originally set sail from the Chester, Pennsylvania naval yard where she was constructed. He had successfully guided her on all her voyages. The men respected Ryan and looked forward to a good cruise.

"Commander Ryan? May I enter?" Master William Conway asked as he knocked on the commander's cabin door.

"Enter, Conway. What's your report?" Ryan asked as he stood to greet his watch officer. Ryan had been pouring over the sea charts between Hampton Roads and the ship's destination. A tall man, he needed to stretch his legs for a moment.

"Everything is in order to set sail, Commander. The men are stowing the last of the supplies right now. Admiral Trenchard signaled to the ship that one more case is to be brought aboard. He indicated it has our final orders and special communiqués for your eyes only," Conway explained. "As soon as that case arrives, we are ready to make way. Boilers are up to pressure and the tide is favorable for leaving port."

"Thank you, Conway. Good work as always. Alert the crew, we'll get under way as soon as the case arrives. I want to get past the shoals off North Carolina and into open sea," Ryan said, dismissing the younger man.

Within a few minutes, Ryan heard commotion on the deck. He realized the case from the admiral was being delivered and walked out on deck to take his ship out of the harbor. He was surprised not only by the crowd on the deck but also by who made up the crowd. His full command of Marines were on the deck, gathered around the delivery, but there was also an equally large group of Marines assigned to the Admiralty. He had expected at the most two longshoremen and a guard or two. Not a squadron of Marines. He did his best to cover his reaction. That sort of security could only mean that whatever was in the case was important, secret and the admiral was concerned for its safety.

"Sergeant Torrence," Ryan said, addressing the leader of the on-board contingent of Marines. "Is everything in order? Have you received the case from the admiral?"

"Yes, sir, I was just accepting the trunk now," Torrence replied, gesturing at the strong box on the deck. "My men have confirmed that everything is in order. We are ready to receive it. I was just about to sign off on the delivery."

"Thank you, sergeant. Please do so and let's send the shore party back to headquarters. It's time for us to get underway and I don't believe the admiral would appreciate it if we took his personal guard along with us," Ryan said with a laugh.

"Yes, sir. They will be off the deck momentarily and we can get underway," Torrence replied, stiff and formally. "I don't believe we have the extra space for the men anyway."

Ryan looked into Torrence's face to see if the Marine was joking or not. He chuckled to himself when he realized the man was stone serious. "You're right, Mr. Torrence, of course."

Turning to let Torrence and his men finish the process of accepting the secure trunk, Ryan scanned the deck space around him. Everything seemed in order, although the last-minute activity on deck would have confused onlookers. Once the manifest showed everything was loaded on board, the commander was free to leave harbor, but that didn't mean that everything was stowed or even that all the men knew where they belonged. While the officers of the ship stayed consistent, it was common for new sailors and Marines to come aboard before leaving on a long cruise. Those men would all need to find their way below decks and stow their own gear in time. That much activity made the top deck look like a bee hive, a confusion of movement with men and cargo going off in every direction. The Huron boasted 16 officers and 118 enlisted men, including 15 Marines that provided security for the ship — especially in port — and to man the cannon in case of conflict.

"Watch officer," Ryan called out from the middle of the top deck to Conway on the bridge. "Let's take her out. Head out under steam power until we clear Cape Henry and then raise the sails. Have the admiral's trunk delivered to my quarters."

A seaman, he felt safer on the water than at the dock. He wanted to get to sea as quickly as he could now that he understood the gravity of the case delivered by the admiral, if not yet the contents.

"Yes, sir," Conway answered, immediately turning to issue the appropriate orders to the crew. The men set to work instantly releasing the lines and pushing the steam ship away from the dock. Ryan could feel the power surge under his feet as the steam was released into the turbines that powered the massive propeller behind the ship. Forward motion was almost imperceptible at first, but quickly the propeller began to bite into the water and he felt the ship – his ship – begin to pull away toward the Atlantic Ocean. It was 10 in the morning.

The Huron passed Cape Henry just after one in the afternoon and turned in a southeasterly direction. Reaching the open ocean, the men set the sails to give the Huron additional speed as it headed toward the Caribbean. The mist from earlier had turned into a steady rain, but nothing out of the ordinary.

"Mr. Simons," Commander Ryan said, getting the attention of his executive officer. The two men were standing on the deck, just outside the Huron's bridge. Ryan had stayed on the bridge during their exit from the harbor and return to sea, although he allowed his officers to handle the effort. "I'm returning to my cabin. I need to review those last minute orders that came down from the admiral. Please maintain our present course and speed. Stay in close to the shore. I don't want to get caught up in the Gulf Stream. It will slow us down too much."

"Yes, sir. I was just about to call for a depth sounding and take a heading off the Currituck Light House up ahead," Simons replied. "I'll let the navigator and chief engineer know your intentions."

"Very well, Simons. Alert me if there is anything unusual," Ryan replied as he walked away. "Looks like this storm might be getting stronger. Let's keep a sharp eye out."

As Ryan passed, a group of sailors who had been milling around quickly tried to look busy. Once a steam ship like the Huron was underway, absent any problems, there wasn't much for the deck crew to do. Of course, there were always things the sailors could be doing, but for now, just a few hours out of dock with the sails set and gear stowed, the men took time to relax. Still, no one wanted to look lazy in front of the Commander. This was the U.S. Navy after all. And if the men didn't look busy, he would be sure to find something for them to do.

What you figure was in them orders that came aboard with all them Marines?" Thomas Carley asked, after the commander passed.

"Not sure as I know," Peter Duffy replied as the men gathered back together from their quickly assumed tasks now that the commander was gone. "When Ryan thinks it's time to let us know, I'm sure he will. For right now, let's just time to keep this lady moving along."

"Think we're heading back to the West Indies?" Michael Durkin asked, stretching out the kinks in his back. "I could sure use some warm air and sunshine. This wind is freezing me to my bones."

"We're headed southeast to get around Cape Hatteras, so it sure looks like we're headed for warmer waters," Denis Deasey replied. "I'm betting we're going to have to go through a storm to get there, though. This mess is getting worse and the wind is blowing right back into our faces. Gonna be a fight tonight to get through it."

"But have you boys seen a group of Marines like that used as errand boys?" Carley asked, bringing the conversation back to the last-minute delivery and their orders. "Those were hard men, not used to driving lock boxes around."

"I didn't see any difference between that group and the group of Marines we have on board to be honest. All those boys have an edge about them," Duffy said. "Good to have around when things get dicey, though."

"Whatever is in the lock box, the admiral must've wanted to make sure no one else got a look at it," Frederick Hoffman said as he walked over to the join the group. "Probably lace curtains for the governor of Jamaica or something. You know how admirals are."

"Don't doubt you've got it right," Carley said laughing.

"You there. Frame, isn't it? You don't have to stand off to the side. Come and join the talk," Duffy said to the only other sailor on the deck — a man with a red scarf around his neck. "If we're going to serve together, you need to get to know the rest of the men."

Before Frame could respond the sailors felt the vibrations from the steam turbine in the engine room slow and stop. Lieutenant Simons stepped back out on the deck.

"Time for a sounding, men. Let's get our depth and make it quick. You've all had enough of a break," the executive officer said.

"Yes, sir, right on it," Duffy replied as he grabbed the sounding line and began lowering the lead weight over the side to determine the depth under the ship. All thoughts of the lock box and the jovial conversation went out of their heads.

"As soon as you and the navigator agree on where we are, we'll get back under way," Simons said with a smirk.

"I'll let Lieutenant Palmer know something as soon as I do," Duffy answered.

Frame, the new sailor, quickly found something else to do. He disappeared from the deck watch without joining in the conversation.

CHAPTER 6

Behind the scenes, the North Carolina Aquarium on Roanoke Island looked like a massive scale version of the game Mouse Trap with its huge array of pipes leading salt water from the exhibit tanks to the filters and then back to the exhibit tanks again. To protect the animals and keep them healthy, the water had to be cleaned continually. That also made it an ideal place to preserve artifacts that had been submerged in the ocean for years.

If the salt water absorbed into an object submerged in the ocean for more than 100 years were allowed to dry out, the water would evaporate and salt crystals would form and potentially destroy the artifact itself. The process to clean and preserve sunken artifacts, up to and including a cast-iron cannon, was to slowly desalinate the water the object rested in until the majority of the salt was removed before it could ever dry out. Depending on the artifact itself, the process could take years. While the aquarium couldn't support long-term projects, its pumps and filtration systems could provide clean salt water that researchers could use to begin the process and stabilize whatever they might find.

Dr. Peter DeSutton was at the aquarium working to stabilize records recovered from another shipwreck off the coast when Andie had called him about the sea chest from the Huron. Interested in the unexpected find, he had called in some favors to move things forward quickly, allowing them to recover the box on the same day it was found. DeSutton was on sabbatical from the marine archeology program at East Carolina University and Andie was the last student he had advised through her master's degree before he stepped away from the classroom. The opportunity for Andie to work with DeSutton again, this time as a peer and contributor, was exciting for her and a little daunting.

It was the morning after they had removed the sea chest from the wreck site when Mike let himself into the backstage area at the aquarium and followed the oversized plumbing around to the makeshift preservation facility. When Mike had the time, which wasn't nearly as often as he preferred, he volunteered as a diver at the aquarium helping to clean the exhibits from the inside. He knew the inner workings of the facility well. Andie and DeSutton were standing over a tank built into a platform talking quietly. Both looked tired, as if neither had slept overnight, but excited as well. Mike was tired himself, having spent the evening enjoying a few celebratory beers from the local microbrewery with Mac and Red.

"Morning, guys, what's up?" Mike said after watching the two researchers for a moment. He marveled that Andie was now grown up and looked like a scientist rather than the young girl he had known for years. Both Andie and DeSutton looked up with a start.

"Oh, hi, Mike. You startled us," Andie said sheepishly, motioning him over. "Come on over and take a look. The box looks great. It's in perfect shape. Being buried under the sand helped keep it clean."

"That looks a lot better than it did just yesterday," Mike said, peering into the tank as the clean water flowed gently past the case. He could see debris and sand leaching away from the box and flowing into the filters.

"You're right, it does," DeSutton said. "You've got great timing. It looks so good that we were just about to see if the trunk lid moves."

"Very cool. But aren't you afraid of ruining whatever's inside?" Mike asked.

"There's no way this box is watertight. Whatever is inside has been exposed to seawater for 130 years. We can't do any more damage to it than that," DeSutton explained. "We're just hoping if there are papers inside they are salvageable and that we can move them out of the strong box and into those preservation trays for cleaning and drying."

"I got ya," Mike said, unslinging his camera bag from his shoulder and setting it up to document the process. He had wanted to continue to photograph the recovery for scientific purposes so the researchers and his friends had evidence of the work they were doing. He had also sent his editor in New York an email about the find and she told him to let them know what they found, to see if it could turn into a story. "Do you mind if I keep doing my job?"

"By all means, please do," DeSutton answered. "We've got a video running as well, but your photographs will be very valuable to the process. You'll be able to get better angles than the static video and if we want to publish anything later, we'll need photographs."

DeSutton turned to Andie. "Are you ready?"

"Sure, Doctor. Just waiting on you two," she replied.

"Get your gloves on and let's see what happens," DeSutton replied.

Andie and DeSutton had already cleaned the hinges on the back of the strong box, brushing away growth and rust from the metal. They took a fine metal saw and cut away a heavily encrusted lock from the box as well.

After a moment's hesitation, "I'm ready when you are," Andie replied.

"By all means, then, let's see if the lid moves and what's inside," DeSutton said, gesturing toward the tank.

Both researchers reached inside and ran their fingers along the crack where the strong ox lid met the base. Andie took a small plastic spatula and carefully worked it into the crack. She began slowly pushing the two pieces apart. Gradually the top began to move. The progress was painstaking and Mike realized none of them were breathing much as they gently opened the case for the first time in more than 130 years – the case that might hold answers as to why the Huron sank.

"It's moving, but pretty slowly," Andie said.

"We can put a little more pressure on it, but let's not force it. We can use fiber optics to look inside the case with that much of an opening," DeSutton replied.

Just then they all three heard a pop and water splashed high into the air. The debris holding the hinge suddenly broke loose and the lid opened all the way, throwing water around the room. Andie and Mike stood looking at each other — shocked — for a moment. Then they broke out laughing as they wiped salt water from their clothes. Doctor DeSutton frowned, but didn't say anything as he reached for a towel to dry himself.

"What on earth are you two laughing at?" Mac Williams said as he approached the scene with his daughter and Mike holding their sides. He was followed by several others, including the aquarium director and members of the local news media. Surrounded by authority figures, Andie was the first to straighten up.

"Morning, Dad," she answered, beaming. "We got the strong box open!"

"What? How did you do that?" Mac asked, excitedly. Then, with a little hesitation, "Should you have done that already?"

"It's all right, Mr. Williams. The box is fine," DeSutton said. "We were just testing it, and it suddenly released. But we're doing everything by protocol."

"Did you find anything? What's inside?" one of the reporters asked.

"Literally it just happened. I have no idea," DeSutton continued. "Andie, please turn the water flow back on, gently. I don't want to wash anything away, but let's get some of this cloudy water out of the tank and see what we can see."

The newcomers gathered around the water tank and stared. It took a while before anyone could see anything, but eventually the water began to clear.

"It looks like stacks of paper," Andie said. "We'll have to dry them out to see if there is anything on them. I hope the salt water hasn't washed all the ink away."

"Even if it has, there are ways to recover some of the information, right, Doctor?" Mike asked.

"There are, but it's a slow process. That's the downside to something like this. It takes time before we find much of anything that is useful, if at all," DeSutton explained to the media and visitors, playing the expert perfectly.

"I've been involved with a couple of archeological projects myself," Mike said. "So often, troves of papers like this end up being routine information with ship's manifests and payrolls. Interesting on one level, but not what we're looking for."

"That's very true, Mike," DeSutton agreed. "I'm sorry I don't know much of the backstory of this wreck. As I said, I recently just learned about my forebear's presence on board and haven't had time to dig into the background. Is there some mystery that I don't know about?"

"Not much evidence of a mystery, only suspicion. But there are questions about what caused this ship to wreck just a few hours out of port. They had weather reports indicating a storm was coming, but they decided to leave port anyway when it would have been safer to wait it out and leave a day or two later. Not many men survived the wreck, but there were rumors about some disagreement between some of the officers right after they set sail. It's all probably just sea stories, but it's intriguing," Mike finished.

"And that explains why Mike is so interested in this wreck. The history behind it," Mac said with a chuckle.

"Mac, that's why I'm interested in everything I do. It's always about the story behind the story," Mike replied.

"There are so many stories like that in archeology, Mike. I hope we find something that helps you answer those questions, but for now Andie and I are going to have to remove these papers one by one and process them to begin drying them out and getting them ready for conservation. It'll be weeks or months before we know what they say," DeSutton said.

"I understand. No worries. It's just cool to be a little closer. Glad I was home for this one," Mike replied.

DeSutton reached into the chest and pulled out a stack of a papers gently and transferred them to a waiting tray of water where Andie would begin the process of separating them and cleaning them to get the salt out. Mike lost interest quickly after photographing the scientists beginning their work. The other visitors started to filter away as they realized there weren't going to be any easy and quick answers.

"Hold on," Mike said as he reached out and grabbed a pair of gloves for himself. "What's that?"

All eyes had been on the papers in the bottom of the strong box as the water cleared. As Mike walked away, he noticed the lid of the box itself. When it flew open, the case had moved on its hinges, falling back underwater. In the process, the lining of the lid had come ajar. Just through the crack in the lining, Mike thought he could see a tube or a box.

"What is it, Mike?" Andie asked.

"Look at the lid to the strong box. I think it was a hidden compartment at one time. It must have broken when the lid popped loose. I think there's something inside there," Mike said.

"What do you have there, Mike?" DeSutton asked, moving closer, a slight edge to his voice.

"Hold on. I think I can get it," Mike said. He gently slid his finger through the opening in the lid and snagged the object. It was round and shaped like a tube. Holding it with his finger tips Mike pulled the tube toward the small opening. Andie reached into the water and took the tube before Mike could drop it. She held up a round tube with sealed ends.

"What do you think it is?" Andie asked.

"Better yet, is it watertight?" Mike asked grinning.

"What do you have there, Andie?" DeSutton asked, taking control of the situation.

"Not sure, Dr. DeSutton. Some sort of hollow cylinder. At least I think it's hollow. It doesn't seem heavy enough to be solid. And I don't hear any water sloshing around inside it, either," she replied, holding the tube up to her ear.

"Please put it on the worktable so we can all look at it," DeSutton said sternly. Mike raised his eyebrows slightly at the tone, but he remained silent while Andie placed the container on the table. DeSutton immediately took over the examination.

"Hmmmm, it appears to be made of bone or animal horn of some sort, about two inches across and eight inches long — he noted for the video camera recording. They hollowed out the horn to keep it watertight. Looks like they did an amazing job, really," DeSutton said as he examined the object. "The ends are sealed as well. They appear to be leaden caps, but sealed with some sort of resin."

"What do you think it's all about, Doc?" Mike asked. "Somebody obviously hid it and took great care to protect whatever it is."

"You're right, Mike. Whatever is in this tube was intended to be kept away from prying eyes and was meant to be a secret. I doubt it was intended to be watertight as much as simply sealed to make sure no one opened it, but they seem to have succeeded anyway," DeSutton explained.

"What's next? Do we open it up? Do you think there might be some sort of trap inside it? Like in that book where a chemical destroys the document if you force it open?" Mac Williams asked.

"Maybe you shouldn't believe everything you read in novels, Mr. Williams, but anything is possible, I guess. Before we try to open it up, I would like to X-ray the tube and see what we can find out that way. And if there is some sort of booby trap inside, that should tell us as well," DeSutton explained.

"That makes sense," Mike agreed. "Where do we get an X-ray machine for something like this?"

"It just so happens we have an X-ray right here at the aquarium. We use it to X-ray the animals from time to time when there is something wrong. That would work, wouldn't it?" the aquarium director said. She had come rushing back when he heard the commotion from Mike's discovery.

"Absolutely. That'll be fine. We should be able to get a good look at whatever is inside the tube with it just fine," DeSutton agreed.

"I'll make some calls and get the techs ready. Shouldn't take too long to get the lab set up," she explained. "I'll let you know when it's ready."

Within an hour the lab technicians had the bone tube set up on the X-ray machine and took a series of scans. The output went straight to computer so DeSutton and the others were able to see what was inside the tube immediately. The lead caps that sealed the ends of the tube obscured portions of the view, but other than that they were able to look at the object from all angles.

"Doesn't look like much is inside," Mike said, leaning over DeSutton's shoulder.

"No, you're right, Mike. About all I can make out on this X-ray is some sort of metallic object inside, almost like a key. There is some light scatter on the X-ray, but that could be from the tube or something else inside. Other than that, it appears to be empty," DeSutton agreed.

"Would paper show up on an X-ray?" Andie asked.

"Probably not. I'm not a radiologist, but I don't think this is a fine enough detail to make that happen," the researcher explained. "There are probably ways, but not with this machine."

"So, it's possible there is a document of some sort inside, we just can't see it?"

"Yes, absolutely. We won't know until we open it up and take a look." DeSutton agreed.

"Sounds like that is the next step, then. Right?" Mike said.

"Yes, Mike. We need to open up the tube. Would you please photograph the process?" Turning his back, and with the assumption Mike would do as he was told, DeSutton picked up a slender scalpel from the medical kit the veterinarian used to treat the aquarium animals. He slowly cut away the resin that held the lead cap on one end of the tube in place while Mike continued photographing the scene.

When DeSutton was through removing the resin, he sat back for a second, to examine his work before removing the end piece.

"Is there any concern about exposing whatever is inside to the air?" Mac asked.

"Maybe a little," DeSutton said. "But not much. If there was some reason to believe there was a virus or something in it maybe, but not in this case. I'm guessing there will be a very old paper in there, but that's about it. This tube probably held some private order or communication that was to remain secret. Once we get it out, we'll need to preserve it, but it doesn't have to happen immediately."

"Sounds like it's time to do the honors then, doc."

Everyone huddled around the worktable. They were all quiet, nervous, excited and barely breathing. They all hoped whatever was in the tube would hold some clue as to what had happened on board the Huron.

DeSutton slowly pulled on the lead cap to free it from the tube. The cap bent in his hand and then came loose. With a pop, the cap was free. Mike was photographing the entire process, shooting nearly continuously. DeSutton upended the tube and the metallic object slid out onto the table. It was vaguely key-shaped, with cuts and marks that would allow it to open a lock somewhere. DeSutton shined a light inside the tube next.

"Yes, there is paper rolled up inside the tube as well," he explained. Using a pair of tweezers to separate the paper from the tube walls, he gently pulled the document out. With his gloved hands, he began unrolling the document and gently flattened it on the table. Everyone stared silently at the document for a few moments.

FbwvpNgcsrtAnbvgzssfjvvlrojbrgwccjcwkkoeyvvfhjzqikwr
bhnzcbhsoyctcqhtsivhksqnuyhDhAzbkogswJgkslbemstvd
byjzsswkpjbkvhwdqoerdboyvvqdmjtinwozqnbuovalqztcys
Zshyszsdysibvwojcwhksntjvhkscjwjovalqzfdhbtsurquonpw
ehksctqbowhsjkrhhfdjrxsEssnbuhkoehfrqnhsjwjzdbotdvb
viafbuwwktqzisyslqsmsumemweubcfssvr

"It's gibberish!" Mac said, breaking the quiet.

"I think it must be in code," DeSutton answered. "You're right; it doesn't make any sense to me either."

"So what do we do now?" Mike asked, feeling mildly deflated. "Seems like we keep getting closer, only to meet with another hurdle."

"I'm not a codebreaker, but I know some people who can help," DeSutton explained. "I'll make some calls. Unfortunately, it will probably be tomorrow before we'll be able to get any help. I think the best thing to do will be to put the document back into the tube, close it up and keep it locked away and safe until we can get a cryptanalyst here to look at what we have."

"Can't we scan the document and send it out to people? That seems a lot faster than waiting on someone to get here," Mike said.

"You're right, of course, but this paper is very fragile. I'm concerned about flattening it out on the scanner and subjecting it to the intense light of the scanning process. We will simply have to wait," DeSutton said, sounding very professorial. He was already gently rolling the paper back up to place it in the tube. "I have a safe in my lab here on site. I will place the tube there until help arrives." Within moments, DeSutton had the tube resealed and walked away to lock it up.

"I guess he told us," Mac said, laughing as he watched the professor walking away.

"Sorry, Dad. Dr. DeSutton can be like that sometimes. But he really is an expert on these things and he knows what he's talking about," Andie explained.

"We've waited for a long time and the crew of the Huron has waited 130 years for this, so one day isn't going to make a big difference. On the other hand, I'm hungry. Let's go get some lunch." Red said as he walked up to his friends.

"Where have you been?" Mac asked.

"I was checking on a couple things with some naval historian friends of mine. I wanted to see if anyone knew anything about the trunk," Red explained.

"What did you find out?" Mac asked.

"I'll tell you over lunch."

"Sounds like a plan to me," Mike agreed. "I must finally be on this time zone. I'm hungry, too. Let's go."

Within 15 minutes, the foursome took a seat at their local Carolina barbecue joint. The smell of wood-smoked pork filled with seasonings hung in the air and an old juke box played softly in the background. After they ordered lunch, the conversation quickly turned back to the tube and the coded message inside.

"Just how complicated can a code from 1877 be? I mean, it should be pretty easy to break, right?" Mac asked over Southern sweet tea.

"There's no doubt that whatever the code is, it will be simpler than the digital encryption we use today, but something tells me this isn't something you work out on the back of a napkin, either," Mike answered. "Cryptography has been around a long, long time. We've learned to automate it, but even back then they had access to some pretty sophisticated ciphers."

"I think the part that really blows my mind is the way the message was hidden in the first place," Andie said. "Think about it. They hid the message in a code and then sealed it into a waterproof tube, and then hid it in the lid of the captain's trunk. Whatever is in the message, someone was trying awfully hard to protect it."

"You're right about that, Andie," Mac agreed. "I've never seen or heard about anything even close to it. This all happened right after the Civil War. There was a lot of intrigue in that period, but this is still pretty tremendous stuff."

"Speaking of intrigue, Red, where did you take off to again?" Mike asked around mouthfuls of food.

"I had only heard rumors about coded messages hidden like that before, but never seen one. I wanted to call a couple naval historian friends to see if they had ever seen one either," Red explained. "Neither one of them had ever seen one in person either, but had pictures of it. It only happened a couple times that anyone knows about. Pretty bulky way to transfer messages around. Seems there was some group called the Consortium around the time the Huron sank that used that technique from time to time."

"Red, is this more of your conspiracy theory stuff?" Mac asked, teasing his friend.

"Well, yes and no. The Consortium was this group of admirals, generals, politicians and industrialists who weren't happy with the ending of the war and they were still trying to stir things up," Red explained.

"Seems like there were a number of groups like that, about that time, weren't there?" Mike asked.

"Heck, there are people today who aren't happy about the outcome of that war, but yes there were several groups like that at the time," Red agreed. "But this one was different, shadowy."

"And here comes the conspiracy theory…" Andie said, smiling and teasing her uncle.

"Sure doesn't seem like a conspiracy now that we just found a tube hidden with a coded message inside in a sea chest on a ship that sunk under mysterious circumstances," Red replied, defensively.

"Okay, that's true. Which brings us back to the coded message in the first place," Mike agreed.

Before the conversation could go any further, Andie's cell phone rang.

"Hello," she answered and then waited for a minute. "Oh, Okay, thanks for that Dr. DeSutton. We'll see you tomorrow then. 8 a.m. sharp. Bye."

"What was that about, Andie?" Mike asked.

"It was Dr. DeSutton. He called in a cryptanalyst and he'll be here first thing in the morning. Dr. DeSutton asked us all to be at the lab when the codebreaker arrives tomorrow, so we can help him understand the history and context of the shipwreck. Dr. DeSutton said this could help figure out the code," Andie explained.

"Okay, that makes sense. No sleeping in, I guess," Mike said, smiling.

"Well, if you want to sleep in, we can probably handle things for you. I don't know that you have to be there," Mac replied with a sly grin.

"You know I'll be there," Mike said.

CHAPTER 7

"Commander, permission to enter?" Lieutenant Simons, the ship's executive officer, said as he knocked on the door to the commander's quarters.

"Come on in, Simons," Commander Ryan said, looking up from his desk. "Is there a problem?"

"No, sir, just came to make a report and inform you that the cook is just about to serve dinner," Simons replied, standing just inside the door. "He said he would bring yours to your cabin."

"That's fine, Simons. You're welcome to join me. We should probably take the time to discuss our orders. Please inform the galley crew that you'll dine in here this evening," Ryan said. The men had served together for more than two years, since the Huron was first commissioned and it was something of a tradition that they often ate together on their first night underway to discuss plans for each cruise, the complement of men, and the state of the ship. Later, both the captain and the executive officer would join the rest of the officers in the officers' mess and even occasionally eat with the crew in the galley, but the first night it was usually just the two of them. While Simons fully expected Ryan would ask him to join him for the evening meal, he didn't assume anything.

"Yes, sir, I'll be right back. Let me just tell the cook," Simons said, stepping back out through the door. He returned just a few moments later and entered the commander's quarters, striding across the floor and taking a seat at the desk, across from the commander.

"How are things looking, Simons?" Ryan asked without preamble.

"The storm is getting worse, sir. We'll probably be in for a rough night, but nothing we can't handle," Simons answered.

"I can feel it and hear it. I'll plan to be on the bridge after dinner and our briefing," Ryan agreed. "How are the men?"

"Mostly the crew you know," Simons answered. "We took on a few new sailors, including a new helmsman. They all seem to be steady men, though. No concerns so far."

"I haven't met all the new men yet, but I will this evening," Ryan answered. He liked to know every man serving under his command.

"Can you tell me about our orders, sir?" Simons asked, just as curious as the men on the deck about their plans for this trip and the mysterious last-minute delivery of the box. "It will help me brief the men on their duties."

Ryan laughed and looked at his executive officer with a smile on his face. "Of course, that's the only reason you want to know – so the men can do their jobs more efficiently," Ryan said.

"Well, no, sir … I mean, yes, sir," Simons stuttered for a second.

"It's all right, Simons. I understand. I'll tell you as much as I know," Ryan answered.

"What do you mean, sir? You don't know what our orders are?"

"Not all of them, Simons. Just the general destination, but not the specifics of where we're going just yet. My orders were specific that I wasn't to open the second set of orders in the lock box until we've cleared Fort Jefferson in the Dry Tortugas," Ryan explained.

"We're headed to the West Indies, then?" Simons asked.

"We're headed to Cuba," Ryan said.

"Interesting," Simons replied. "But why go past Fort Jefferson if we're going to Havana? That takes us out of the way. We could cut straight away from Key Biscayne and head straight there. Going past Fort Jefferson takes us another 70 miles past Key West and well out of our way."

"You would be absolutely correct if we were headed to Havana, but we're not. We're going around the island and approaching from the south side. We're headed to the Isle of Pines," Ryan said.

"And what are we going to do when we get there?" Simons asked.

Before Ryan could answer there was a knock on the door and a crewman delivered dinner. As the men settled in to eat, it took a few more minutes before they got back on track in their conversation. Simons knew Ryan had not forgotten his question and would get back to it, so he didn't press although he was exceedingly curious. Still, Simons didn't want to wait too long and decided to redirect the conversation when he found the opportunity.

"Isle of Pines. That was a pirate island, right?" Simons asked.

"That's the history of the place. Plenty of stories of pirates and treasure from the days of the buccaneers," Ryan said.

"But why are we headed there?"

"We've been ordered to the Isle of Pines to survey the coast for mapping," Ryan explained.

"Correct me if I'm wrong sir, and I'm sorry if this is none of my business, but isn't Cuba in the middle of a revolution? Why are we headed there now? I thought the Havana harbor was blockaded by the Spanish," Simons asked, trying to understand their intent.

"You are absolutely correct. I can tell you didn't waste your time in port spending all your time in the bars," Ryan said with a laugh. "They've been fighting against Spain for almost 10 years now. I understand it's going pretty badly for the Spanish, actually."

For more than 50 years, since the 1820s, the U.S. government had been concerned about Cuba. In his 1823 Monroe Doctrine, President James Monroe staked out the entire Western hemisphere as part of the United States' sphere of influence, claiming both Puerto Rico and Cuba as natural extensions of the North American continent. On several occasions, the U.S. had attempted to purchase Cuba from Spain, offering $130 million at one point. Factions within the U.S. government wanted to support the Cuban rebels and help Cuba become free from Spain, while other groups refused to support what became known as "Cuban belligerency". They didn't want Cuba to gain their freedom from Spain directly. Rather, they hoped to absorb Cuba into the United States.

For many years Cuba's trade with the United States had far exceeded the island's trade with Spain. A major sticking point, though, was the fact that slavery still existed in Cuba. By the 1870s, it was illegal to import new slave to Cuba, but it still happened. The island's single largest work-force was made up of African slaves. The island's key crop was labor-intensive sugar cane farming. They needed thousands of men to perform the hard, back-breaking labor and slaves were the easiest, most economical method to do that. Easiest for the Spanish, that is.

"Groups of Cubans have been trying to get us involved in the island for years," Ryan continued. "They want us to come in and liberate Cuba, and free them from the Spaniards. There are groups in the U.S. who want us to go in there, too, but they want us to take over the island and make it a new state. And still other groups, mostly in the southern states, want us to run it as a slave state," Ryan continued.

"Which one of those groups do we fall into, Commander?" Simons asked.

"As far as I'm concerned, none of them," Ryan answered. "My orders are to head that direction for now. Nothing more. When we pass by Fort Jefferson, we're going to stop and pick up an adviser and then make our way around to the Isle of Pines. When that adviser is on board, we'll open the rest of our orders and find out what we are supposed to do next. That's about all I know at the moment."

"Very mysterious if you ask me. What would stop us from going ahead and opening the orders now?" Simons asked. "We could always reseal them."

"Simons, I understand you're curious, but you do understand what you just suggested would be disobeying a direct order, don't you?" Ryan asked with an arched eyebrow. "Besides, I'm not sure where the orders are. I've been through the lock box the Marines brought on board, and I can't find anything unusual. Considering the nature of the way these orders were dropped off and the fact that they are hidden somewhere in the case, I would also guess they will be in some sort of code. The adviser we're picking up at Fort Jefferson will probably have the code key."

"All spies and mystery, sir. And I apologize for suggesting that we open the orders, sir. I didn't mean to suggest that…" Simons began.

"I understand your curiosity, Simons, and because of that, will ignore it, but I don't want to hear any of that talk in front of the men. You can relay our orders that we are headed for Fort Jefferson, but nothing more for now," Ryan said, cutting the younger man off.

"Yes, sir. I understand, sir."

CHAPTER 8

Mike pulled into the aquarium parking lot feeling a little better this morning than he had the day before. And better than the day before that. He was almost back on Eastern Daylight Time and would have been sleeping well again if it weren't for the fact that his imagination was completely on fire. He couldn't wait to meet the cryptanalyst and find out what was in the secret message in the tube.

Mike's career had taken him all over the world and he had been involved in solving mysteries, sometimes involving archeology, and unraveling hidden meanings to help understand stories. He was always interested in the human element in stories and looked beyond the surface to try to fully understand what was going on. Mike had a long-standing curiosity about the story behind the story of the Huron. He wanted to understand what could cause a group of professional sailors and officers to be so far off course that they would run into an island the size of Hatteras. There were treacherous shoals and currents all over the North Carolina coast that had taken nearly 2,000 ships to their final destination, earning this piece of coast line the nickname "Graveyard of the Atlantic." But Mike was confident there had to be something more human, more personal that had caused the

Huron to go down.

"Hey, guys," Mike said with a laugh as he approached Andie, Mac and Red, waiting at the aquarium's side door. "And I thought I was early."

"Hey, Mike," Andie replied. "We're waiting on the codebreaker. He should be here any minute and we didn't want him to get lost wandering around inside."

"No doubt you're all just worried about the analyst. That's your only reason for getting out of bed so early this morning," Mike's sarcasm was evident. Mac and Red laughed at the exchange.

"Well, I...

"Hold on, Andie, I think our guest is here," Mac said, interrupting Andie before she could finish her retort. "Let's go say Hi."

The foursome walked across the small side parking lot and greeted the young man getting out of the car. The scientist stood a little over six feet tall, with long brown hair that was tied back in a pony tail, and he didn't look much older than Andie. His bright green eyes were the first thing most people noticed in his handsome face.

"Dr. Parrot?" Andie asked.

"Ummm, hello. Do I, um, know you?" the man asked, fumbling for a minute as he was caught off guard by the attractive young woman.

"No, sir, but Dr. DeSutton was my graduate adviser and he described you to me," Andie explained.

"Well, it's very nice to meet you," Parrot said, recovering quickly and smiling into Andie's eyes. Andie smiled back and was seemingly caught off guard by the connection. There was a long pause until suddenly Mac cleared his throat. Andie recovered quickly.

"Let me introduce the rest of the welcoming committee," Andie said, gesturing to the others.

"It's a pleasure to meet you all. First, call me Phil. Second, Mike, I'm a big fan of your work. I really enjoyed that story on that archeological find on the Adriatic Coast of Italy. That was amazing. When Dr. DeSutton called and asked me to consult on this project, I was hesitant, but when he mentioned you were involved, I jumped at the chance," Phil said.

"Thank you, Dr. Parrot, er, I mean, Phil. I'm sorry I can't say I know much about you, but I'm here to help any way I can," Mike replied, slightly off balance.

"I'm a big history buff but I'm a diver, too. So whenever I run across stories like that one I follow them pretty closely. It happens that you seem to be involved with a lot of stories I find interesting," Phil explained.

"That's all right, Phil," Andie said, taking back control of the conversation as she took the cryptanalyst by the arm to lead him into the building. "We all feel that way about our local celebrity."

Shaking his head and laughing at Andie's less-than-subtle interest in the visiting scientist, Mike fell into step behind the others as they walked into the aquarium building.

"Hold on," Red said as he entered the dark lab. "I'm surprised the lights aren't on in here. I assumed Dr. DeSutton would be in here waiting on us. I think the switch is over here."

When the lights came on, they all stood quietly shocked by the scene in front of them. The room was a wreck. Water tanks were overturned. Papers were strewn about the place as if someone had searched through the laboratory looking for something.

DeSutton was gone, too. His car was in the parking lot, but there was no sign of him anywhere.

Mike immediately pulled out his camera and began photographing the scene while Mac reached for his mobile phone to call the police. The rest of the morning was a blur as each of the visitors gave statements to the local sheriff's department investigators. It took a while before any of them got to speak to the others.

Mike met up with his friends sitting at a picnic table outside the aquarium.

"The police are treating this as a robbery and a missing person. The aquarium's alarm system was deactivated, but Dr. DeSutton could have turned it off when he came in to do some work. Do any of you know how to reach Dr. DeSutton?" Mike asked once he was done speaking to the police. "Andie, do you know where he's staying?"

"I tried to call his cell phone, but it went straight to voicemail," Andie said. "I gave all of that information to the police and someone was going to check out his house."

"It's gone, too, isn't it?" Mike asked.

"I couldn't find any sign of it. And the cabinet Dr. DeSutton put it in was broken open," Mac agreed. "It's gone."

"What's gone? The document? The one you discovered?" Phil asked, realizing the full meaning of the morning. "Dr. DeSutton is gone and so is the document? Who could have done this? Why?"

"That's the question of the day, of course," Mike replied. "I'm going to dig around and see what else I can find out, though. I don't think the local police quite understand what's going on here. I think someone wanted the coded message. They took it and Dr. DeSutton. I just don't know why. "

"Did anyone scan the document with the code you wanted me to break? Maybe if I can figure out what it says, that'll give us a clue as to who could have stolen it," Phil said.

"Dr. DeSutton wouldn't let us scan it. He was afraid something might happen to it and wanted to wait until you got here," Andie explained.

"Oh. That's a little odd. And disappointing," Phil said, looking down.

"Hold on, though. I photographed DeSutton opening the tube and unrolling the document. Maybe I got enough of the message that we can piece it together," Mike said.

"Do you have those images with you?" Phil said, immediately excited again.

"No, I backed them up last night, but didn't bring that memory card with me this morning in my camera," Mike said. "Let's go back to my place. I've got a high resolution monitor and Photoshop on my computer. We can take a close look at the images and see what you can see."

"That's great, Mike. Lead the way," Phil said.

"What do you want us to do?" Mac asked as Red nodded.

"I know the police are going to be digging around, but make some calls and see if you can find anyone who saw anything. You guys have this island wired. See if there were any strangers hanging around, that sort of thing. If we find anything, I'll call you, but if not, let's plan to meet at my place for dinner tonight," Mike said, taking charge.

"Sounds good, Mike. See you this evening," Mac agreed.

"Oh, and Mac? Bring beer," Mike said.

CHAPTER 9

The man the other sailors knew as Frame stood watch on the bridge. He was a helmsman who had just transferred to the Huron. New to the ship, he drew the first four hour shift from 4 to 8 p.m. after leaving dock. It was the least favorite watch for most of the men because it meant supper would be cold by the time they got to head to the galley. Still, they were luckier than most. The ship's cook, Joseph Murphy, did his best to provide for all of the sailors and made sure those coming off watch didn't just get leftovers. The men worked in four-hour shifts, on for four and off for eight, around the clock.

"Mr. Conway, it appears the storm coming from the southeast is getting worse, sir," Frame said to the watch officer. "It's growing harder to hold our heading."

"And of course our orders are to head straight into it," Conway commented under his breath. "Keep a careful eye out, Frame. There are shoals all around here. These are treacherous waters and we need to keep straight on to the course the navigator laid down or we'll get in trouble. Slipping over a degree is all it would take to put us on the rocks in a wind like this."

"Yes, sir. I know," Frame replied quietly. "I'm new to the Huron, sir, but I've sailed through here many, many times."

"Sure you are, sailor," Conway answered. "No slight intended. Just saying it to remind us all to be on our toes."

The two men and the rest of the bridge crew settled into a tense silence, watching the storm coming at them as the waters churned up and the winds blew harder. Without warning, a sail on the first of the ship's three masts blew loose and the seamen on deck jumped into action. Conway stepped outside the bridge to oversee their efforts.

"Secure that sail, men, before she tears to shreds," Conway shouted over the roar of the increasing wind. "Set the fore storm stay-sail and take in that spanker. I want to see a single reef in fore trisail, and a double reef in the main trisail. This storm is going to get worse before it gets better and we're heading right into the face of it."

Conway stepped back inside the ship's bridge. "Frame, alert the engine room that we're going to heave to for a minute and take a sounding while we reset the sails."

"Yes, sir," Frame replied as he took the stopper from the brass pipe the bridge crew used to communicate to the boiler room. It took a couple shouts to get the attention of an engineer and get the crew to disengage the turbine.

As the men moved to carry out their assignments, Frame was left alone on the bridge. He kept the ship on an even keel, holding the ship's wheel steady. Frame knew how to steer the ship as well as any man in the navy. He had served in the Confederate Navy during the War of Northern Aggression. After, since Lee's surrender at Appomattox Courthouse in Virginia, he changed his name, moved north and re-enlisted in the combined United States Navy. The time was full of turmoil and a man with obvious experience, claiming to have lost his paper wasn't questioned.

Frame's job at this moment was to keep the ship from trouble and guide it along the navigator's chosen path. He also knew, though, that secretly he had a different set of orders. He followed the lead of men he respected more than any admiral in Washington, D.C. He alone on board the Huron knew what the Huron's task in Cuba would be, and the men he looked to had ordered him to do whatever he could to make sure the ship didn't make it there. Frame had planned to sabotage the engines and force the Huron into port in Charleston, but this storm gave him another idea, a better one that would take the ship out of service all together.

Standing alone on the bridge of the Huron, Frame let the ship drift a few degrees to the West. Then, he reached over and adjusted the ship's compass in its case so it read back to the ship's original heading. Within moments the sails were set to right and the rest of the bridge crew returned to their posts. Frame never changed his expression. Instead, he continued concentrating on his duties as helmsman.

"There's the Currituck lighthouse on the starboard quarter," Frame reported to the navigator and watch officer Conway at eight p.m.

"Thank you, Mr. Frame," Commander Ryan said as he entered the bridge. It was time for shift change and he walked through to make sure everything was going as expected. "Mr. Conway, how are we progressing?"

"We're making about 5 and a half knots, sir," the watch officer responded. "Engineering reports everything is in order below and the sails are holding fine. They are one-third into the wind on the port tack. Barometer is 30 inches and steady for the last three hours."

"Mr. Palmer," Ryan said getting the navigator's attention. "Keep on this heading. I don't want to get too far away from the coast. If we get out into the Gulf Stream with this wind and storm, it'll push us backward. I'm afraid we're going to have to pick our way down the coast until we get clear of it."

"Yes, sir. I've got the course plotted out, making our way down the coast line," Palmer replied.

"Good men. I'll be in my cabin, but come get me if you need me. I'll not plan to turn in until we make the Cape Hatteras Light, or daylight, whichever comes first. It is going to be a long night," Ryan said, leaving the bridge.

CHAPTER 10

"Okay, Phil, all I see is gibberish," Mike said as he and cryptanalyst looked at the images Mike had taken while DeSutton opened the tube hidden inside the Huron's lock box.

"Sure, Mike, what did you expect, 'The secret of life is…'?" Phil asked with a laugh.

"All right, all right, I knew it was in code. I realized that when we opened it up in the first place. I guess I was stating the obvious, but now the ball is in your court. What does it say? How do you go about reading something like this?"

The two men had pieced together the encrypted message using several different images. Lining up the letters and edges of the paper, they rebuilt the document. But that was only the first part of their task. Mike and Phil then spent the next few hours trying to figure out ways to decipher the text and find out what it said.

FbwvpNgcsrtAnbvgzssfjvvlrojbrgwccjcwkkoeyvvfhjzqikwr
bhnzcbhsoyctcqhtsivhksqnuyhDhAzbkogswJgkslbemstvd
byjzsswkpjbkvhwdqoerdboyvvqdmjtinwozqnbuovalqztcys

Zshyszsdysibvwojcwhksntjvhkscjwjovalqzfdhbtsurquonpw
ehksctqbowhsjkrhhfdjrxsEssnbuhkoehfrqnhsjwjzdbotdvb
viafbuwwktqzisyslqsmsumemweubcfssvr

"First, we have to consider the era. What year did the Huron sink again?" Phil asked.

"It went down in November of 1877," Mike replied.

"So, this is a Civil War era cipher. That's actually good news. There were some pretty sophisticated ciphers during that period, but World War I and II both brought about huge advances in cryptography. This is probably some sort of substitution cipher," Phil explained.

"So you can decode it?"

"Eventually yes, but it's not quite as easy as all that. I can't tell you what it says in the next 15 minutes. There are computer programs that can analyze the letters in the code and determine the frequency of the letters used, making some guesses and then improving the accuracy as it moves forward," Phil said.

"I've not had much experience with ciphers and codes. How does this work? How did they set up this code?" Mike asked.

Phil explained that substitution ciphers of this era used what was called a vigenere square. It was made up of 26 rows, spelling out the alphabet, but changing it cyclically. The first row begins with A, the second B, the third C and so on. From there, the code uses different alphabets from different rows and the corresponding columns.

"I've got one of the best programs on my computer, using an algorithm I created, and I'll put the message in and see what comes up. But, that can take a while," the cryptanalyst cautioned.

"Fair enough. We'll just have to wait, I guess. Obviously, whatever is on this list was important enough to get Dr. DeSutton kidnapped so there is more to it than just someone's laundry list," Mike said, agreeing. "We need to do everything we can to figure this out and do it fast."

"This is a little outside my element. I understand how people make ciphers like this and can figure them out, but I'm a little confused why they would do it," Phil said. "Was it common for U.S. naval vessels to encrypt special orders or messages like this?"

"Not that I can think of," Mike replied. "This had to be some sort of special message, not the orders for operating the ship. Some sort of covert mission, I guess."

"Even more so when you remember that whoever received this message had to be able to decipher it as well. So they had to have the knowledge to work the cipher," Phil explained. "There are two sides to this."

"That's interesting. I never really thought about that," Mike replied.

"Ciphers like this use a key word as part of the encryption. The person who got this message would have to know how to use the vigenere square and would have to know the key word as well. If we had the key word, we could get the answer in just a few minutes, probably, but without it, it's a lot of guessing and running through different variables," Phil said. "When they prepared this message, they used that keyword to further scramble the letter substitutions. And then they could have done it as a vigenere cipher, or used a variation of that cipher, making it more complex than that."

"What would the key word be?" Mike asked.

"Unfortunately, it could be anything. It could be the encrypter's daughter's middle name. Or the ship captain's favorite pudding. It can be any length, too. The way the substitution works is you repeat the word over and over until it is the same length as the message itself. It could be a two-letter word or a 10-word phrase. Doesn't really matter," Phil said.

"Does your program allow you to enter key words?" Mike asked, trying to find a way around the problem.

"Sure. I can do a couple different things with the message. Once I get it all entered, I'll set the program to try to break it down using letter frequency. But then we can put in a key word. I can also set it up to search through random words, trying those as keywords as well. Obviously, though, there are billions of possibilities for that so don't get your hopes up," Phil finished.

Before Mike could continue, his doorbell rang. It was Mac, Red and Andie, and they had brought pizza and beer.

"Is it dinner time already?" Mike said as he opened the door.

"We've been trying to call for an hour to see if you two were ready to eat," Mac answered as he walked into Mike's living room, carrying beer from the local brewery. "The beer was getting warm, so I finally decided to come on over."

"That's the last thing any of us want to happen. Get it in the fridge right now," Mike said, laughing at his friends.

"Don't let him fool you, Mike," Andie said as she carried in pizzas. "He was worried sick that something had happened to you two after Dr. DeSutton's kidnapping, so he insisted on coming right over."

"Sorry guys. I guess time got away from us," Mike replied, sheepishly. "I didn't realize it had gotten so late in the day. I must have turned off the ringer on my phone."

"Me either," Phil said entering the living room from Mike's office, smiling when he saw Andie. "But now that you guys are here, I'm suddenly starved."

"Mike, don't you feed your guests?" Andie said, with a playful swat on Mike's shoulder. She went into the kitchen and came back with plates.

"Nope, I only feed them when they produce results," Mike replied, teasing the cryptanalyst as he handed him a plate and motioned toward the food.

"So I guess that means you haven't been able to break the code?" Red asked.

"Unfortunately, no. We got the whole document pieced together from my photographs, but haven't made any real progress since then," Mike answered. "Did you guys find out anything from your calls? Did anyone notice any strangers hanging around?"

"No one noticed anything strange. We talked to everyone we could find and came up with nothing," Mac answered. "It is a tourist island so there are always strangers hanging around. I think the locals just block out the strangers unless they're acting weird."

"Damn. I was hoping your contacts could help. We're not any closer to finding out what happened to Dr. DeSutton," Mike said. "I can't imagine how it all fits together, yet, but I know his kidnapping has to do with finding the hidden message on the Huron. They took it, too, of course. But how does a 19th century shipwreck get a 21st century scientist kidnapped? Particularly when only a few people know about finding the note in the first place."

"Doesn't make any sense to me, either," Red agreed. "We'll keep looking and asking around."

"It seems like the answer lies in what we found on the shipwreck. I think we should leave solving the kidnapping to the police and concentrate on the hidden message. If you're right, Mike, we'll get to the answer and hopefully help Dr. DeSutton at the same time," Mac said.

"Sounds like a plan to me," Mike agreed. "Let me show you what we found and bring you guys up to speed."

While Phil showed the new arrivals how the cipher chart worked, substituting one letter for another, Mike printed off copies of the document they had reassembled.

"Looks like gibberish to me," Mac said.

"Don't get Phil started," Mike said, laughing. "I said that earlier and got a detailed primer on the process." While the two men had just met, they had quickly become friends. Mike knew Phil was going to fit in well with the group. They were all quiet for a while as they ate and stared at the print outs.

"Phil," Andie asked around bites of pizza. "What are these numbers on the second page? Could that be your code key?"

"Hmmm, let me see that, Andie. A traditional cipher isn't really designed to use numbers. When they include numbers in the message, they spell them out. Like I said, it is cycles of the alphabet. But that is interesting that those numbers are even on there," Phil said, looking at the string of numbers.

"Maybe it's some sort of substitution for letters in the alphabet," Red offered, scratching his chin.

"No, it can't be. That would defeat the purpose of the cipher in the first place," Phil answered.

"Mac, you know what those numbers look like, don't you?" Mike asked, suddenly grinning from ear to ear.

"You know, I believe I do," Mac said with a laugh. "You have charts around here anywhere?"

"On the drafting table in my office. You know where they are," Mike replied.

"Are you two going to share? Or are you going to keep this a little inside secret?" Andie asked, getting frustrated with her father and Mike.

"You know, boys, I think you've got it with this one," Red chimed in. "Good job on seeing that one."

"Okay, I'm with Andie on this one. What am I missing?" Phil said. "Doesn't look like any code I've seen."

"Because it's not a code. Look at the numbers again. He read them off.

213342823252. Its 12 numbers. Break it into pairs of 2 each, and what does it look like?" Mac continued, enjoying his chance to be the expert for a minute. "21, 33, 42 and 82, 32, 52."

"Are those coordinates?" Andie asked, the light coming on. "Where is it?"

"Hold on. Someone needs to catch me up. I'm not sure what you're talking about and I don't like being the one left out," Phil said with a laugh. "People come to me to have them explain things to them, not the other way around."

"It's all right, doc. We all get that way around here from time to time. This just goes back a lot longer than the 1870s and was created to make things easier to understand, not harder," Mike explained. "If our guess is right, those latitude and longitude coordinates as shown in Hours, Minutes and Seconds."

"Doc, have we told you where the Huron was headed before it went down? Or haven't we had time for that?" Mac asked, as he looked at a sea chart.

"Honestly, I don't guess so. I know you guys were going to give me the history, but after we discovered the break in and Dr. DeSutton being kidnapped, we never got back around to it," Phil said.

"The Huron was headed to Cuba to perform environmental surveys around the island," Mike explained. "The interesting thing is Cuba was in the middle of the first Cuban revolution, trying to expel Spain and the Spanish fleet. They were asking the United States to intercede and help them overthrow the crown. Havana Harbor was actually blockaded at the time."

"That's a pretty strange atmosphere to be working on environmental surveys, isn't it?" Phil asked.

"Which is why I've always been fascinated with this wreck. There is a bigger story going on here," Mike said. "We've just never been able to find any proof of what it was."

"What does it have to do with latitude and longitude coordinates?" Phil asked.

"It just so happens that those are the coordinates for a place called 'Punta del Este' on the Isla de la Juventud," Mac interjected as he grinned at the map on the dining room table, his finger tapping on the spot.

"Where in the world is that?" Andie asked.

"Truth be told, it's only been called that for the last 50 years or so. Before that, and when this note was written, it was called the Isle of Pines. It's the island on the southern side of Cuba," Mac explained. "They also called it Treasure Island."

"You're kidding? That's pretty wild. Is it THE Treasure Island?" Phil asked.

"Actually it is THE Treasure Island. Robert Louis Stevenson based part of his book on it," Mike said. "Let's think about this for a second. That list of numbers was on a second page in the tube. The encrypted message was on one and the coordinates on the other. So, the captain could open up the tube when he got to Cuba, but wouldn't be able to read the message. What if the coordinates were the location for a place to meet whoever he was supposed to deliver the message to?"

"Interesting theory, Mike," Mac said. "How do we prove it? I mean, those people are long since dead."

"Personally, I think we need to do a little research and take a look around where this meeting was supposed to happen?" Mike said with a wry smile.

"You're kidding. You want to go to Cuba to try to figure this out?" Andie said. "How does running off to Cuba solve Dr. DeSutton's kidnapping?"

"My gut tells me that's where the answers are," Mike replied. "They kidnapped him and took the original copy of the message. No one knew we would be able to put together a copy of it, so they wanted to hide it and have the only copy. The police haven't turned up any threats against Dr. DeSutton so far. All that tells me the key to whatever is happening here is hidden in the note we found in the tube. Since the Huron never made it to Cuba, maybe whatever they were going to Treasure Island for is still there. They might be forcing Dr. DeSutton to help them find it."

"What could be so important to instigate a spur-of-the-moment kidnapping? Obviously, they didn't have time to plan it. All this came together in just a few hours," Andie asked.

"You're right, Andie. Someone heard about finding the hidden message and reacted quickly. They came in and took Dr. DeSutton with no preparation," Mike agreed. "Whoever it was had to have some sort of information on what was hidden in Cuba. The only thing that could still be valuable 130 years later is gold and jewels. Maybe someone was trying to finance the revolution back then."

"So, we're going to Treasure Island to find treasure?" Mac asked with a laugh.

"Sure looks that way."

CHAPTER 11

Spray from the storm and the darkness of the night made it impossible to see more than a few feet for the men on the midnight watch. The Huron's engines continued to plow through the heavy surf and the sails still aloft were about one third filled with gale winds as they made their way down the coast. It was slow going, but the stout ship battered its way past North Carolina.

At 1 o'clock, Master French, the midnight watch officer ordered the ship to heave to for a moment to check the depth under the keel and confirm their location. Within moments the crew reported 10 fathoms and French duly relayed the number to Commander Ryan who was standing at the door to the bridge.

"Thank you, French," Ryan said.

"Why don't you get some rest, sir?" French asked.

"Once we clear this storm I will, French. Not yet, though. This area is treacherous."

"Very well, sir," French said. He knew the commander was simply keeping watch on his ship, not doubting French's abilities. With that acknowledgement, French turned to the helmsman and ordered the Huron into motion.

"Let's get her moving again Mr. Denig. Four bells to the engine room, please. I want to pull through these seas," French ordered.

"Helmsman, let her come off a point on the helm. I'd like to get out a bit from the beach just to make sure," the navigator Lieutenant Palmer ordered.

The matter-of-fact business of the bridge made it all the more surprising when the Huron struck bottom, violently throwing men and loose equipment forward.

"Hard down!" Ryan shouted as he struggled to stand back up after being thrown against the navigator's table. There was a collective gasp as a wave passed below the ship, lifting it off the bottom for a brief moment, only to be followed by the second crash as the keel landed on the bottom causing her to begin to roll onto her starboard side. The ship was in instant chaos as men shouted and attempted to reach the upper decks, vainly trying to discover what happened.

"Are we aground?"

"What happened?"

"Help me I'm stuck!"

"Get the commander!"

With each wave that passed, the jarring of the hull against the bottom was lessened — only because the ship was run further aground and was lifted less and less.

"Stop the engines!" Ryan ordered from the bridge. "Palmer, find out if we still have steam in the boilers. I want to see if we can back her out of here before the hull gets holed."

Master French pulled back on the throttle, signaling the engineer to stop the engines. Palmer left his station to yell down the hatch to the engine room below.

"Can you back her, engineer?" Palmer asked.

"We've got full steam on all the engines. Yes, we can," Chief Engineer Loomis replied.

"Make it happen, Mr. Loomis," Palmer ordered.

"Mr. French, save the ship's log. We've probably foundered on Nags Head. Mr. Palmer, please sound the distress whistle. We're going to need some help," Ryan said, taking charge of the bridge. "Get all hands on deck and batten down the hatches. Get those sails lowered."

Within moments, French reported back to the bridge that the captain's office where the ship's log was stored was filled with water, being on the starboard side.

"Very well," Ryan acknowledged. "Lieutenant Simons, order the fore mast cut away, please. Maybe we can right this ship without the added weight."

"I will make it happen immediately," Simons said, leaving across the angled deck to organize the men. The Huron was over on her side, at about 40 degrees.

Night swallowed the dying ship as the storm tossed wind and waves over the deck. The clouds above obscured any moonlight leaving it pitch black. Lanterns on the ship were extinguished to prevent fire in the heaving wood.

"Mr. Palmer, where are we? I need to know how far from land we are to gauge when help will arrive," Ryan asked.

"Commander, my charts showed us well off the coast, but one of the men reported two rocks directly ahead of our position. They are saying we are solid on the beach," Palmer reported.

"Where? Show me, Mr. Palmer."

Ryan and Palmer ventured forward through the gangway to look past the ship toward what they were just realizing was the beach.

"My God! How did we get in here?" Ryan asked.

"I'm not sure, sir. All of our navigation shows us well out to sea," Palmer replied.

The men could see the white foam of wind-tossed waves crashing on the beach less than 200 yards away, the thick spray making it hard to see.

"The good thing about this is help should arrive quickly. We may lose the ship, but we shouldn't lose any lives over this," Ryan said, shaking his head. "It's a terrible loss. What time is it, Mr. Palmer?"

"It's about 2 a.m. sir."

"Tell the men to hang on. Help should be coming soon, but let's see if we can get some of the men to safety. Lower the cutter and try to get a line to shore to send men across."

When the Huron went down on her starboard side, the port life boats were tangled in the rigging making them useless. The ship itself crushed the starboard side boats. Within just a few moments, Master Conway reported to the captain the status of the one functioning boat.

"Sir, the cutter is in the water and ready to go. We've tied her fast with a line. I would like permission to take her into the shore," Conway said.

"Go ahead, Conway," Ryan agreed. "But be careful. The surf is getting rougher."

"Yes, sir," Conway agreed. He turned and made his way along the slanted deck calling for volunteers to help him row the small cutter to the shore. He quickly organized five men to help him and they assembled at the railing. Conway reached out for the small craft to bring it in close so the men could board. As he did, a wave broke over the port side of the Huron, knocking men down and throwing the ship further on her side for a moment. Just as quickly as the wave hit, the small cutter swamped and disappeared below the waves.

The tide was coming in and making the sea more dangerous. Water was creeping up the deck as well. When the Huron first went down on her side, the water was at the edge of the railing, but as time went on, the sea climbed higher. Waves continued to batter the ship. Just before sunrise, the men had had too much and the pounding of the waves was not lessening. Men began to be swept from the deck and into the churning black water below them. No help had yet arrived from the lifesaving service on the beach.

"You there," Conway shouted to a seaman on the deck. "Give me your life preserver. I will try to swim in and get help. "

"I can't do that Master Conway. I can't swim!" the man shouted over the waves and out of fear.

"If this keeps up, none of us will make it…" Conway's reply was drowned out by a blast of ocean wave that broke across the deck, knocking him from the rigging and into the water below.

Conway barely had time to grab a breath before he was plunged into the cold ocean and dragged immediately under the black surface. He was unsure of which way was up, simply struggling against the pressure holding him down. His heart was pounding as adrenaline surged in his veins. Before being tossed into the water he was on the edge of exhaustion — cold and tired from the night's torment. He knew one thing in his mind, he wasn't going to die. Or at least not without a fight.

His head broke the surface and he struggled to breathe as he wiped the salt from his face. He tried to get his bearings as a wave crashed on top of him, crushing him back below the surface and tossing him head over heels. He felt his clothes ripped from his body as he continued to tumble. Panic was rising in his mind as his breath ran short. He had to get to the surface, he needed air. He began to fight, and struggle, kicking with every ounce of energy he had left. His head swam from the exertion and lack of air in his lungs. His body ached and his mind grew sluggish.

It didn't register at first when his knees hit the sand and he realized his head was out of the water. He had been tossed onto the beach by the waves. Men grabbed his arms, lifting him up and dragging his naked body across the sand. Local fishermen carried him to a small hut where he found three other sailors from the Huron.

"Mr. Conway," one of the sailors reported to the watch officer after the fishermen loaned him some clothes. "The locals tell us there is a lifesaving station about three miles down the beach from here. But, it's closed for the season and they say they won't break into it."

"What of the Commander? Any sign of Commander Ryan or the other officers?" Conway asked.

"None at all, Mr. Conway. I heard they tried to make it to shore, but no one has seen them come up the beach."

"Very well then, Mr. Young. Take whatever men you can find and break down the doors. Get the mortar and get back here. Men are being swept from the ship and lost. We have to get them help," Conway replied to the young ensign. "I'll do what I can from here. I'll drag the men out of the surf."

"It's a miracle you made it through the surf, Mr. Conway. The undertow is so strong," Young replied.

"If any of the men are at all exhausted, there is no way they will live. Get that lifesaving equipment and get back here as quickly as you can," Conway said as he started down the beach toward the water's edge.

The sun was beginning to rise over the water by the time the men made it back to the wreck site with the lifesaving mortar, designed to fire a safety line with a grappling hook from the beach to the ship. Any men still on board could have used a harness and made their way to safety. The men never fired the mortar, though. No one was left on board alive.

Helmsman Frame was never seen again.

CHAPTER 12

Dr. Ian Fallow was in his office on board the research vessel Espial, sorting through papers and making plans to get back out to sea when his phone rang. It was a blocked number. He guessed who was on the other end and answered it.

"Dr. Fallow, I need you to do something," the voice said.

"I'm afraid it will have to wait," Fallow replied. "We are taking the Espial out on a science cruise in a few days and I need to get things ready. There is a lot of work to be done before the science teams get here."

"I am fully aware of that, Dr. Fallow," the voice continued. "I need you to include a new team to your cruise. They need to go to Cuba."

"I'm sorry, but I can't do that. We are full. There aren't any spare berths on board. We're going to be close to Cuba, but we weren't planning to enter Cuba waters for our research. I'm afraid it just can't be done," Fallow argued.

"Dr. Fallow, I think you might be mistaking my tone to seem that you have a choice in this matter," the voice said, still as calm and quiet as it was before. "The ship you use? We own that. The crew that runs that ship? They work for us. And we own you, too. You will do what I say and I won't tolerate any more equivocation."

Fallow was quiet for a moment. He wanted to argue and tell the man on the line that no one owned him, that he was a respected scientist and that he was in charge of the Espial. But none of that was true. They did own him.

"What do you need me to do?"

"A group of four people will be arriving in the airport tomorrow. Have someone from your staff meet them and bring them to the ship. And then I want you to set sail immediately," the voice said. "The leader of this group is Mike Scott. He is a journalist. His editor will contact you with the coordinates of where they need to go. Give them every convenience and make the resources of the ship available to them."

"Why now? We had plans to do some good work on this trip?" Fallow asked, his voice nearly a whine.

"When we saved you from yourself, you were given total control of the Espial, unless we needed the ship. Until now, we have left you alone to do your research and pretend that you are a man of integrity," the voice replied. "But now it is time for you to honor your side of the bargain."

Fallow had been a full, tenured professor at a prestigious university until he lost it. At the time he didn't believe anyone would notice the paper he published under his own name had been published once before in an obscure journal by a scientist no one had ever heard of before. The original paper was published in Chinese. He just needed to publish something that year to justify his budget and his research hadn't gone as well as he had expected. It must have been a slow news day, because a national news channel ran a brief story on "his" research. And others picked it up. And suddenly the research he published just to fill the pipeline was getting attention all over the country. He was asked to speak on his findings and Fallow's ego almost had him believing that he had actually written the paper and done the research. Until someone noticed the similarity in his paper and the one from China. And then realized it wasn't just similar, but word for word.

Fallow was ruined almost as quickly as his star had risen. Stripped of his tenure and so thoroughly embarrassed that he couldn't find a job, even at a small junior college, Fallow was about to take his own life when the phone rang. He couldn't believe his ears. He was being given another chance and he had immediately jumped at it.

CHAPTER 13

Being an international journalist and the recipient of various awards, including a couple Pulitzer prizes, made entrance into Cuba fairly easy for Mike. It didn't take much effort for him to bring a couple others along as well as his "assistants". Red stayed behind to keep watch on the dive shop, but Mac, Andy and Phil came along. He had called his editor in New York to help him work out the details.

Things came together quickly after Mike explained to his editor what they had found and how it had been stolen. She realized Mike was onto something and gave him the leeway to find out what was happening; another advantage of bringing home prestigious awards from time to time. For better or worse, Mike got a lot of rope; he was just hoping he didn't hang himself in the process.

Mike's editor found an environmental group working with the Cuban government, conducting surveys and assessing the quality of the marine life around the island. They were planning to leave from Key West in a couple days and head to Cuba, skirting the island and passing around the south side where they planned to do most of their work. Mike's editor was able to apply a little leverage with the group's sponsoring organization and Mike and his group got the last cabin on board the chartered research vessel. The four of them were going to have to bunk together, but at least they had four separate beds. They packed light, but did bring their dive gear and Mike's cameras and housing as well.

The foursome caught a series of uneventful flights from Raleigh-Durham International, through Atlanta on to Miami and then grabbed a smaller commuter plane directly to Key West.

"What's the plan, now, Mike?" Phil asked Mike as they retrieved their bags in the small airport at the end of Florida.

"We'll go straight on over to the research ship. I want to get settled in. They plan to leave in the morning so there's no point in grabbing a hotel for one night. We'll see how things come together and then see about some dinner. There are lots of great places to eat on Duval Street," Mike said.

"Good," Andie said. "I'm starving."

"When aren't you hungry?" Mac asked, in his fatherly, good-natured way.

"It's my youthful metabolism, Dad" Andie said with a wink. "Too bad you and Mike don't remember what I'm talking about."

"Hey, hey, leave me out of this," Mike said as he looked around the tiny airport and then changed the subject. "They said they were going to have someone come over and pick us up. I'm surprised there isn't anyone to meet us."

Just then Mike heard a voice come from behind him. "It's a good thing I'm here then."

Mike froze for a second when he recognized the voice. Sarah. He hadn't seen her in more than a year, but he knew he would never forget the sound of her voice.

"Ummmm, hi," he stammered. "This is some surprise," Mike said as he turned to face her, trying to find his footing. Sarah would qualify as "the one that got away" in Mike's world. He fell for her when they first met a while back, but life and careers had kept them apart. The last time they had seen each other, things hadn't ended well. They had both been frustrated and let their emotions get the better of them.

"Good to see you, too, Mike," Sarah said with a smile, although she was a little hesitant, too. The two locked eyes and everything else disappeared around them. Sarah was of medium height for a woman, about 5'6" and fit. Her long, curly brown hair was one of her most distinctive features. She was beautiful, not in a classic sense, but striking just the same. Mike felt the same instant attraction every time he ran into her. His chest felt tight and breathing was a little difficult.

"I had no idea you were on this project."

"Would it have made a difference?"

"No, probably not, but, I guess, but, wow. It's great to see you."

"Umm, who is your friend, Mike?" Andie asked, interrupting as she stepped forward between the two breaking the connection.

"Oh, umm, yeah, sorry guys. Sarah, this is Andie, Mac and Phil. They're working with me on a project. Guys, this is Sarah," Mike said beginning the introductions as they all shook hands.

"So, Sarah, what's your role on this little excursion?" Andie asked, bristling a bit at the female competition. She could tell Sarah affected Mike and she wasn't sure she liked it.

"I'm the second in command, if you will, of our research project. Dr. Ian Fallow is the principal investigator on our program, but he brought me on to handle the logistics. So, I'm in charge of making sure everything runs on time and that everyone gets where they need to be," Sarah replied. "Bringing in the four of you has thrown a few wrinkles into my plans, but nothing we can't handle. Dr. Fallow is happy to have you along, Mike. He said he knows of much of your work including a certain story that came out of the Keys you put together a couple years ago. He hopes you'll be able to direct your attention to what we're working on as well."

Mike noted that she didn't say SHE was happy to have him along. She obviously knew he was coming so had had a day or so to prepare for it. He was totally caught off-guard. It just so happened that the story from the Keys she mentioned, was where he had met her as well. They had seen each other several times since then, but careers and life had always gotten in the way of them making a relationship of it.

"That's very flattering, Sarah. Please tell Dr. Fallow I look forward to working with the two of you and I'm anxious to learn more about your research."

"We're all interested to hear about what you're working on in Cuba as well," she said, her question obvious. She was curious what he was working on that would get him added at the last minute to an ocean research vessel.

"Let's get our stuff and get loaded up, then," Mike replied, changing the subject. He wasn't sure how much he wanted to share of what was going on. He had no reason to suspect Sarah of anything, but at least until they left port, he wanted to keep things as quiet as possible. He knew his editor would have kept the story pretty simple and straightforward. He also knew she would have offered that Mike would be interested in learning about the research project the scientists were working on, so that all made sense.

Seeing Sarah for the first time in so long had him a little off-balance and he was still trying to recover. He was also suddenly struck by the dream he had, just a couple mornings before when Mac had called about finding debris from the Huron. Sarah was in that, too. Coincidence? Premonition?

"Andie, can you find us a cart to help carry our things?" Mac asked.

"Sure, dad," Andie replied and she walked away a little sulkily.

"So what are you driving, Sarah?" Mac asked, breaking through some of the building tension. "I guess you could say that you and I have similar tasks. You have to get your group where they are supposed to be and I get to shepherd these three along and get them where they need to be."

Mike simply smiled at his friend, realizing exactly what Mac was doing.

"It's right over there, Mac. We've got a big van. Should be more than enough space for your gear. When we get to the research ship, things will be a little tight, though."

"Oh, don't you worry about that. We're all used to spending time on boats. We'll make do right quick and get everyone settled. We'll stay out of your way as much as we can, too," Mac said, putting on his best awww-shucks routine and taking Sarah by the arm.

Mike stood still for a minute and watched Sarah walk away with Mac. He always liked to watch her walk. Then he shook his head and got back to business. Andie walked up pushing a cart and the three of them loaded their equipment and followed Mac and Sarah out the door.

"What's the story between the two of you?" Phil asked.

"I'm sorry, what's that?" Mike stumbled.

"Sorry if it's none of my business, but obviously you two have some sort of history. I was just curious."

"Oh. Was it that obvious?" Mike asked, blushing slightly.

"It was totally obvious," Andie joined in.

After a moment's pause, Mike replied "We met down in the Keys a couple years ago. I was vacationing and she stormed in with this story of a conspiracy. Turned out she was right. Ended up breaking up a smuggling ring that was doing some real environmental damage to reefs in the Keys. We were attracted to each other, but it never worked out. Travel and careers got in the way. We've run into each other a couple times since then, but it was never the right time."

"Ah, sorry. Didn't mean to bring up difficult memories," Phil replied.

"It's okay. It is what it is. My life is amazing and I wouldn't change a bit of it, but the travel makes it pretty hard to maintain a relationship. It can get a bit lonely at times," Mike answered, talking more to himself than Phil or Andie.

CHAPTER 14

"So, Mike, I really appreciate you bringing me along on this trip, I mean it's very cool to come with you guys and visit Cuba, but I'm not sure why I'm here. I could continue to work on the cipher at home and email you what I find," Phil said once they had gotten their gear stowed on board the research vessel. Mac and Andie had gone off to explore the ship and check out the dive locker, leaving Mike and Phil looking over the railing of the ship at the ship's berth outside of the Florida Keys Community College in Key West.

"As I see it, the problem is we don't have a clue what the key word is for the cipher. You said it could be anything. Yes, you could sit back in your office and pour over records and do research, but you might not come up with anything. I'm just playing a hunch here, but I feel it in my gut that the answer is in Cuba. Somehow the Huron's original mission and Cuba are all connected, I just know it is. Mac, Andie and I are really close to this story. We've sat up many nights drinking beer and trying to solve the riddle of exactly what the Huron was up to. I'm hoping that having you here as we dig into this, you'll see that one clue the rest of us miss," Mike explained. "And then, we don't have to worry about delays or hesitating to suggest a clue to you that might unlock the cipher. You'll be here so we can just tell you. You can test it out and tell us to keep searching or that you solved it. Remember, we're trying to solve the mystery and find out what the Huron was up to, but we're also trying to find some clue to who kidnapped Dr. DeSutton. We don't have time to waste."

"I'm glad you don't have any unreasonable expectations of me or anything," Phil said with a laugh. "I'm an office nerd, you know. I'm a cryptanalyst. Not exactly cut out to be James Bond."

"If it makes you feel any better, I've met several spooks over the years when I was covering war zones and sticking my nose in places that it didn't really belong. Most of them aren't James Bond either. Just like you, they thrive on gathering information and staying out of the way. You do that and you'll do just fine," Mike said patting the younger man on the shoulder.

"Do just fine at what?" Andie asked, as she and her father walked up.

"Oh come on, Andie. You know. I told Phil here that if he played his cards right, he would get a date with you," Mike said teasing her. Mike expected a mouthy retort, but what he got was a surprise when he saw Andie blush, then turn and walk away.

Mike turned and gave Mac a look as if to ask, "What did I do?" but Mac simply shrugged his shoulder and moved on.

"Dive locker on this tub looks first rate, Mike. They'll be able to supply us with any special diving gases we want and they have plenty of tanks on board. The diving safety officer said they really weren't planning to do much diving, although it was a contingency. They're planning to carry out most of their surveys using cameras mounted on ROVs and conducting water sampling," Mac explained. "Looks like we'll pretty much have the run of the place."

The US Research Vessel Espial was a gleaming white example of naval engineering and science combined. She was 224 feet long and 45 feet wide.

She featured a crew of 17 with room for 22 more scientists. The ship's laboratory space is what made it special, though. She had more than 700 square feet of lab space, both wet and dry, and could carry towed sonar arrays as well as remotely operated vehicles, ROVs, for deep ocean work. Even her name suggested research. Espial means "to spy" or in this case "to watch and observe" in old English. The ship was privately owned, but it rented out research space to smaller organizations and companies that needed to be at sea, but couldn't afford to pay for an entire ship and crew.

"That's cool except for one thing. If they're doing all of their surveying while underway, it will be harder for us to jump in the water or go exploring on the island when we get close to where we want to be," Mike realized.

"It's amazing how all this is working out, actually. They plan to use the Isle of Pines as their base of operations. They'll shelter in a natural cove there and do all of their surveys from that base. We'll be able to get off the boat and dive or explore the island whenever we want for as long as we want," Mac explained. "The Espial has several run-a-bout boats. We'll be able to use one of them and go do whatever we need to do."

"Mac, you weren't gone that long. How did you find all this out?" Mike asked laughing at his friend's natural ability to talk to anyone.

"Just so happens the Diving Safety Officer is a North Carolina boy. I recognized his accent. We started talking about barbecue and he was suddenly my best friend," Mac said with a laugh. "He'll give us anything we want. Doesn't hurt that he's young and I had Andie with me, of course."

"Well, no, that never hurts," Mike agreed laughing. "I don't know that we'll be doing that much diving. We'll probably use that more as our cover than anything else. If there was something hidden on the island in 1877, they wouldn't have been able to hide it underwater."

"I know. No worries, but I wanted to check it out just in case. And it makes sense if we're going to be on an ocean research ship, we would be interested in diving," Mac agreed. "The other thing I heard, more rumor than anything else, was that Dr. Fallow was on the outs with his university."

"Hmmm, that is interesting. I would have thought the head researcher on a ship like this, even if it is privately-owned, would have some university connection," Mike said, puzzled. "I guess it doesn't matter a lot in our world, though. His research is not that important to me."

"Agreed," Mac said.

"So, we're going to have pretty much unlimited access to the island? That's a pretty amazing coincidence that this ship was leaving and planning to visit exactly where we needed to go," Phil said after listening to the conversation.

"I wish you hadn't said that."

"What?"

"Coincidence. I don't believe in them," Mike explained. "I knew this was all working out to be too easy, but I was doing my best to ignore it. But now you brought it up, so I can't conveniently ignore it anymore. Let's just continue believing everything is falling into place for a reason. But keep your eyes open and let me know if you see anything that looks suspicious."

"Fair enough, Mike. Hey, let me grab Andie and let's go get some dinner in town tonight. I think your lady friend, Sarah, said we were going to leave in the morning, right?" Mac asked.

"That's what she said, Mac, but I think we're too late. Looks like they're making ready to get underway tonight. They just pulled in the gangplank and I can feel the diesels running," Mike replied. "Look over there. Those men are hauling in the starboard lines. Yep, we're free."

"Odd. Must have decided since we were here there was no point in waiting any longer, but still strange for them to change their plans so suddenly," Mac said, shaking his head.

"Does that count as suspicious?" Phil asked.

CHAPTER 15

Mike and the team hung around on the upper deck for a while watching the crew do their job getting the Espial underway and enjoying the warm ocean breezes as they headed out of Key West and turned west toward Ft. Jefferson. They didn't have any role to play on the actual operation of the research ship so they decided it was best to stay out of the way.

As things settled down, they realized they hadn't ever gotten around to eating dinner. They agreed to head back to their cabin and then find the galley. They were given a single cabin with two sets of bunk beds. Sarah apologized to Andie for having to share a room with the three men, but she laughed it off. She assured Sarah that their stateroom had more space than their dive boat at home. She had spent many nights on board with the crew as they looked for ship wrecks.

As they made their way through the ship, the few crew members they passed did their best to ignore them. They even caught a few glares as walked toward the galley.

"I know we're not here to make friends, but has anyone else noticed the looks we're getting?" Andie asked her dad and Mike. "I've smiled at a couple of the guys and they aren't smiling back at all."

"And that is definitely out of the ordinary for you, isn't it?" Mike said, teasing the young blonde. "I mean, they are sailors after all."

"Mike, I'm serious. The crew is not happy to have us on board at all," Andie said, uncharacteristically concerned.

"Hmmm. Not sure why they would treat us any differently than the other scientists. I mean the crew is always going to look at the researchers a little funny, but they're used to having groups on board. It is a research vessel," Mike said, as he thought back on the men and women they had passed in the passageways. He realized Andie was right, no one greeted them or even acknowledged them. "Let's get to the galley and see how people act. I'll ask Sarah if there is something going on we don't know about."

They entered the galley to find it about half full as the ship's researchers and crew not involved in taking the Espial out were getting dinner as well. The room was comfortable, if utilitarian. Tables lined the walls with bench seats on either side. The tables had rims on them to keep plates and glasses from sliding off. The kitchen crew served the food commissary-style from a series of hot trays on the left side of the rectangle room. The food was simple, but good.

Still, no one spoke to them. Not even the cooks. When they entered the room, the conversation dropped off. Mike, Mac, Andie and Phil realized every eye in the room was watching them. After they got their food, the foursome found an empty table and settled down to eat.

"This is a pretty good burger," Mac said as he took a bite of the sandwich on his tray, but I'm a little surprised that the food isn't a little more elaborate than this. Ships like this usually put out a pretty good spread."

"You're right, Mac," Sarah said as she approached their table. "The food is really good here. The chef is a real chef. He makes some incredible meals, to be honest. This is just what they were able to pull together at the last minute. They did the best with no warning that they were even going to be cooking tonight. Usually everyone goes out for one last meal in town before beginning a voyage." She said the last with a sneer in her voice.

"What changed the plans?" Mike asked. "Why did ya'll decide to take off early?"

"Are you kidding me?" Sarah asked as she turned to face Mike, frustration apparent in her face.

"Not at all," he replied a little taken aback. "Did we miss an announcement or something? You said we weren't leaving until the morning. We were about to go ashore and get some dinner ourselves."

"You're serious, aren't you?" Sarah replied, calmer, but with a look of confusion on her face.

"Yes."

"We got the order through the company that you all insisted we leave immediately. We didn't even have time to put everything away. The order said as soon as you were on board that we had to get underway. We're actually going to meet a fast boat at Fort Jefferson. They're running out a last-minute piece of equipment and a new crew member."

"Sarah, I don't know who gave that order, but we certainly didn't. We're guests here. We aren't making any demands on anyone," Mike said, raising his voice a bit hoping some of the others in the room would hear. "We were just as surprised as you when the ship pulled away from the dock."

"If you didn't insist on us leaving early, who did? I thought it was the famous Mike Scott sense of priorities," she said, her eyes narrowing at him one last time. Their shared history gave her more ammunition in an argument and also made her a bit more sensitive to some situations.

"I had nothing to do with this," Mike said, ignoring the jab. On a couple different occasions they had argued about his chasing off on a story just when things were getting good between them. "We need to get to work but we're not on any special time table, I promise."

"I don't like this at all. I'm going to have to find out what's going on," Sarah said. "If I'm supposed to be in charge of the logistics of this trip, it's not starting out well."

"Sorry, Sarah, but really we didn't ask to leave early," Mike said, opening his hands in a gesture of innocence. "We were looking forward to dinner on Duval Street as much as you guys were."

"All right, Mike, I believe you. Sorry. I'll talk to you all later. I'm going to have to try and find out what's going on," she said as she turned to leave. "If you do decide to change our plans," she said with a heavy emphasis on the word DO, "please let me know first."

"That explains the warm and friendly reception we've been getting," Phil said as he watched Sarah walk away.

"You got that right," Mac agreed as he looked at Mike. "Everyone thought we changed their plans and upset everything. Any clue what's going on here? Could your editor have said something when she made the arrangements to join the group?"

"It's possible, but I doubt it. She knows better than to do something like that. It would raise suspicions about us. She's spent way too much time in the field herself to do something that would alienate the entire crew without a really good reason. I'm going to call and check into it, though."

"Does this qualify as one more thing that seems suspicious?" Phil asked.

"Unfortunately it does, Phil. Unfortunately it does."

"I think we need to keep on our toes and watch our backs," Mac said. "I'm with Mike. I don't like it when things are too easy or when things don't seem right."

"I hate to sound paranoid, but I'm glad we're all sleeping in the same room," Phil said, scanning the faces in the room around them.

CHAPTER 16

The morning dawned directly behind the research vessel as it made its way toward the Dry Tortugas before turning southwest to cross the strait between Florida and Cuba. From there they would head around the western tip of the still-communist island and then head east toward Isla de la Juventud — what was once known as Treasure Island. Even in the calm of the morning, the air was steamy and thick. Among the group, they agreed to call it Isle of Pines, rather than struggle with the Spanish pronunciation.

"What's that over there, Mike?" Phil asked as approached the handrail outside their stateroom. Mike had been up for a while watching the sea.

"Those are the Dry Tortugas. We're about 90 miles or so from Key West. Judging from the time, we're making about 10 knots which isn't bad for a ship this size," Mike said. "The structure you see out there is Fort Jefferson. That was where the Huron was headed before it went on to Cuba. It seems like we're following pretty closely the path they were supposed to take."

Fort Jefferson is the largest masonry structure in the Western Hemisphere, built with 16 million bricks — mostly by slave labor. Construction on the fort began in 1846 but it was never finished. The civil war, and the changes in weapon technology that came with it, rendered the fort obsolete. The hexagonal structure was built in three tiers with gun rooms built directly into the walls to allow cannon fire in any direction while keeping the gunners safe.

"Should we go look at the fort and see if there are any clues there?" Phil asked.

"That's the strange thing. The army abandoned the fort about three years before the Huron sank in 1877. After the Civil War, it was being used as a federal prison, not a military installation at all," Mike explained. "Whatever, or whoever, was there to meet the Huron wasn't part of the official fort. I'm sure there's nothing left to see. It's been a national park since 1935."

"Okay, that makes sense."

"Morning gentlemen," Mac said as he and Andie walked up. "Any clue why we're heading west instead of making our way south toward Cuba?"

"Good morning guys. No official word, but I can make a guess," Mike replied.

"Give it your best shot."

"Two reasons: Remember Sarah said yesterday we were meeting a fast boat to bring on some piece of equipment and a last minute crew member. But I'd also say the captain is delaying entering Cuban waters until he absolutely has to. We'll probably head south soon to come around the western tip of the island, but I'm betting our early departure has run afoul of the Cuban government. We can't enter their territorial waters without their permission. I don't care if this is a research vessel or not," Mike explained.

"That makes sense," Mac agreed.

"Isn't there a US Army base on Cuba somewhere?" Andie asked.

"Guantanamo Bay is on the far end of the island. We're going around the western end, but it is on the eastern end. We'll be several hundred miles from the base," Mike answered her.

"I probably shouldn't ask this, Mike, but why do you know so much about Cuba?"

"I've actually been down here a couple times in my official capacity working on stories," Mike said. "It's an interesting, intriguing place."

"Any idea how long it will take us to get to the Isle of Pines?" Phil asked.

"As I said earlier, looks like we're making around 10 knots, that's about 11.5 miles per hour. From the maps I looked at online, and judging by the route we're taking, it's about a 500 mile run all together," Mike said. "Probably another 40 hours or so before we get to where we're headed. That's after we get back underway from this little transfer. My guess is it will happen pretty quickly, though."

"And that's if we don't have to stand off shore while the politicians and diplomats work out our permission to come within 12 miles," Mac added.

"I'm just afraid this is taking too long. How are we helping Dr. DeSutton sitting out here in the Caribbean?" Andie asked.

"Not much we can do at the moment," Mike agreed. "I'm worried about him too, Andie, but the police are investigating. I'm still sure this will pay off and help out in the end. We'll just have to be patient."

"Let's take a walk down to the stern. I want to get a look at some of the equipment this ship is sporting and then we can get some breakfast," Mac said. "Come on people, we committed to this course of action. Twelve hours later is not the time to start second guessing ourselves."

"You're right, dad. Lead the way," Andie said.

The foursome headed down a set of external stairs from the deck where their cabin was located to the Espial's main deck. They had just reached the work area where the ship's winches were stored as a smaller, faster boat pulled alongside. Crewmen were readying a winch to lift some crated equipment on board the larger research vessel.

One man from the small boat mounted a ladder that was lowered over the side of the Espial and made his way aboard with a medium-sized sea bag while the other two men on the boat attached the winch hook to a set of straps that would hold the box in place while it was lifted aboard.

Everything was going as expected; right up until all hell broke loose. In the blink of an eye, the box slipped in its rigging just as the winch operator swung the crate over the deck of the Espial. The momentum of the swing and the shifting rigging was all it took for the box to slip and break free. Mike saw what was about to happen. He didn't have time to shout or think; he simply launched himself toward two crewmen who were standing in the way of the falling crate. He hit them both with a flying tackle, knocking them clear of the crash site. The box hit the steel deck and shattered sending pieces of the broken crate flying.

"Is everyone okay? Are you guys okay?" Mike shouted, his body surging with adrenaline.

"Yeah, I'm fine," the first crewman said.

"I think I'm okay, the box didn't hit me, but I can't feel my leg," the second one said, strangely quiet.

Mike rolled over and began to stand up from the deck. He saw what was wrong immediately. A large shard of broken crate was sticking out of the back of the second crewman's thigh. He was bleeding heavily.

"Hold on, man, lay still," Mike said as he rushed to stop the bleeding. "Is there a medic on board, or a medical kit? We need it here, now!"

Mike was trained as a combat medic, something he took pride in from his time in war zones. On more than one occasion he had given aid to injured soldiers when he was embedded with companies of soldiers and marines.

"Oh man, look at that!" another crewman said. "Pull that thing out of his leg. That's got to hurt."

"I want you to lay still and relax," Mike said in his calmest voice. "You've got something sticking out of the back of your leg. We're going to stop the bleeding, but the last thing we're going to do is to pull it out. Okay? You with me?"

The injured crewman started to swoon from the blood loss as the medical kit arrived. Mike gloved up and began applying pressure to the wound. He was shoving the man's muscles and skin toward the bone in his leg, squeezing the opening where the board had cut through blood vessels. The pressure was closing off the torn openings and allowing the body's own clotting mechanisms to take over.

"Don't we need to put a tourniquet on or something?" a bystander asked.

"I don't think so. I think we can handle this without one," Mike replied.

"You're right. We can control the bleeding without a tourniquet. They come with their own problems," a woman said as she knelt down beside Mike and began to don a set of gloves. "I'm Rae Lesley. I'm part of the research staff, but I'm also a MD and the ship's doctor."

"Oh great, I'm glad you're here, Dr. Lesley. Do you want to take over?" Mike asked, a little hopefully.

"Not at all. You're doing great. And call me Rae," she said. "There are too many people called Doctor on the ship already. Just keep that pressure up. The bleeding seems to be slowing down nicely. She opened the medical kit and took out an IV bag.

"Ned, I'm going to give you an IV to replace some of the fluids you've lost from the bleeding and I'll add in some medicine for the pain. I'll give you some antibiotics as well," she explained to the injured crewman as she drew clear liquid from a vial and injected it into the IV bag. "Someone please alert the captain and don't let that delivery boat leave. We'll need them to run Ned back to Key West. We might want to arrange for a helicopter pick up as well, but it will all depend on how quickly the Coast Guard can get out here."

Mike maintained the pressure on the man's wound as Rae cut away the man's work pants and dressed the wound. She kept Mike in place so she was free to maneuver and make arrangements for the man's care. They quickly decided to transfer him to the smaller boat and send him back to Key West. The Coast Guard would send a helicopter out to pick him up but it would be delayed for about an hour. It made more sense to meet the helicopter half way.

It seemed like everything happened in the blink of an eye, but it was two hours before the injured crewman was bandaged up and ready to leave the boat. Ned was transferred to a stretcher and lowered over the side to the delivery boat. They used winch straps from the Espial, not from the delivery boat this time. Crewmen not involved in caring for Ned were already investigating the accident to determine what had happened to make the crate fall.

Mike was stiff and tired from kneeling on the boat deck by the time he was able to stand up.

"Guys, let me go back to the stateroom and get cleaned up. Then let's get breakfast. I'm starving," Mike said to Mac and Andie.

"Good luck on getting breakfast. I think they stopped serving it a little while ago. It's almost lunch time," Andie said.

"That would explain why I'm so hungry," Mike replied with a smirk.

"It's pretty amazing what adrenaline does for the body. But it really sucks when it goes away, doesn't it?" Mac said.

"You got that right, pal."

"Where did Phil wander off to?" Mike asked, surveying his group. He was a little nervous not to see everyone together…probably a leftover from the adrenaline rush.

"As soon as things calmed down he said he was going to check out the ship's laboratory facilities," Mac explained. "There wasn't much to do here."

Phil turned up a few minutes later, after Mike had changed clothes and met them going to the galley to get some lunch.

"You guys won't believe the lab facilities here," the cryptanalyst said. "Pretty amazing stuff. I know a bunch of people who would kill to have a lab like that."

"Having a little lab envy?" Mac asked him with a smile.

"Most of it isn't my field, but it's still impressive. Some pretty serious computing horsepower on board, too. I've already spoken to them about tapping into it to crunch some numbers," Phil explained.

"You didn't tell them what for did you?" Mike asked, suddenly alarmed. It had never occurred to him that others on the boat might find it odd that he had brought along a cryptanalyst. Phil wasn't the typical researcher you would find on a ship doing ocean research. His presence might raise some eyebrows, especially going to Cuba.

"No, I didn't. I kept that pretty quiet. I just told them I was along to handle some database work for you. They seemed to buy it," Phil said, already understanding where Mike's mind had just gone.

"That's good. Thanks," Mike replied.

"Who did you say owns this ship? It's not a NOAA vessel is it?" Phil asked.

"No, it's not. They contract out to NOAA and some other groups, but it's privately owned."

When they entered the galley to get lunch, they discovered everything had changed for them. It began with a standing ovation. Mike, Mac, Andie

101

and Phil stood there dumbfounded and more than a little bit embarrassed.

"I guess you've been accepted," Sarah said to them when they finally sat down with their food. It had taken a while to actually get their food, as they had received thank yous, hearty handshakes and smiles all the way through.

"Well that was a big change," Mike said.

"They appreciate what you did for Ned, jumping in to help like that. Everyone on board is talking about how you saved his life and Rae told everyone you probably saved his leg, too," Sarah explained. She was smiling at Mike this time, in direct contrast to their confrontation the night before.

"Well, I don't know about that..." Mike began only to meet a raised hand in his face from Andie.

"I know what you're going to say, but don't. Don't be modest. I know you just did what you saw had to be done, but you did help save a man's life and got us accepted into the crew at the same time. I would call that a win-win!" Andie said with a laugh. "Now accept the thank yous like you know you're supposed to do."

"Ummm, thank you?" Mike said.

"See, that's much better," Andie replied, kissing Mike on the cheek and then pointedly looking at Sarah. Andie wanted to remind Sarah that she and Mike were close, too. It was Sarah's turn to be uncomfortable. They all stood still and quiet momentarily until Mac came to the rescue again.

"Sarah, Phil tells us you have a first rate lab on board. I would like to see it myself when we get a chance," he said.

"Any time you want, Mac. Anything we can do to help you out, just say the word," she replied. "What exactly is the nature of your research?"

"Oh, you know me," Mike interjected. "Always chasing off after some story. I don't know that we'll need a lot of your lab time."

"I do know how YOU are, Mike," she replied. The smile left her face for a minute. Unfortunately, more than once, she had been left behind when Mike had chased off on a story.

"What are you and Dr. Fallows working on?" Mac continued to avoid the tension that constantly seemed to be building between Mike and Sarah.

"Well, there are several different things going on. Our team is looking at fish populations in several different locations around the Caribbean. But there are actually a couple different research projects going on at the same time," Sarah explained. "Dr. Fallows is the lead investigator on board, but this is a privately-funded research ship. We both work for the parent company, but they lease out lab space to smaller organizations that are doing important research, but can't afford to charter their own boat. Or really wouldn't need to."

"So, that's how we joined you," Phil said, coming full circle.

"Exactly. We had enough room and were leaving about the time you needed to go," she answered.

"You don't really know everyone on board, then?" Phil continued.

"I've met many of them at one time or another, but no, I don't know everyone. Think of a trip like this as a scientific co-op. We share space and lab facilities, but each team has their own agenda and projects."

"Pretty amazing that all of these groups needed to head to Cuba as well," Phil commented.

"Actually, we weren't. That general area was on our list, but it wasn't our first stop. When your team decided to join us, we got the word from the corporate office that we were headed for Cuba. A couple of the research projects had to shift gears a bit to fit that into their schedule," Sarah said, standing. "All right. Duty calls. But thank you again for your help today. Let me know when you need to get into the lab and we will work it out."

Mike was quiet as he watched her walk away.

You thinking about what might have been, Mike?" Andie asked.

"Not at all," he said when he turned back to face his team. "I was thinking that there is definitely something else going on here and I don't like it."

"What do you mean?"

"Someone pulled strings for us to get on this boat, and then for it to go exactly where we wanted and even to have us leave earlier than expected," Mike said. "It feels like we've stepped into something much bigger than we knew. Add to that Dr. DeSutton's kidnapping and this is getting really messy."

"So this is some sort of set up?" Phil asked.

"I don't know what's going on. Someone wants us on board this boat and headed to Cuba," Mike said. "We just need to stay on our toes and watch our backs. I told you before, I don't believe in coincidences."

"Since we're being paranoid, what if the accident this morning wasn't an accident at all? What if you were the target of that crate?" Andie asked.

They all turned and looked at the people around them. Some were quietly eating, others talking animatedly to their friends. No one seemed to be paying special attention to them.

CHAPTER 17

"When're they gonna get here, Jonas?"

"They was supposed to be here two days ago, Clem," Jonas answered him with a sigh. "I told you that already."

"I know ya did, Jonas. But how long are we going to keep waiting on them?" Clem asked, whining. "We been on this rock for days. We're gonna run outta food. We didn't bring enough supplies to last too long."

"It's a good thing I brought along those fishing poles, isn't it?" Jonas asked.

The men were waiting on the USS Huron to arrive. They were under orders to wait in the Dry Tortugas for the ship to arrive and to give the captain a set of orders. What the two men didn't know yet was that the Huron had sunk two days before. It was November 26, 1877.

The men were holed up in the recently abandoned Fort Jefferson. The fort had been built but never served to defend the United States. More recently it had served as a prison, housing federal prisoners including the men involved in the assassination of President Abraham Lincoln. The pair had taken over an east facing watch tower built into the fort wall and were keeping watch toward Key West looking for the USS Huron to come into sight.

"Yeah, it's a good thing you wanted to bring them poles, Jonas," Clem agreed. "But how long are we gonna stay out here?"

"A few more days, at least," Jonas said. "We got to. Do you want to tell them that we weren't here when the ship came?"

"No, no you're right," Clem agreed. "I sure don't want to tell them that. Any idea what's in the box we brought out here?"

"No, Clem, I don't have any idea. I'm like you. Men with stars on their shoulders give me orders and I follow them. Same as you should be doing now," Jonas said, putting as much meaning into his words as he could. He needed Clem to help him keep watch, but he really didn't like the other man.

Jonas was a member of a group that collectively called itself the Consortium. They were a group of like-minded industrialists and military leaders interested in taking advantage of the unrest in Cuba. The Spanish were on the verge of losing the island to the rebels currently staging a revolution. The men of the Consortium wanted to influence the outcome of that revolution. They wanted to make sure things went their way.

Revolutionaries on the Spanish colonial island had contacted the government of the United States, still recovering from the Civil War, about interceding on their behalf. They wanted the US to take the island from the Spanish and to make it a state. The leaders in the US, though, had not been able to gain the support they needed in Congress to take that action. The members of the Consortium had used their influence to push the US into the middle of the conflict whether they wanted to be there or not.

Clem simply looked at Jonas blankly for a moment, taking a moment to process what the other man was telling him.

"You're right, Jonas. I think I'll go look for the ship. See if it's coming," Clem said. He picked up a fishing pole as he walked down toward the water. Jonas knew Clem was just trying to fight the boredom. They obviously had a better view from the watch tower, but Jonas was happy for the time alone.

As a member of the Consortium, he wasn't used to duty like this either. He was used to giving orders, not waiting endless hours. At the same time, he wasn't a member of the inner circle. He answered to men greater than himself. Still, he was pleased that the great men of the Consortium trusted him with this duty. The captain of the Huron didn't know what his orders included. They weren't sure how the career US Navy man would react when he learned them. But that was the point of giving them to him once he was already underway and well away from the Admiralty in Washington. They needed him to feel like he was on his own and couldn't turn around and ask for clarification. There was an element in Washington that was opposed to the Consortium's efforts. They were likely to do anything they could to stop moves to connect the US government with the revolutionaries.

Jonas was to pass off a simple set of instructions for the Huron's captain. He was to give him the code word that would allow him to decrypt the orders he already carried. But most importantly, Jonas was to decide if the captain would follow those orders. If he wasn't, he was to make sure the Huron was under the command of someone who would follow orders when it left the Dry Tortugas. And that meant him.

Jonas went back to scanning the flat, calm horizon with his binoculars. He needed the Huron to arrive. He wanted to get back to his life as much as Clem did. That was one thing they could agree on. Just then, Clem shouted "I see sails coming this way! There's a boat coming!"

"Finally," Jonas breathed as he turned his binoculars to scan the horizon in the direction Clem was pointing. He quickly found the approaching boat. From that distance, he could only make out the shape of a sailing ship.

Nothing more. They would have to wait.

Jonas waited in the shade for a little while, allowing the boat to get closer, but finally he got up to join Clem on the dock where they both knew the boat would approach. It took another hour for the boat to get there, but before it had docked both men knew it wasn't the Huron. They kept their thoughts to themselves about who it was.

The old sailing ship dropped anchor just off shore from the fort. After the crew got things squared away, they lowered a long boat and several men entered to row ashore. Clem and Jonas remained nervously quiet. Both knew they would find out what was going on soon enough. There was no point in guessing.

The long boat approached the small dock and three men came ashore; an officer and two soldiers. One man stayed with the long boat.

"Can we help you, sir?" Jonas asked. Clem and Jonas had set their uniforms aside while they waited and neither had thought to retrieve them while they waited. The three men were quiet until they reached the hard-packed dirt.

"You two were ordered to wait here for the USS Huron, is that correct?" the officer asked without preamble.

"Umm, yes sir," Jonas replied, confused. He knew their orders were secret and he didn't know who this man was. But he was caught off-guard by the man's directness.

"I've been sent to inform you that the USS Huron went down off the coast of North Carolina two days ago in a storm. The ship is a total loss."

"So, our man was successful then?" Clem asked.

"Yes sir, he was," the officer replied.

"Clem, what are you talking about?" Jonas turned to the man beside him. "Do you know this man? And what do you mean 'successful'? That is terrible news. We'll have to order another ship to Cuba immediately."

"No, Jonas. Your plot is over. There won't be another ship headed to Cuba. The revolutionaries are on their own," Clem answered, standing straighter and more authoritatively than Jonas had seen him.

"What? I don't understand. What are you talking about? We were here to pass along orders to the Huron. You don't know who I really am. I'm not some lackey," Jonas said, shouting. He was confused and suddenly angry, so he was saying things he normally would have kept to himself.

"You are wrong about that, Jonas. I know exactly who you are and exactly what your orders for the Huron were. We know all about your plot. I received my orders to come here and stop you in case the Huron made it through," Clem replied. "You've lost."

"Who are you?" Jonas asked quietly, the realization that Clem was not an uneducated solider coming slowly.

"It doesn't matter who I am or who these men are. All that matters is that your plot has been stopped," Clem answered and then he turned to the other three men. "Gentlemen, carry out the rest of your orders."

Jonas was too slow to see the two Army soldiers draw their Smith and Wesson American revolvers from their holsters. Without hesitation, they both fired, their guns roaring. The .44 caliber bullets struck Jonas hard in the head and chest. He was dead before he hit the ground.

"Should we bury him, sir?" the officer asked Clem.

"No, I don't want any evidence of this. Throw him into the water, the fish and the crabs will make short work of him," Clem replied. "Have your men get our supplies from the watch tower and burn everything. After that, we'll leave."

"Yes, sir. I will see to it immediately. We'll row back to the ship in just a few minutes."

The two soldiers picked up Jonas' body and carried to the water's edge.

"I need to report to our friends in Washington that all is done. The message never made it through," Clem replied. "Good work, Captain. Thank your men for me."

"Thank you, General."

Washington was awash with intrigue after the Civil War as winners and losers jockeyed for position in the post-war United States. While the Consortium that had created the plot to support the Cuban rebels included admirals, generals and politicians, so did an equally powerful group that was working to head off their schemes. They didn't want the United States to intercede in the Cuban revolution. Rather, they hoped the Cubans would lose. They planned to buy the island from the cash-strapped Spanish afterward.

CHAPTER 18

Once the excitement of the morning settled down, there really wasn't much for Mike and his team to do except study. They had approximately two more days at sea before they got to where they were heading. Mac and Andie spent time in the dive locker making sure their dive equipment was set up and well cared for, but that didn't take long as it was in perfect shape before they left, and the dive locker had everything they needed on board as well. They didn't expect to dive much, if at all, but it was a habit and a hard one to break.

Beyond that, Mac, Mike and Andie spent time looking over charts and satellite images of the island to find likely places where whatever they were looking for was hidden. Without knowing exactly what they were looking for, it was a lot of guesswork. They also went back over everything they knew about the Huron, its mission papers, the official inquiry into the wreck.

While they were all accustomed to research and understood the necessity of it, all three of them were more accustomed to "doing" things. They were getting a little edgy.

Phil, on the other hand, was totally in his element. He explained to them that the more he knew about the events of the day, the Huron and their destination, the more information he could enter into the cryptographic software that he hoped would decode the message they found in the wreck. He was constantly asking the other three questions and entering key words and phrases into his computer. He had also patched into the on-board mainframe computer to speed up his processing time.

"This boat really is amazing," Phil said to break the silence in the stateroom where the four of them had holed up, reading various files, charts and maps. Even he could feel the tension in the room.

"First, one note about terminology, Phil. Anything this big, that carries several small boats itself, is called a ship. Second, what's got you impressed?" Mac asked.

"Thanks for the clarification, Mac," Phil said with a laugh. "I'm just amazed we are so far out in the middle of the Caribbean Sea, and I still have internet access, along with some serious computing power backing me up."

"All the comforts of home?"

"Sums it up nicely!" Phil agreed.

"What are you working on, now?" Mike said as he stood to stretch his back.

"I was searching for information about the revolution going on in Cuba about the same time as the Huron was coming to visit. I've found digital copies of the journals kept by one of the revolutionary leaders. I searched for Isle of Pines and Google brought this up. Not how they are connected or how much it will help in the long run, but it's really helping me to understand what was happening on the island at the time," Phil explained.

"That's pretty cool," Mike agreed. "Maybe the author was on the island or something."

"I've been skimming through it so far, looking for anything that might be relevant. A lot of what he wrote about was the day-to-day operations of the revolution. He mentions greater plans from time to time, but nothing very specific so far," Phil said.

"Keep reading. That sort of background can really help us when we are looking for places to search on the island," Mac chimed in. "We're not coming up with much right now."

"How are we going to narrow this down, Dad?" Andie asked.

"I'm not sure, honey. I agree with Mike that the answer to our questions is probably on the island, but there won't be an X marking the spot or spot lights lighting up the sky," Mac said. "I know you're worried about your professor. I am, too. I don't like the idea that anyone could be kidnapped from my island."

"Listen to this," Phil said. "I might have found something. The leader's name is Rodolfo. He says he and some of his men are hiding out on the Isle of Pines. Let me read it to you."

"Men are restless. They want to get off this tiny island and back to the fighting. They complain that the Spanish army is marching on their homes, while they do nothing. I am trying to keep them calm. I can't tell them exactly what is coming, because I am not sure myself, but I tell them help is coming from America. I want the men to trust that help is coming, but I am beginning to wonder myself. I don't trust these foreigners. They tell me they are bringing money and weapons to help us throw the Spanish out of our land, but I wonder what will happen when the Spanish are gone. Will we have to fight these Americans for our land, too? Are we shaking off the yoke of one overlord simply to carry the weight of another? And this one is closer to our home. Will they try to enslave us like they did before the war they fought on their own land. I just don't know. Have my leaders made a deal with the devil? These are the questions that haunt me while I try to keep my spirits up in presence of the men. I must believe that we will win this war and we will overcome. I just hope they get here soon. They are late."

Rodolfo was a mulatto school teacher before the revolution. His father was Spanish and his mother an African slave. His Spanish blood helped him receive an education. His literacy brought him to the attention of the revolutionary commanders from the beginning. While Rodolfo loved his father, and in spite of the fact that he had personally benefitted from the Spanish rule, he often said he could no longer support the world that brought the Spanish to Cuba.

"The date on this entry is November 30, 1877," Phil said. "He has got to be talking about the Huron."

"Wow, Phil. That is amazing," Mike breathed. "I just know you're right."

"Phil, let me help you. I can go over that with you," Andie volunteered. "I think we need to read that journal word by word and see if there are any other mentions, before that one or after it, that might give us a clue. I've pretty much memorized the maps of the Isle of Pines so I will be able to compare that to anything that mentions where we should be searching."

"Sure, Andie. Let me go back to the beginning," Phil agreed.

"While you two work on that, I'm going to stretch my legs a bit and get some fresh air," Mike said. "I want to talk to the captain and the head researcher, Sarah's boss, to see what they are up to. I need to grease those wheels a bit since we're on their boat."

"Sounds like a plan to me, Mike," Mac agreed. "I'll come with you."

Mac and Mike stepped outside their cabin door and nearly ran into a crewman who was walking past. They stepped past each other and moved on.

"Huh," Mac said.

"Huh, what?"

"Just huh. I think that was the new guy that came on board. You know, during the accident," Mac said.

"I was a little busy at the time," Mike said with a shake of his head. "I didn't notice. But why is that worth a 'huh'?"

"Just that this section of the ship is made up of the staterooms occupied by the scientists and egg-heads on board. The crew is on the other side and to the back, except for the captain and bridge crew who are forward of here," Mac explained. "There aren't any operational stations on this deck and side."

"So, you're trying to figure out why he is walking this way?" Mike asked. "Man, I'm not even that paranoid. He probably just got lost. You said he just came on board."

"I'm sure you're right," Mac laughed. "It's not like we've known anyone who was kidnapped recently right from under our noses or anything. I can't imagine why I would be a little suspicious," rolling his eyes.

"All right, you got me on that one," Mike agreed, turning serious. "Keep an eye out and keep being paranoid. Now, let's go find the researcher and make nice."

Mac and Mike walked toward the bridge first. Their stateroom was on the same deck as the bridge so they decided to see if the head researcher, Dr. Fallow was there. The captain welcomed them aboard, and thanked Mike for his help with the accident on deck, and for helping to stabilize Ned, but said he hadn't seen Dr. Fallow recently. In fact, Captain Hank Nelson told them he hadn't seen the man all day. He added that he rarely saw the man in person. Usually, he simply got messages when Dr. Fallow needed something specific or if he had a change to their itinerary.

Thanking the captain, they headed down below toward the lab areas. Mac had already explored the area, but it was Mike's first time into that part of the ship. He was extremely impressed by the quality of the equipment and the spaciousness of the labs.

In the back of his head, though, he was preparing himself to run into Sarah again. He still wasn't sure how he felt about that. He knew they could have a professional relationship, but there was always a little bit of a "what if" in the back of his mind. They had met in the Florida Keys. Mike was on vacation and Sarah was there trying to stop men from harvesting conch. Mike ended up helping her out and they got to know each other. But their careers had taken them different directions immediately. They had tried a couple other times to get together and they had spent time together, but then the phone rang and one or the other of them ended up jetting off to somewhere — often both of them. The last time they had seen each other, it had ended badly. They were both frustrated with the situation and had said things neither of them really meant. There was an intense physical attraction between them, along with a great respect and friendship. They just couldn't make their professional lives agree with their personal desires.

Mike was so completely distracted as he remembered his time with Sarah that he didn't watch where he was going. He didn't even see the man in the hallway until he almost crashed into him. "Oh, excuse me," Mike said, as he danced around the man in the corridor.

"Please watch where you are going," the man said stiffly as he swerved in the other direction. A thin, pale man, with white-gray hair that seemed to blend into his white lab coat, it was a member of the science team carrying a tray of water samples to the lab.

"Sorry about that," Mike continued, trying to be friendly. "Have you seen Dr. Fallow? My friend and I are looking for him."

"Why do you want the director?"

"My name is Mike Scott and this is my friend Mac Williams. Can you tell us where we can find him please," Mike said in a far-less friendly tone.

Responding to both the information and the tone of voice, the man replied with a New England accent, "You have found him, Mr. Scott. I am Dr. Fallow. Follow me, please."

With a brusque turn, the researcher continued down the corridor, following the path he was on before Mike interrupted him.

"He said, please, but I don't get the feeling it was actually an invitation as much as a command do you?" Mike said with a smile.

"Me either. I get the feeling he's used to people doing what he tells them to do," Mac replied.

The pair followed Dr. Fallow, but they hung back a little, moving more slowly than then researcher in a slightly passive-aggressive way of telling the man they didn't work for him and didn't follow his orders. When they reached his office, Dr. Fallow was standing inside impatiently holding the door for the two men.

"It's nice to meet you, Dr. Fallow," Mike said as he walked in. "My editor tells me you're doing some interesting work. I look forward to learning more about it."

"I don't think I am ready to go public with what we are working on, yet," Fallow replied. "I don't think I can give you the story you are looking for. And frankly I'm not happy to have you on board."

"Oh, ummm, okay. I was led to believe you were actually pleased to have us along. Has something changed that I don't know about?" Mike was suddenly on his guard but he didn't want to throw Sarah under the bus. He left it open-ended who had told them that.

"No, nothing has changed. We're just not in the position to talk to the media about what we are doing yet. Everything will have to be peer-reviewed before I publish anything," Fallow said. "Your publication doesn't have the stature that I need to release my findings."

"Well, I'm sorry you feel that way, Dr. Fallow," Mike began as he pushed forward on his chair, his eyes narrowing. "You do of course realize your research is not our primary purpose for being here either. You might be on the verge of discovering a cure for cancer for all I know, but that isn't why I'm here. So, my main purpose for seeking you out at the moment was mainly out of courtesy. I would be happy to make myself available to you, as a favor for allowing us along on this voyage, but I'm not here at your beck and call. If you don't want to tell me about your research, that's fine with me. We'll stay out of your way for the rest of the cruise."

Mike stood and Mac followed him.

"Hold on, Mr. Scott," Fallow said to their backs. The two men paused at the office door and turned back around.

"I apologize for my abrupt nature," Fallow began. "I could have handled that more gracefully. I am under some pressure here to get some things done. I trust you will have a good and successful voyage. I am sure I will see you around."

"Have a good day, Dr. Fallow," Mike said with a nod.

Mike and Mac walked in silence for a few minutes as they worked their way back to the stern.

"Well, that was interesting," Mac said, breaking the silence.

"No kidding," Mike said, with a quick laugh, releasing the tension in his shoulders.

"I've never seen you talk to anyone like that before," Mac said. "Even when Dr. DeSutton was condescending to us back at the aquarium, you handled it a lot more gracefully than that."

"I can't tell you the last time I had to," Mike replied. "Even on assignments where people aren't happy to have me around, they aren't usually rude. Even when they are, I would much rather convince them to tolerate me."

"But the Mike Scott charm wasn't going to work on this one?"

"I didn't think so. It's funny, now that you mention it, DeSutton did get kind of strange right after we found the tube in the chest and opened it up to find the hidden message," Mike said, stopping to think. "He went from being friendly, if a bit pompous, to rude and demanding. Actually, he acted a lot like Fallow just did."

"I wondered if I was the only one who noticed that," Mac replied.

"I guess I had put it aside with the excitement of the moment," Mike said. "Now that you bring it up, though, you're right."

"Something is going on, here, Mac," Mike said. "I don't have a clue what it is, but there is more than meets the eye with this ship, our quick exit from Key West, Dr. Fallow and the research. I'm even beginning to think it's not a coincidence that Sarah is on board. I just don't know what it is yet."

"Remember what I was saying about being paranoid just a little bit ago," Mac asked.

"Yeah?"

"Welcome to my world," Mac replied.

"Let's go find the other two and see if they have found anything that will be useful."

As they walked down the hallway toward the deck where their stateroom was located, they passed the crewman they had seen near their room earlier that day. They looked at each other and began walking faster.

CHAPTER 19

The supply train was ambling along, rolling over the ruts and stones, each driver trying not to break an axle, since it would make that wagon and even the whole supply train a sitting target for the rebels.

Their relatively gentle handling of their cargo didn't change the path ahead, though or what would happen next, The rebels were lying in wait They knew the supply train would come this way, they just had to be patient. Knowing when to spring the trap was the important part. They needed to make sure the wagons couldn't turn and run easily or mount a defense so they always look for narrow spots in the road with good cover for the attack. Years of successfully supplying themselves by attacking the supply trains had ensured that they each knew their roles.

Four men were hiding under the bridge. Two more were up in the trees, ready to rain fire down from above. The rest of the men were hiding in the fields along the road, huddled down underneath straw, and in the tree line, twenty yards away. They had arrived just before dawn to take up their positions. A few small wagons had come through, but the men had held their positions. They wanted the big Spanish supply train. The men of the revolution needed to supply themselves to keep fighting and they knew the

Spanish couldn't continue their own push if they didn't have the food and ammunition.

The first wagon came into view around a small bend in the road, followed by four more. This was it. This was the first shipment of supplies for the Spanish men waging war against the people of Cuba.

Rodolfo knew the Spanish would be prepared for an ambush. There would be security. He and his men had been successful too many times before for this to be easy. He wasn't surprised, when he realized the carts were all being driven by Cuban men. He could just see a Spanish solider inside the covered wagon aiming a gun at the prisoner driving the wagon. Rodolfo knew his men would be reluctant to fire on their countrymen.

Making a quick decision, he stood up and stepped quickly out into the middle of the bridge before the first wagon began to cross. The first driver pulled his horses to a halt and called out for the wagon drivers behind him to do the same. As the wagons slowed to a halt, they all sat silent for a moment.

"My friends, thank you for bringing these wagons to us. We appreciate your support of the revolution," Rodolfo called out to the man 20 feet away. At first there was no response to Rodolfo's call and he began to repeat himself when the man inside the wagon moved forward to where he could reply.

"You are under arrest for treason against his majesty King Alfonso. I order you to stand aside from the road and tell your men to throw down their arms," the Spanish officer replied.

"I am but a poor, lone man here in the road," Rodolfo said with a laugh. "Do you see men with me? Have you been drinking? It's not like my men are surrounding you and are ready to cut you down without hesitation."

"Maybe I will simply kill you, then!" the Spanish officer roared back.

"I don't think that would be a good move on your part. Then you would be a murderer. I know God would not forgive you for that. You would certainly go to Hell for that," Rodolfo replied. He was simply delaying the inevitable when the Spanish officer decided to act, but he knew his own men were circling around through the trees. The Spanish had begun loading troops into the first wagon to be prepared to respond to any problems. His men had already taken the three wagons in the back without firing a shot. There was just one soldier on each and one Cuban driver. Normally, the snipers in the trees would take out the drivers and his men would concentrate their fire on the first wagon. But Rodolfo was tired of seeing good Cuban men die.

"God doesn't care about you," the Spanish officer replied. "I would be doing him a favor."

"Do you speak for him now? I guess I should stand aside then," Rodolfo said as he quickly jumped off the road.

His own men had moved into position. They opened fire into the first wagon. The snipers from the trees concentrated their fire at the officer in the front. Two of the men hiding below the bridge charged forward and grabbed the Cuban driver where he had leapt from the wagon.

The Spanish soldiers in the wagon were killed without firing a return shot. The skirmish was over before any of them knew what happened.

"I guess he can discuss things with his God in person, now," Rodolfo said as he climbed back onto the road to face the carnage. "Let's get this cleaned up and get away from here as quickly as we can. The sound of the gunfire might have attracted more soldiers. Take their bodies into the field and cover them with cane straw. Search them for papers or anything important and keep their guns as well. We will use it all in the fight to free ourselves from their king."

In just a few minutes, the raiders had removed the Spanish dead. They quickly interrogated the Cuban drivers and found men they knew in common. They were confident the four men were prisoners and not working for the Spanish of their own free will. Half of Rodolfo's men jumped into the wagons and moved them out; the rest returned to their horses hidden among the trees. They shadowed the wagons just off the road to provide support in case they ran into trouble. They weren't always so lucky, but this time they made it to their camp without a problem. The men in the camp unloaded the supplies and stored them away.

Approaching the revolution's field headquarters, Rodolfo began to relax. The revolutionary army had built a fort based on what some of their officers had seen in America. More than one revolutionary officer had served in the American armed forces during the civil war and had chosen to support the revolution in Cuba as a way to continue fighting and using the skills they had developed on the American frontier. The Cubans had fought against their occupiers for nearly 10 years at this point and had developed a hierarchy and a military structure. They had public officials and a revolutionary government that imposed law in the towns and villages they had occupied.

Just after they came through the gates at the revolutionary fort, Rodolfo received a summons from the revolution leaders. He was never sure if that was a good thing or a bad thing, but considering his recent successes, he felt confident things would go well.

"Let our friend pass," Commander Maceo called out to the guard as Rodolfo approached the command tent. "He is just back from another successful excursion."

"Congratulations, Rodolfo!" Commander Maceo said as Rodolfo ducked to enter the tent. "Without you and your raiders, we would have lost this war a long time ago."

"Thank you, Commander. I do my best to serve," Rodolfo replied. "Are things that bad, sir?"

"Yes. Yes, they are, my friend. Sit down. Be at ease," Maceo said gesturing toward a chair. "I have an assignment for you, but I don't think you will like it. That's why I have asked you to come and talk to me. If you are successful, it will turn the tide of the war and I believe we will win. If you are unsuccessful, in spite of all of our other plans and efforts, there is no way we can win."

"I am sorry to hear things are so dire. I had no idea," Rodolfo answered, steeling himself for what he thought was the inevitable. "I will accept any challenge you ask of me. Just tell me what I am to do. If it means my death and that of my men, we will gladly answer the call if it means success for our cause."

"I know you will, Rodolfo. I know you will," Commander Maceo said. "Fortunately, I don't have to ask you to lay down your life this time."

"I don't understand, sir."

"I need you to go away."

"Away sir? Haven't I served you and the revolution well?" Rodolfo asked, hurt.

"You have served extremely well. That is why you must handle this assignment. You and your raiders are expert at staying hidden while carrying out your duties. You slip through enemy lines and wreak havoc and then slip back without being detected. Didn't I just hear that you killed more than a dozen men and brought back four supply wagons without a single casualty?"

"That is all true, sir, but…"

"But I need men who are so used to working together that it is second nature. Men who can follow orders without them being given. I need your men to do something."

"Yes sir. We will follow any order."

"I need you to go to the Isle of Pines, here," Maceo said, pointing to a location on the map of Cuba and the smaller island to the south. "An American warship is coming to meet you. It will bring support for the revolution. Without it, we cannot survive. With it, I am sure we can win this fight. To get there, though, you will need to cross Spanish lines. And you will need to bring back their support."

"What are they bringing?"

"I am not sure exactly. It may be guns, ammunition," Maceo replied. "It may be gold to buy supplies. I don't know what is coming. But that support will make the difference. I am sure of it."

"We will go then," Rodolfo replied. "You can count on my men to get the job done."

"I knew I could, my friend," Maceo said. "Go with God and good luck to you. Remember one thing; your good name will be the key to us winning the war."

Looking back now on that conversation that happened two weeks before, Rodolfo was still struggling. It had been a difficult journey crossing the island and making their way in small boats to the Isle of Pines. They had remained hidden and safe. They had avoided opportunities to engage the enemy, even though they wanted to, because Rodolfo knew it would put their mission in danger. But now, the waiting was the problem. This must have been the part Commander Maceo knew he wouldn't like. His men, too, were frustrated. They wanted action, not to be delivery men. Rodolfo had no one to turn to so that he could voice his own frustrations. He simply wrote them in his journal and then set them aside. What he really wanted was for the Spanish to go away so he could return to his school house. He loved to read and write and loved to teach others to do the same. While he had been successful as a leader of his raiders, in his heart he was a man of peace.

Rodolfo put his journal away. That journal, a few pieces of clothing and the weapons he carried were the last few things he owned. They were all stashed in a small trunk under his bed. He was frustrated that whatever help was coming wasn't there yet.

One war ship could not stop the entire Spanish Navy that was blockading Havana harbor, so he didn't know whether to be excited or resigned to his fate. After nearly 10 years the revolution was stalled. His men had fought their best, but without help from the outside, they just could not overcome the Spanish forces. The better trained and equipped men of the Spanish army were too much to handle — at least when they attempted to meet them gun for gun on a battlefield.

"Good morning, captain," one of Rodolfo's men said as soon as the leader stepped outside of his tent.

"Miguel, you know I hold no such rank," Rodolfo replied with a smile. His men would follow him through hell and back. They had decided among themselves to give Rodolfo the title even if the revolutionary commanders had not.

"Si, captain, but that does not matter to the men. You are our captain!"

"Thank you, Miguel. Any news from the night?" Rodolfo asked. He knew his men would have woken him up had something happened, but he still asked the question every day.

"No sir," the man said. "I am sorry, but I have nothing to report. No orders from the scouts and no sign of the American ship."

"Thank you, Miguel," Rodolfo said with a fatherly tone. "You're a good man and I am pleased to have you by my side. Please have the squad leaders come to my tent after breakfast. We must decide how much longer we will stay on this tiny spit of land. I feel we need to be back to the battle."

"Yes sir! I will pass the word and have everyone here soon," Miguel saluted and ran off from his post near Rodolfo's tent.

Rodolfo had stationed his men on the southern side of the Isle of Pines, itself on the southern side of his beloved Cuba. He felt like he and his men had run away from the fight. They found a bluff on the island with a good view of the sea all around to keep watch. They had their orders. They would stay under cover and watch for an American warship to sail by, close to the island. They would light a signal fire and wait. If the ship responded by coming closer, dropping anchor and sending a long boat ashore, they were to meet it and accept whatever support they would receive. That was all Rodolfo knew. The support could mean anything. He hoped he would lead a force of men and cannon back to Cuba, but he doubted it. Still, any support was better than nothing.

While he didn't know the greater strategy as put forward by the revolutionary leaders, he did know that the longer they drew this fight out, the better off things would be. He had heard that the Spaniards themselves were facing a revolution at home, partly because of the fight in Cuba. The longer they had to maintain a fight half a world away, the harder it would be for King Alfonso XII of Spain to maintain his new monarchy.

CHAPTER 20

Las Ramblas was one of the proudest, most vibrant streets in Barcelona, Spain. Or, rather, it was a string of five pedestrian walkways placed end to end, filled with musicians, merchants and street performers, ending at the harbor where Cristobal Columba (Christopher Columbus) left in search of the new world, gold and glory for his king nearly 400 years before. The street itself was dotted with tapas restaurants where Catalans met for coffee and bite-sized tastes of local fare.

It was also home to the Carlist movement in Spain. The Carlists believed the wrong person was made the monarch in Spain with the death of King Ferdinand VII in 1833. Until 1830 Salic law was the law of the land in Catholic Spain, dictating that the heir to the throne had to be male. When the king found himself sick and feared that he would die without an heir, he decreed that the child of his pregnant wife would be his heir, regardless of whether it was a boy or a girl. Isabella was born later that year. When Ferdinand died in 1833, she became Queen. The king's decree had placed his child ahead of his younger brother, Carlos, in line for the throne. The Carlists felt this change in succession was illegal and went to war in support of their king. They also questioned whether the power of the king came from God or from man.

It was ironic that Barcelona, and its harbor, were the jumping off point for Columbus since the Carlists believed that undermining one of the Spanish colonies in the New World was the key to undermining the reigning Bourbon monarchy and bringing the true king to the throne.

So it was not unusual that the four men knew each other socially and professionally in the port city. But it was unusual that when they met to discuss the revolution, they used other names, each one representing a region of Spain, because during a civil war they could never know who was listening. As was his practice, Senor Andalus was the first to arrive at the table in the dark tapas restaurant. He liked to be there first to watch the others come in to make sure they weren't followed or compromised. Senor Catalan was next. He tended to be the most explosive of the four; given to outbursts — something Senor Andalus tried to reign in. The last thing the foursome wanted was to attract attention. Srs. Castile and Aragon were the last two to arrive at the small table. The men were seated so closely together their knees nearly touched, but none of them said a word until after the server poured their coffee and left.

Senor Andalus was first to break the silence.

"Do we know anything of the efforts in Cuba?" he asked without preamble.

"Everything we put in place has been made ready," Aragon answered. "We are just waiting on the Americans to do their part."

"Why are we putting so much faith in those upstarts again? The country is only 100 years old," Catalan growled, his temper already showing.

"Senor Catalan, we've been over this before," Andalus replied quietly. "We can't be seen to be directly involved with the rebellion there. If we were, the king would charge us with treason and have every reason to initiate an inquisition much harsher than anything this country has ever seen before. We would be hunted down and destroyed. It would take away any of the credibility we have with our supporters. They would give us up in mere moments."

"I understand, but I still don't like it. I don't trust them," Catalan replied.

"Who is it that you do not trust?" Senor Castile asked. "Is it the Americans or our brothers the Cuba revolutionaries fighting Spanish soldiers?"

"I don't trust either of them, to be frank," Catalan replied. "Tell me again what is to happen now."

"As you know, Senor Catalan, we have placed a store of gold on the Isle of Pines, just south of Cuba that was gained from the plunder of pro-monarchist homes and leaders. But we couldn't just give it to the revolutionaries. We need the Americans to be involved. We need their support and their willingness to provide arms for the fighters. We can supply money for their cause from here, but we can't give them the arms and supplies they need or else we would be found out," Senor Andalus said. "So, we hid the gold and supplies, the treasure if you will, on the island. A separate emissary went to a faction within the US that will make contact with the revolutionaries and will tell them where they can find the gifts."

"I don't understand why we have to make some Americans rich and give them Cuba," Catalan argued. "We are undermining the greatness of Spain as we fight to protect it."

"Remember, we have to make sacrifices if we are to bring socialism to Spain," Senor Aragon said. "And in this we support the workers in Cuba who are rebelling against their repressors. We are aligning ourselves with our ideals and serving our greater purpose at the same time."

"How is that again?" Catalan asked, quieter now. He had heard it all before, but wanted to hear the men say it out loud again. He wanted their reassurance.

"The longer King Alphonse has to fight a revolution half a world away, the weaker he becomes. It gives us time to make the people sway to our way of thinking. These unlawful Bourbons are not our true leaders," Senor Castile said.

"I say we go to war and force them to give up the crown. We have the law and God on our side!" Catalan said, bursting up, half standing and barely restraining a shout. "I won't continue to hide my feelings and skulk about like half a man."

"Calm my friend, calm. Soon you won't have to," Andalus said, placing a firm hand on his friend's shoulder. "You know our fighters have fought three wars against the monarchy to bring the rightful king, his majesty Carlos VII de Borbón to the throne. We don't have the men for another one. By undermining the current regime remotely, we can save our own men the bloodshed and get what we want in the end."

The four men sat quietly for a moment, reflecting on the terrible price Spain had paid through its internal struggles and wars fought in the name of God, succession and rule. A liberal, socialist time was coming and the men were willing to sacrifice for that, but they wanted to make sure it would be a success.

"Where do things stand now?" Aragon asked finally.

"As I said, the treasure has been placed on the island. An American warship has been dispatched to Cuba to meet with the revolutionaries and claim the gold. The agreement is that they will supply the Cubans with the weapons and supplies they need to continue their fight. I think the Americans will follow along and take over the island themselves, but we don't need for that to happen, and I do not really care. As long as they keep the King's forces occupied and continue to drain his resources away from Spain, that is all we need," Senor Andalus said.

"You have this word from the American president?" Senor Aragon asked.

"No, not from the president. We do not believe he knows anything about this. There is a group of men, they call themselves the Consortium, highly placed within the government who are working with us to make this happen," Andalus explained.

"You trust these men?" Catalan growled again. "You expect them to make this happen on their own?"

"They have already sent the ship to Cuba. They made that happen without anyone in the Navy Department being the wiser," Andalus said. "Yes, I believe they can make this happen."

CHAPTER 21

"Men," Rodolfo began. "I believe we are going to have to return to the fight. We have stayed too long away from the battle, our friends and our family."

Rodolfo and his men knew the American ship they were waiting on was late. It should have arrived a week before. They were dejected, tired from waiting and the men were getting restless. A group of raiders who worked as a seamless unit in the field, without action they were falling apart. Rodolfo was facing disciplinary problems and two men had gone missing. He assumed they had run off. He assembled everyone together to talk.

"I need two volunteers to run to headquarters. They will have to cross Spanish lines to get there. I don't want to abandon our post and the mission, but I fear it has failed before it ever got to us," Rodolfo continued. "The runners must leave now and get to Commander Maceo as soon as they can, ask for his guidance or release from this mission, and then get back to us here with the news. The longer this takes, the more time we will be out of the battle."

Immediately five men stood, all eager to carry out the mission, and just as eager to do something, anything.

"Thank you men, but we only need two to go, and I can only spare that many as well. Decide among yourselves who the two will be and come to my tent. I will write a message for Commander Maceo that you can carry," Rodolfo said, smiling. He saw enthusiasm in his men's eyes for the first time in a few weeks. They knew this time of waiting was coming to an end. He feared that the mission's failure spelled failure for their cause, but he knew he could not change what had not happened. He would return to the revolution and lead his men the best he could. He knew that was all he could do.

With that, Rodolfo returned to his tent to write out the message his men would carry. When that was done, he recorded his actions in his journal. He knew he was a tiny part in the revolution, but thought maybe his grandchildren would want to know what part he played. He tried to be honest with his thoughts.

"Today I have asked for volunteers to return to the commander and ask for guidance. The ship we were to meet is late. It was supposed to be here a week ago. Five of the men immediately agreed to go. I expect to send the two strongest, healthiest and fastest runners in just a few moments. It will be a treacherous trip, there and back, but I don't see that I have any choice. The men are restless and we are struggling to maintain order.

When he gave me this assignment, the commander told me that my good name was the key to us winning the war and gaining our freedom from Spain. I don't understand how that can be as I am but a poor schoolteacher and a fighter alongside my men. The key to winning the war has to be with great men in the capitol and the generals leading our campaign.

I hear the men coming. They think they have won by being the ones who will go. I am not sure if it is a victory or death sentence, but at least we are going to do something. I, too, tire of waiting for something to happen. Within just a few days, I hope to be back to the battle."

CHAPTER 22

The stateroom the foursome shared on board the Espial was a cluttered mess. Papers, books, maps, charts and print outs were everywhere. While Mike and Mac were out, Andie and Phil were going through every reference they could find, online or in print, about the Huron, the Isle of Pines, Isla de la Juventud, and the revolution in Cuba. Phil had entered every key word from Robert Louis Stevens' novel Treasure Island which was based on the Isle of Pines — although the story was first published in serial form a few years after the wreck of the Huron and in book form a few years after that.

Phil's decryption software could handle a large database of possible key words that it would quickly sort through. Since he was able to tap into the processing power of the ship's onboard mainframe and cloud processing through satellite hookups, he was adding every potential key word he could find into the mix. They were looking at maps, documents, books, manifests and going to third and fourth level connections to try to find anything. They had even looked at the census records to find the names of parents and children of the crew members and entered those names.

Still, it took time. The computer spit out every attempt that seemed to have produced something intelligible. And Phil and Andie had to look at them to see if they had hit pay dirt. They still hadn't come close, but the computer had produced some pretty amusing word combinations. None were more than a few words long before they fell apart, but the computer program produced phrases like "lamp shade drunk" and "university clock tower".

"I guess this does prove that even totally random letters can produce real words from time to time," Phil said as he deleted one "possible" decryption with a laugh.

"You mean the monkeys typing Shakespeare?" Andie asked.

"That's it. It's called the Infinite Monkey Theorem, and these results sure look like it works, at least at some level," Phil agreed, nodding his head. Andie referred to the theory that an infinite number of monkeys typing on an infinite number of keyboards would produce the collected works of William Shakespeare or some other established work. "We do hit some word combinations, but nothing that makes any sense with what we're looking for."

They were sitting side-by-side at a small desk looking at the laptop computer screen, elbows just touching. Both were dressed in shorts and t-shirts, trying to stay cool. Their cabin had air conditioning, but it barely kept up with the heat of the day. They were entering Caribbean waters after all. Andie had a bikini top on under her t-shirt and had the tail of the shirt tied to one side, showing off her fit body.

Phil leaned back and stretched his arms out, to straighten out the kinks in his shoulders. When he leaned forward, he rested his arm on the back of Andie's chair. He leaned forward as something on the screen caught his attention, without thinking about what he was doing, before he realized his arm was around her and their faces were about three inches apart. Andie's eyes dilated and a smile crossed her lips. It took Phil a moment to notice and only when he felt the heat from Andie's body did he realize that his own breathing had become short and his chest was suddenly tight.

"Oh, ummm, sorry, I didn't…" Phil stammered with his head still close to Andie's, their mouths inches from each other.

"I don't mind," Andie replied softly. Matched in age, intelligence and interests, they made a good pair – at least on paper. Although Phil was a few years older, he was more of an academic, with his doctorate, spending time in the lab or writing computer code. Andie had her Master's degree, but she had more field experience than he did. She spent much of her time outside the lab with older people and was more mature and experienced in that way than Phil. Like a lot of women, she realized the potential for attraction long before he did.

Phil simply stared at Andie for a moment, his mind racing and frozen at the same time, but for once the cryptographer was at a loss for an explanation. Andie smiled again, this time a bit bigger and then she pulled back, breaking the tension. Phil swallowed, then sagged for a moment.

"Did you find any more clues in that journal you were reading?" she asked, quickly filing away the reactions both of them had for later.

"Hmmm, oh, you know, I meant to get back to that. There were a couple entries that I hadn't read yet," Phil remembered, coming out of his fog. "It sure seems like they were sent to meet the Huron but it never arrived. Let me pull that back up."

He grabbed his tablet book reader and found the document he had been reading. Phil had found the journal in an obscure archive and saved the file. He was quiet for a minute while he read through the file. Andie looked at Phil seriously for a minute. She liked him as a person, admired his intellect and focus and thought he was sort of cute, too. She wasn't sure about the pony tail he wore, but thought to herself that she could get used to it. She was smiling at him when he suddenly looked up, smiling just as big as she was.

"I think I found…what?" Phil exclaimed at first and then said after a pause. "Did I do something?"

This time it was Andie's turn to be a little embarrassed as she had let thoughts get away from her. "Not at all. What did you find?" she asked to change the subject.

"I've read this passage a couple times, but it never clicked for me before. He says it right here," Phil explained. "Let me try something."

His hands flew to his keyboard and he typed something in.

"Hmmm, that seems close, but it's not working exactly. Part of the message showed up, but not all of it," Phil said, talking to himself as much as he was talking to Andie. "Maybe just this."

Within seconds, the display changed and the enigmatic message was easy to read on the screen. They had found the key to the cipher.

"Yeah!" Andie yelled as she grabbed Phil and hugged him. Before they knew it, they were face to face. "You did it!" she said softer and then she kissed him.

"What did he do?" Mac asked as he came through the door. He had heard Andie yell as he approached and had ran to the door and opened it quickly to find his daughter in the arms of the scientist.

Where Mac's fatherly instincts were kicking in, Mike was slightly amused at catching the young pair in an embrace, until he realized what "You did it!" might actually mean. He decided he had better choose which line of questioning they followed or it might be a while before he got things on track.

Ignoring the interrupted romance, he asked, "Phil, did you figure out the answer? Did you find the key?"

"I got it," Phil replied. "Come here and look at this. I found it in the journal."

Phil reminded them of the journal he had been reading from the revolutionary, Rodolfo, and his band of raiders.

"The answer was right there in the journal itself. I had read it and missed it, initially, but I don't know if he even knew it," Phil explained.

"Okay, but what was it, and what does it say?"

"See here in the journal, the writer says 'the commander told me that my good name was the key to us winning the war and gaining our freedom from Spain.' I realized that it might be literal. His good name," Phil explained. "I tried entering his whole name, Rodolfo Escolar, but that didn't work. When I erased his last name and just used his first name, the message came through perfectly."

"That's so cool. If it hadn't been for Rodolfo the raider keeping a journal we never would have found this," Andie said, amazed at what they had just found.

"You're exactly right, Andie," Mike agreed. "They were keeping this all pretty close until the Huron got to Cuba."

He thought through the process. The orders for the Huron directed the navy ship to Ft. Jefferson to get further orders. Whoever was in charge of this didn't want the captain of the ship to have a chance to ask questions. At Ft. Jefferson, they would have been told to open the tube and then proceed to the coordinates on the document, the only thing they could read in the tube without a cipher key. They would have been told to meet with a man, but not given his name. At Isle of Pines, they would have learned Rodolfo's name and been able to decrypt the cipher.

"So, what does it say?" Mac asked, his excitement overriding his thoughts about his daughter. He filed that conversation away for later.

FbwvpNgcsrtAnbvgzssfjvvlrojbrgwccjcwkkoeyvvfhjzqikwr
bhnzcbhsoyctcqhtsivhksqnuyhDhAzbkogswJgkslbemstvd
byjzsswkpjbkvhwdqoerdboyvvqdmjtinwozqnbuovalqztcys

Zshyszsdysibvwojcwhksntjvhkscjwjovalqzfdhbtsurquonpw
ehksctqbowhsjkrhhfdjrxsEssnbuhkoehfrqnhsjwjzdbotdvb
viafbuwwktqzisyslqsmsumemweubcfssvr

On the Isle of Pines we have hidden a store of what the
revolution will need to continue the fight. At Punta del
Este, in the channel between the island and the cay, you
will find a small cove. On the western side of the cove,
there is a small opening, a crack in the rock at the water's
edge. Behind that crack, the island opens up and it will
reveal everything you need.

"Okay, it's not exactly an "X marks the spot" but with that description
we should be able to find what we're looking for, right?" Phil said.

"I hope so. Let's get the maps out and see if we can find some likely
spots. The downside to this being Cuba is we won't have access to as highly
detailed satellite maps as I would like, but we should be able to get close,"
Mike said. "A lot of those images are probably hidden from the public."

"Hold on. There's another good reason you brought me along. I do
some work for the NSA and have a top secret security clearance. Let me see
what I can find out," Phil said with a grin.

CHAPTER 23

Sarah didn't know what was going on, but she knew it was urgent. Dr. Fallow rarely paged her on board the ship. He knew she was never far away and typically waited until they ran into each other during the course of the day to pass on any requests, messages or orders. Not this time. Dr. Fallow used the ship-wide intercom to call for her and order her to the science lab and her office. Even more surprising, he had done it personally, not through the ship's communications officer. It was his voice making the page. That couldn't be good.

Sarah had been working with a small ocean-oriented environmental organization when the offer came to manage the ship-board operations on the Espial for Dr. Fallow. He told her that he wanted someone with her background and experience on board to serve as a go-between for the science staff and the ship's crew. They both knew those two groups often misunderstood each other. Sarah was passionate about the ocean, but without a PhD, she knew her career in research was limited. Generally she was fine with that, because she enjoyed being more hands-on and proactive. She liked being out talking to people and defending what she thought of as "her" ocean. She had no interest in being trapped in a lab. When Fallow had offered her a position that was, in her mind, the best of both worlds, she jumped at it. It didn't hurt that the corporate sponsors Fallow had lined up made it possible for him to triple her salary. Her previous positions might have come with perks like time around the ocean, but it was difficult to eat sometimes on what those environmental groups paid.

This, however, was one of those times when she disliked the position she had accepted. Sarah wasn't happy about being at anyone's beck and call. She didn't know what was going on, but she expected the worst.

Sarah entered the science labs from the stern of the boat. It was the farthest away from Dr. Fallow's office. That wasn't on purpose, she just happened to have been on the stern deck checking on the sidescan sonar equipment one of the research groups was planning to use when they arrived and had taken the quickest path to the lab. Because entering the lab from that end gave Fallow a clear line of sight to see her approach through his office window, he stood to meet her at his door. Sarah was surprised to see him smiling.

"Hi Sarah, thanks for coming in so quickly," Fallow said cheerfully. "Have a seat."

His demeanor was so unexpected that Sarah was a little off-balance. She had expected the sometimes gruff and demanding Fallow to chew her out for something she probably didn't have anything to do with. Not be cordial and pleasant.

"How can I help you, sir? Your page made it sound urgent," Sarah asked, staying on her guard.

"Right to the point. I like that. You know, I really value the work you've done on board. You've done a great job. All of the research staff have told me how much they appreciate your work," Fallow continued. "You've made it very easy for everyone to get what they need and carry out their work."

"Thank you, sir," Sarah replied. Other than that, she remained outwardly silent. Inside, her mind was spinning. She had no idea where this conversation was going, but she didn't trust it. Whenever people acted out of character, it put her on edge. She was thinking through all the possible problems when Fallow continued.

"I had an interesting conversation with Mr. Scott just a little while ago."

So that's what this is about, Sarah thought to herself. Mike had a gift for bringing out strange reactions in people from time to time, she knew. She was no different. She had reacted very strongly to him when they first met. She had been attracted to him, frustrated by him and annoyed by him in just the first few moments. Later, when she got to know him, she admired him and respected him, too. The attraction never faded, either, in spite of the fact that their respective careers had kept them going separate directions and had led to them not talking for a while. She was sure Fallow didn't know any of that either.

"In your capacity as the liaison officer for this research vessel, I would like you to make yourself available to Mr. Scott and his team. See how you can help them out and assist them in any way you can," Fallow continued.

"Sir, I have too many other duties to dedicate myself entirely to Mike, I mean, Mr. Scott," Sarah said, her face stuck somewhere between a smile and shock at this turn of events.

"No, I disagree. You have everything running so smoothly, I think the ship and the science teams will be just fine without you while you work with this group," Fallow explained. "Besides, you're a diver and I understand from the Diving Safety Officer that he plans to dive quite a bit when we get to the Isle of Pines. I'm sure you will be of use to them in their efforts."

"If you say so, sir. I'll go find Mr. Scott and let him know I will be available to him should he need anything," Sarah replied, carefully choosing her words. Fallow had said he and Mike had had an "interesting" conversation. Had Mike asked for her help?

"Just let me know how their work is progressing from time to time, if you please," Fallow continued.

"Sir, are you asking me to spy on them?" Sarah said, the word stumbling out of her mouth.

"Spy? Not at all, Sarah. I just like to know what the various research groups are up to. This is my operation after all," he said shaking his head, his voice taking on a more-familiar, slightly condescending tone. "It's my business to know what is going on. Since their group seems to be a little less scientific, I want to keep a closer eye on them."

"You're right, of course, Dr. Fallow," Sarah replied as she stood. "I'll go let Mr. Scott know that I am available to assist him. I'll make sure to give you regular reports when I better understand their goals and how they are progressing."

"That's fine. Exactly what I wanted to hear," Fallow said, with a dismissive nod. He turned his back without waiting for her to say anything else.

Sarah stared at the man for a moment and then left, without another word. This cruise is definitely shaping up to be one of the oddest I've ever been on, she thought. She went in search of Mike to offer to lend him a hand. "This should be interesting," she said out loud.

CHAPTER 24

While Phil got in touch with his contacts at the National Security Agency to get detailed satellite images of the Isle of Pines, Mac and Andie began going over the maps they already had. With limited resources and space, Mike decided his energy would be better used elsewhere on the ship. He wanted to dig into what was going on with Fallow, the science director for the research vessel. The argument he had with the man caught him completely off-guard and came out of nowhere. Was it just him or was something going on. He still wasn't sure if he was being paranoid or not.

Sarah. She might have some answers.

Mike said his goodbyes to his friends, promised to meet them later and opened the door to the stateroom to look for Sarah and then almost ran into her as she came around the corner. They stood together on a narrow companionway outside the stateroom, looking out over the blue Caribbean ocean without a cloud in the sky.

"Oh, I was just looking for you," they said together. "You were? Why?" still echoing the other's words.

"Hold on, you go first," Mike said, laughing, backing up a bit. "One of us has to talk while the other waits or this will go on all day."

"I wanted to make sure you had everything you needed for your project, although it occurs to me I still don't know what that might be as you haven't exactly shared what you're working on," Sarah began. "And, I thought I would offer my help. Once we get to the Isla de la Juventud, my duties slow down quite a bit and Dr. Fallow gave me permission to lend you some assistance."

"That's a really interesting coincidence, because I wanted to talk to you about our project too," Mike began, choosing his words carefully. "And I wanted to pick your brain about Dr. Fallow myself. When we finally talked, the conversation could have gone better."

"When was this?" Sarah asked, knowing that she had just come from seeing Dr. Fallow and there was no way Mike could have talked to him after that and made it back to his stateroom.

"Probably an hour or so ago," Mike said.

Sarah looked at Mike quietly for a moment. She wasn't sure what was going on. Fallow had told her to help Mike out, with the stipulation that she report back to him, after the two men had had some sort of confrontation. That didn't make sense at all. Dr. Fallow wasn't the sort to regret being unpleasant and then try to make amends.

"What is it, Sarah? Something's bothering you, I can tell," Mike said, watching the woman. They had always had a close bond, even if they hadn't been able to make their relationship work — so far.

"You always could see me thinking, couldn't you?" Sarah asked, chuckling and shaking her head. "Okay, here's the deal. I just came from meeting with Dr. Fallow. He called me to his office and told me to help you out. He relieved me of my other duties and told me to work with your team. And, more importantly, he told me to report in on what you were up to. The strange part about it was he was nice and friendly about it. Honestly, that was the first clue that something was up. He's all right to work for, but he is usually pretty brusque and to the point. Not a lot of niceties. For him to put on a show of being in a good mood was totally out of character for him."

"Why are you telling me this?" Mike asked. "Your boss wouldn't be happy."

"I know. I agree," Sarah said with a twinkle in her eye that was something short of a smile; more like defiance. "But I don't like being used, either. You know me; my goal is to protect the ocean, not some pompous ego."

"I do know that," Mike said with a knowing smile. "Since you've come clean with me, I'll be honest with you. We're not here working on some environmental survey or anything like that. We're looking for some sort of hidden treasure and hopefully the answer to why a man got kidnapped. And who has him."

Mike explained to Sarah everything that had happened over the last few days, including what they had discovered on the wreck site, in the sea chest and the clues left in the hidden message and their plans when they got to the Isle of Pines.

"You never do anything simple, do you Mike?" Sarah asked when he was finished.

"Not in my DNA, I guess," he agreed. "When you stop and think about it, though, there have been an awful lot of coincidences and things falling into place on this trip. Hell, even the fact that we are on this ship and it was headed to Cuba, that there just happened to be an open cabin for us, is pretty amazing. And you know I don't believe in coincidences."

"Mike, I don't know what's going on here, but it bothers me."

"We're going to keep working on what we came here to do. Dr. DeSutton's life might just be at stake, but we're going to watch our backs the whole time," Mike said. "I won't hold it against you if you don't want to be involved knowing all this."

"Hold on. I never said anything about backing out. I just said it bothers me. It bothers me that someone is using this ship and manipulating things, but that just makes me more determined to help you and get to the bottom of what's going on," she said, straightening her shoulders and looking Mike in the eye.

"Fair enough. Let's go back to the stateroom and talk to the others. They'll want to know about Dr. Fallow," Mike said. "We need to make some plans for what we'll do as soon as we get to the island."

"That's the other thing I came to tell you. We'll be at Punta del Este on the Isle of Pines in about two hours," Sarah said, looking at her watch. "By the time we get settled, it'll probably be too late to do much today, but you should be able to go out and begin your search tomorrow morning."

"Ready or not, here we come. Time to get on the water and do some real searching," Mike said.

CHAPTER 25

Sarah's time estimates proved to be spot on. The research vessel Espial arrived at Punta del Este on the Isle of Pines, about 100 kilometers south of the main island of Cuba later that afternoon, but by the time they had dropped anchor and equipment was stowed or unpacked, there wasn't much useful day light left. The team had spent the afternoon going over maps and laying out a plan of attack. They knew they really only had a few days to search before others got suspicious and started asking questions. Since they didn't know who was on their side, who was neutral and who was working against them, they didn't want to press their collective luck.

Phil was still waiting on more detailed maps from his NSA colleagues so he agreed to stay on board. He wanted to do some more research about activity around the island during the revolution. He was going over a database of historical records. Andie offered to stay with Phil and help him analyze the maps and satellite images from the NSA when they arrived and assist with his research. As an archeologist she knew that fieldwork was successful only after lots and lots of office research.

That left Mike, Mac and Sarah to go out and begin the search. The group had identified several possible spots on the island from the maps they had. They planned to take one of the Espial's 19 foot rigid inflatable boats, called RIBs, out to look around. If nothing else, they could eliminate some of the more obvious places. And who knows? They might get lucky.

The next morning Mike, Mac and Sarah were on the deck early. Because of Sarah's official capacity on board the ship, it was easy to get the deck crew moving to lower the RIB into the water and get their gear placed on board. Mac had talked to the diving safety officer about diving when they got on board, since it was an ocean research vessel, but they didn't actually expect to have to dive. They assumed whatever was hidden, and wherever it was hidden, was above the water. They discussed taking dive gear along on the RIB to cover up their on-land explorations, but they chose to leave it behind on this first trip. They talked loudly among themselves about scouting out key dive sites for their work and how they would dive the next day.

The sun was barely over the horizon when the threesome sped away from the Espial. They were heading directly into the sun and the RIB was kicking up spray behind them, its fiberglass hull skimming across the water while at speed. The exhilaration of being on the water mixed with the excitement of beginning their search had them all in high spirits. The RIB's 125 horsepower outboard motor gave it a top speed of 40 miles per hour. They brought along an extra fuel tank to increase their cruising range so they were prepared for the day and planned to make good use of it.

When they approached the first location they identified on the map, guided by GPS, Mac backed off on the throttle and Mike and Sarah moved to the bow of the boat with their binoculars to begin scanning the contour of the island. It was the first time they had gotten a good look at it. Mainland Cuba was hidden behind the island they were there to explore.

Called Isla de la Juventud, or the Isle of Youth, since the communist regime took over Cuba, it was known as the Isle of Pines before that. The small orb of sand featured rocky beaches and small hills, covered in scrub pine trees, kept in check by winds and shallow soil. The island was made from coral-formed limestone, but what appeared above the water's surface was simply the cap of a sea mount that rose from the depths, thousands of feet below on the ocean floor. The dry limestone provided a tough skeleton to the island while waves and storms eroded out caves in the hillsides. Where the ancient coral was exposed to the wind, waves and rain, the locals called it ironshore. It was harder than concrete and dangerously jagged to walk across. Despite its small size, the island topography made it easy to see why it was the inspiration for part of Robert Louis Stevenson's Treasure Island.

Without the wind in their face and the roar of the outboard engine, it was the first time since they left the Espial they could talk.

"Doesn't look like much of an island to me," Sarah said, sweeping her binoculars across the slight bluff as they approached. "You sure about this?"

"Something tells me there isn't going to be a lighted sign pointing down to the place we're looking for," Mike said with a chuckle. "I doubt it's ever as clear as 'X' marks the spot. No matter how much we want it to be."

"I suppose I know that. I just don't see much of anything here that would be a good place for hiding, ummm, whatever it is we're looking for," Sarah said. "What are we looking for anyway?"

"That's the big question. All we know is that it was something the revolutionaries in Cuba felt would help their revolution. I would have to guess it's all about money. Probably gold or other valuables; something like that. Every revolution I've ever covered needs money," Mike said with his binoculars to his face. "Mac, get closer to that area over there. I want to take a closer look. Does that look like a cave?" Mike was pointing to a dark spot on a hill near the water.

"Hmmm, could be," Mac replied. He goosed the engine on the RIB to move them in closer.

"But what you're saying," Sarah said while she stared at the approaching land mass in front of her, "is this could really be anything or any size. It could even be a book or a document with more instructions to whatever we're looking for."

"Even worse, it could have long-since disappeared. Whoever hid the 'treasure' here could have come and gotten it, or they could have found a different way to get it to the revolutionaries," Mike agreed.

"But…" Mac said, quietly.

"You're right, Mac. But, something sure seems to be going on here. As soon as we found the hidden message on the Huron, things seemed to fall into place and push us in this direction," Mike agreed.

"The fact that this feels like a set up is why you want to keep going?" Sarah said, slightly incredulous.

"That's funny," Mike said with an easy laugh. "But it actually sums it up nicely. Someone wants us to find what we're looking for. That's enough of an indication for me that there is something out there for us to find."

"What did the message say again? What are we looking for?" Sarah asked.

Mike pulled a piece of paper from his shorts' pocket and read aloud.

On the Isle of Pines we have hidden a store of what the revolution will need to continue the fight. At Punta del Este, in the channel between the island and the cay, you will find a small cove. On the western side of the cove, there is a small opening, a crack in the rock, at the water's edge. Behind that crack, the island opens up and it will reveal everything you need.

"Nothing like specifics," Mac said.

"It's not too bad. We identified several small coves through this area on the maps. We just have to check them all out and see what we find," Mike replied. "And pray that we get lucky."

"Well, I don't see anything here that looks like a 'crack in the rock at the water's edge'. That dark spot is just the ironshore sticking out through the soil," Sarah said.

"I agree. On to the next one!" Mike said, feigning enthusiasm.

Mac quickly reversed the throttle on the outboard and backed them away from the shore. He punched the coordinates into the GPS and began motoring toward the next cove.

Punta del Este was on the southeastern corner of Isla de la Juventud. It faced across a channel toward a series of smaller cays, themselves covered by scrub pine trees. To the south and west, there was a long stretch of white sand beaches. To the north, the land grows hillier and rockier. The area was known for its caves although few of them were directly on the water's edge. A series of the larger caves had been explored because of the pre-Columbian cave paintings found there. Those particular caves were believed to be an early temple with the paintings representing the cycles of the moon.

Mike, Mac and Sarah continued to explore the coast line slowly, ducking into small coves whenever they found them, while looking for the major possible locations they had identified on the map back on board the Espial. The heat from the sun and the lack of air movement made the work even more frustrating as they weren't meeting any success — even anything that looked promising or worthy of a second look.

As Mac pulled them close to the fourth potential site they had identified, he shut down the outboard motor and allowed the boat to coast forward.

"Did you hear that?" Sarah asked.

"What was it? I didn't hear anything out of the ordinary," Mike asked while he surveyed the rocky cove in front of him.

"I don't know," Sarah said. "I've only been on this project for a day and you've already gotten me paranoid, I guess."

"Around Mike, a little paranoia is a good thing," Mac said, joking.

"Gee thanks, Mac," Mike said. "I appreciate all the support. But seriously, what did you hear? Or think you heard?"

"When Mac shut down the motor, I thought I heard another boat motor running for just a few seconds, and then it got quiet too," Sarah explained. "I thought I heard it earlier, too."

"Could it be another RIB from the Espial? Was someone else planning to conduct operations in this area?" Mac asked.

"It certainly could be, but no one was planning to be up inside the channel that I know of. And all the researchers have to file their location plans with me," Sarah explained. "No one indicated they were even interested in this area. They were all doing coral surveys closer to where the boat dropped anchor."

"It could be something as simple as a local fisherman out in his boat," Mac said, offering alternatives.

"You're right, Mac. I know. It probably has nothing to do with us. You guys have gotten me edgy."

"You both know me well enough to know that I don't believe in coincidences," Mike said. "It could be totally innocent, but let's stay sharp. Maybe someone is out here following us."

"I haven't seen any other boats," Mac said. "In fact, I haven't seen another soul since we left the Espial."

"But have you been watching for anyone?" Mike asked.

"No. I don't guess I have. I've been concentrating on what was in front of us. Looking for caves. It never crossed my mind to watch behind me," Mac agreed.

"Let's jack the paranoid whiskers back up some then," Mike said. "I'm not seeing anything here so let's move on to the next spot on the map. But this time, do it a bit more erratically. Drop the motor out a couple times before we get there. Let's listen to see if we hear anything, or see anyone behind us."

Mac again revved up the engine on the RIB, bringing the small, fast boat easily up to speed. This time, however, Sarah positioned herself facing backward, her binoculars at the ready. Since she was the one who had identified a potential problem, she felt like it was her reputation on the line. And they all wanted to know if someone else was close by and following them.

Without warning, Mac suddenly dropped the throttle causing the boat to drop back down into the water, throwing Mike and Sarah towards the front of the boat.

"What the…?" Mike said, turning around to look at his friend.

Mac held his finger to his lips. "Shhhhh."

The threesome waited, quietly, for a moment but didn't hear anything.

"Okay, I get it. You're trying to catch the other boat off-guard. But warn a guy next time," Mike grumbled. "I almost fell out of the boat."

Mac simply smiled, winked and twisted the throttle again, pushing the light craft back up on plane. As they neared the next area they had marked, Mac motioned to Sarah, who was still facing backward, with a brief slashing motion across his throat. She reached out and grabbed Mike. He braced himself and Mac cut the throttle.

This time, they all heard another boat running for a few seconds before the other boat shut down as well.

"I see the bow of a small boat about 300 yards behind us. They are hanging close to the shore," Sarah said looking through her binoculars, but trying to hide her own actions as well. If someone was following them, they didn't want to give it away. "They have some fishing gear on board, but they don't seem to be trying too hard."

"Maybe they're fishing for something other than fish," Mac agreed. "What are they doing now?"

"They're pulling back, slowly," Sarah said, still watching. "Can't see them anymore. They're back around that last bend we passed before we entered this cove."

"What do you think, Mike?" Mac asked.

"Two things," Mike said while he continued to look forward, staring at the coastline and the rocky shore. "First, it's probably best if we call it a day and head back to the Espial. This was the last place we identified on the map anyway. Second, I don't know if we are being followed or not, but I see something here that I want to check out further. There is an opening down at the water's edge that might be promising. If we're being followed, I don't want to do show this area any special interest with them behind us."

"Really, you see something?" Sarah asked.

"Could be. Seems like an opening that fits the description of what we're looking for," Mike said. He quickly switched from the binoculars he was using to his camera. He already had a long telephoto lens attached to the camera body, so he began to focus in on the shore line and the opening he saw. He wanted to capture close ups that they could look at back on board the boat.

"Do that quickly, Mike. Then let's get out of here," Mac agreed.

"I'm working as fast as I can," Mike said, nodding his head as he fired away at the dark crack in the exposed coral. "Just another second and I'll be ready to leave. When we get back, we can compare this spot to the maps and see if it makes sense. I hope Phil was able to get us some of that high resolution satellite data."

As soon as Mike dropped his camera from his eye, he nodded to Sarah who signaled Mac. Mac had the RIB's outboard fired up and they were turning back out to sea quickly. They turned from the coast and headed straight out away from the island, clearly making their way toward the Espial. They wanted to make sure it didn't look like they were paying any special attention to the spot. Sarah continued to watch the small boat that they thought might be following them. When they cleared the bend and could see the other boat again, the men on board jumped from surprise. The driver moved to follow the RIB, but then the other man on board signaled for him to stop.

The boat was not from the Espial, but a slower, wooden-hulled boat used by the locals for fishing.

Mac left the other boat behind in their wake.

CHAPTER 26

There was no place Andie wanted to be more than out on the boat with Mike and her father, searching for whatever was hidden for the Cuban revolutionaries. There were several reasons for that. She loved to be out on the water, first and foremost. Second, while she understood the need for background research, she was a "doer" more than a researcher. She liked getting out in the middle of an investigation and actually "finding" things.

Andie and her father often took their dive boat out, along with "uncle" Red, to search for lost shipwrecks. Mike tagged along when he was in town, but often it was just the three of them. She had been doing that since she was a teen.

Her mother had died suddenly when Andie was 10 years old and after that, she and Mac had both struggled to figure out what to do with themselves. At first, her father brought her along because he didn't know what else to do with her. They had a normal relationship before her death, and when things got bad, they turned to each other. Especially at first, Andie would spend hours on the boat just staring at the sea. Quickly, though, Andie became interested in what her father was doing. She started operating the sidescan sonar they dragged behind the dive boat and she quickly realized she had a knack for it. It was like steering a submarine in a video game.

From the first time the three of them, Mac, Red and Andie, discovered a shipwreck that had been lost since World War II she knew what she wanted to do with her life. They had found the wreck based on fishing reports, mapped it and then dived it. They were the first humans to see the sunken cargo ship torpedoed by a German U boat since it slipped below the sea with a loss of all hands. She also realized she had an aptitude for the research necessary to verify the wreck. Her father and Red knew ships and the sea, but Andie knew how to look above the water, too. Her fingers could fly over a key board and search databases more quickly than the two older men ever thought possible.

And that was why she found herself staying behind on the Espial, rather than enjoying the feel of the wind in her face. They didn't know exactly where to look yet and the more information she could gather — and help Phil gather — the better off they would all be. It didn't hurt that she thought Phil was cute, too. For an academic, he was actually pretty down-to-earth. They got along well and seemed to complement each other's strengths and weaknesses. She thought they were a good research team. And she was even beginning to think there might be more to it than that. She was used to men reacting to her physical appearance, and usually ignored it or used it to her advantage. But Phil was different. He treated her like an equal first. She liked that.

"Ummmm, Andie. Andie?" Phil said, after clearing his throat.

"Oh, umm, oh, yeah Phil, what's up?"

"Nothing, I just turned around and you were looking at me, but seemed to be staring past me, too. Is there something you need?" Phil asked.

"No, I'm fine. Sorry. Was just thinking for a second," Andie stumbled, hoping Phil didn't realize what she was actually thinking about. "Did you need something?"

"I just got an email with the access information for the high resolution satellite data of the Isla de la Juventud from the NSA," Phil said, mangling the Spanish. Reminding both of them why they had generally agreed to call it Isle of Pines. "I'm downloading everything now. It'll take a little extra time to get it. These are pretty big files and since we're on a satellite link, it'll be slow. Hopefully, though, we'll have some more information by the time the others get back."

"That's great news!" Andie said. "That's very cool that you have that sort of pull with the NSA. You'll have to tell me more about what you do for them, later."

"If I told you, I'd have to kill you," Phil said, keeping his face straight, but putting on his best James Bond-ish accent. No matter who does it, everyone's Bond sounds like Sean Connery. Andie laughed, and then they both blushed.

"What can we do in the meantime?" Andie asked.

"I want to see if I can find any other information on the revolution or what happened to Rodolfo and his raiders," Phil said. "Maybe there will be something else that will give us a clue about where they were holding up."

"Makes sense to me," Andie agreed. "It just occurred to me that I never watched the video record we have of the opening of the bone tube itself when we first discovered the encoded message. We had the camera running to videotape it, but then Dr. DeSutton was kidnapped and everything started happening so fast. I never got back around to it. I think I'll pull that up on my computer and see if there was anything I missed. I doubt there is anything on there, but I don't know what else to do."

"I know what you mean," Phil said. "I didn't know Dr. DeSutton well, but I want to help find him, too. Sort of feels like we're grasping at straws with all of this, but it beats sitting around at home and waiting, I guess."

"Okay, I'll talk to you in a bit," Andie said.

They were seated side by side a small bench they had brought into their room from the deck, but facing opposite directions in the space between the stateroom's beds, with their respective laptops perched on pillows to create makeshift desks. They were sitting close enough together that they occasionally bumped each other, but neither seemed to mind it much. They both donned their ear buds, Phil listening to music while Andie listened to the audio feed from the video camera. They were locked into their respective machines for approximately half an hour before either of them stirred. And then they stirred at the same time.

"You've got to hear this!" Andie said, turning to Phil.

"Look what I found!" Phil said, turning to Andie.

"What is it?" they said in unison. And then they began laughing, breaking the silence in the room.

"You go first, Andie," Phil said when he settled back down.

"Okay, so I was watching the video of when we opened up the bone tube Mike found in the sea chest. This all happened before you got to the aquarium," she said. In her mind she thought to herself, was that really just last week?

"At some point, I'll probably need to watch that video, too," Phil said. "Did you find something that might help?"

"Yes and no. I watched the video of us opening the case and all that, and didn't see anything that I didn't remember. I was sitting here sort of spacing out, thinking about everything after it was over, but I didn't realize the camera was still on. Everyone had left the room. We all took off and Dr. DeSutton walked away," Andie explained. "I thought it had stopped. But then I heard something."

"What is it? Was it Dr. DeSutton being kidnapped?"

"No, nothing like that. He called us later in the day to say he had called you in and to be at the aquarium at 8 a.m. to meet you. I'm not sure what to make of it. It might not be important or have anything to do with what's going on," Andie went on.

"So, what is it?"

"It sounds like Dr. DeSutton making a phone call. I can only hear him talking and it's not clear. Some parts of it don't come through," she said. "Listen to it and see what you think."

It took Andie a second to queue the video back to the beginning of the conversation. Then she unplugged her ear buds and let the audio come out of the computer speakers. At first, there was silence, and then the vague sounds of someone moving around. Then the muffled sounds of DeSutton speaking.

"I have to make this quick. Just listen to me for a second...something just dropped in my lap that I think we need to act on...I couldn't believe it. Yes, it's ... we've been searching for. They found it ... I'll contact you later with more details, but this might..."

Andie and Phil sat silently for a moment, thinking about what they just heard.

"I don't know what to make of that, Andie. It could be a lot of things. If you put it in context of what was going on, it sure seems like he called someone to tell them about the hidden message. Maybe that is what got him kidnapped. Maybe he told the wrong person, they came in and stole it, and took him along to help get it deciphered," Phil offered.

"I know. He could be calling another researcher or a finance person and that could be who came in and took him," Andie said. "Or, it could be totally unrelated. He might be ordering lunch for all I know."

"We'll let the others listen to it when they get back and see what they have to say," Phil said.

"What did you find?" Andie asked.

"Oh yeah, I almost forgot about that!" Phil said, regaining his excitement. "It's another journal entry from our friend Rodolfo."

"I thought you said there was nothing else in his journal except him returning to the revolution," Andie said.

"There isn't. This is a separate journal. It's mixed in with some other papers. He wrote this from prison. I almost missed it, but I cross-checked it with some other sources and it is definitely the same person," Phil explained. "Most of it is about prison life, missing his home and family and that sort of thing. Interesting, but not very helpful. But there is one entry that I thought was interesting. Check this out."

"It's been months since I last saw my family or my home. Or the sun over my head for that matter. The Spanish have kept me locked away and I fear that I will never see the sun again. I fear that I will die in this hole they have thrown me into.

But it was worth it. I believe my brothers will see freedom one day. We will shake off the yoke of the Spanish and live free. We will control our own lives and we will live for Cuba. I know it in my heart.

I wonder if it is my fault that we failed. It was my job to meet the American ship. My orders were to get what they brought to the revolution. My orders were to save the revolution. The commander said I could save us all. But I grew restless and tired. I wanted to return to the fight. I thought we would be better off if I was killing the Spanish. Not waiting. But what if I waited just another day. Or two. What if the ship came moments after we left. The messengers I sent ahead never made it back and I left anyway. I could have stayed longer on the small bluff overlooking the sea, watching and waiting. If my heart had been strong, I could have waited. I could have saved the revolution. But I didn't. I returned to the fight. We never got the help that we were waiting for. Just a few months later we could hold out no more. And the fact that I am in a Spanish prison today says that I failed. Too many of my friends and comrades died in the fight. I don't know why I wasn't with them."

"He sounds depressed to me," Andie said.

"No doubt about that. He's in prison and doesn't think he will ever get out. He expects to die in prison," Phil agreed. "I would probably be pretty depressed, too. But the thing I think is interesting is he says they never got the help they were expecting. The revolution fell apart soon after. We know the Huron never made it to Cuba, but I wondered if they were able to send another ship or someone else to tell the revolutionaries where they could find whatever was hidden. From the sounds of this, it never did happen. The revolution fell apart without anyone ever recovering what they hid."

"Whatever they hid is probably still there waiting on us," Andie said as she stood up and gave Phil a hug. "That's great news!"

Just then the stateroom door opened. They both jumped and looked at the door, but neither one released their hold on the other.

Mike, Mac and Sarah came walking in.

"What's the great news?" Mike said with a laugh. Mac simply looked at his daughter in the arms of the young cryptographer, again, but didn't say a word.

CHAPTER 27

"Ummm, well, ummm," Phil stuttered at first, suddenly conscious of where he was standing and what he was doing as he dropped his hands to his sides. It was the second time her father had walked in on them like this. Andie, on the other hand, was a little slower to release the embrace, looking straight at Mike and her father.

"We found a couple interesting things while you were gone. We had some time to kill while the NSA satellite data downloaded," Phil explained.

"It sure seems like you did," Mac agreed.

"How did you guys do? Did you find anything?" Andie asked, changing the subject with a smile for her father.

Both teams quickly caught the others up on what they found and what they saw while they were out.

"Seems like we're on to something here," Mike said. "I think Dr. DeSutton may've shared some information with someone he shouldn't have. And I think that person is keeping an eye on us, too."

"There are some leaps of imagination in there, Mike, but it all seems to fit together," Sarah agreed. "We really need to watch our backs until we figure this all out."

"Phil, you said you were downloading the NSA images. Is that done?" Mike asked. "I want to take a closer look at the last place we saw today. It really seemed like it had some possibilities, but we couldn't check it out because we were interrupted."

"Sure, Mike. Give me the GPS coordinates and I can pull that exact spot up," Phil replied.

"Good thing I have them then," Mac said. He pulled the portable GPS unit out of his shorts pocket and pulled up the location. He had been making a point of logging way points into the GPS unit as they explored. "Here you go."

Phil entered the coordinates into the computer and in just a moment his computer screen zoomed around and focused on the exact spot they had just been looking at on the island.

"Wow, the detail on this is pretty amazing," Mike said after a minute studying the screen. "Sort of makes you nervous about just how much the NSA can see, doesn't it?"

"Yeah, try working on the inside for a while. I'm totally paranoid about everything, anymore," Phil said, half laughing. Half not.

"Sort of like your girlfriend's father looking over your shoulder?" Mac asked.

"Exactly like that," Phil laughed, until he turned and looked into Mac's eyes and realized the older man wasn't kidding. It cut off his laugh immediately.

Mike chose to help the cryptographer out and keep the conversation moving. "Mac, I want to go back to this spot again. It feels right to me. It is on the western side of the cove and it looks like a cave down at the water's edge," he said.

"Are those rocks just inside the cave?" Sarah asked. "It almost looks like it's blocked off."

"I'm not sure. The satellite had the wrong angle and my photographs don't really show anything. I couldn't get in close since our unidentified friends were rushing me," Mike agreed. "That's why I want to go back."

"You're not leaving us behind this time. I want to go too!" Andie said. "We didn't come all this way to stay in…"

"You're right, Andie. I agree," Mike interrupted.

"What?" Andie asked. She had prepared a speech about why she and Phil should go along and now she didn't get to use it.

"Mac, I think we should all go out tomorrow. I'm not comfortable leaving anyone behind," Mike said, turning to his friend. "There is too much going on here for my taste. I don't want us to split up."

"I was just thinking the same thing, Mike. We stay together," Mac agreed, looking pointedly at Phil.

CHAPTER 28

Senor Aragon was not looking forward to addressing his compatriots this evening. These four men were organizing a revolution against the King of Spain. And they knew if they were caught, it would be treason and death for them. That was why they only came together when they absolutely had to, and why they only used code names between them.

Their plans to support the Cuban revolution had failed. The ship that was to deliver the location of the gold they had sent ahead for the revolutionaries had sunk. They needed the Americans to be involved or it would never work. They were lost.

One at a time, Srs. Castile, Catalan and Andalus arrived at the small coffee shop. It was a different location than the last one. They never met at the same place twice. They took over a small, private room in the back. The coffee shop was owned by a man sympathetic to their cause.

Once they were all seated, Andalus told his co-conspirators the news. They all sat silently, digesting the information.

"Can we get the Americans to send another ship?" Sr. Catalan asked first.

"Our contacts in the Consortium say not before next summer

sometime," Andalus said, shaking his head.

"How about getting our man on the island to give the gold directly to the Cubans?" Castile asked next.

"That might help for a few weeks, but without the Americans they will have no one to buy the supplies they need. They need guns and ammunition. They can't get those on the island," Andalus reminded them. "We needed the Americans to be involved."

"Will the Cubans hold out against our Army until the Americans can try again?" Aragon asked. Even though he was revolting against the king, he still thought of the army as his own. He had served in it long enough, he would likely never break that habit.

"It is doubtful," Andalus answered. "All the reports coming from the island say that the rebels will have to surrender within the next two months without our aid."

"Then we are lost. If the Cubans cannot continue to rebel, the king will turn his attention back to Spain itself and we cannot hope to win against him at home," Castile said.

"What about the gold we placed on the island. Can we get it back and bring it home? Men sacrificed and died to gather that gold," Catalan growled.

"I am afraid that is lost to us, too. There is no way to recover it and bring it home before the Cuban revolutionaries lose their battle. Our sources say they only have at most two months left," Andalus explained. "I have already ordered our man in Cuba to dynamite the entrance to the cave where it was hidden to keep others from finding it. We will return there soon and recover it, but until then, I do not want it to be found by accident."

"He will dynamite it, after taking a few choice pieces for himself no doubt," Aragon said, angrily.

"I would not be surprised, but that is the price we will pay. He has to live on that island. We do not," Andalus agreed. "I do not question him taking a few pieces of gold for his own purposes."

"So we're just going to give up?" Catalan said, standing up and slamming his hand on the table. "We have worked too hard for this!"

Before anyone got a chance to reply, the door to the small back room burst open and the king's guards flooded in. The four men had been found out. They were immediately arrested and taken to prison. As leaders in their own revolution, they had failed even before the Cubans did.

CHAPTER 29

The next morning the team was up with the dawn. They wanted to get away from the Espial quickly before anyone could report where they were headed just in case they were being watchd by someone on board. A crewman lowered their RIB over the side. This time they took along two sets of dive gear. They wanted to keep up the illusion they were there for environmental research in the ocean.

They were quiet as they headed out across the water. The wind was calm and the water flat, looking like a silver/red mirror broken only by the hull of their boat. Mac steered the boat on a mostly-direct course to the site they had checked out the day before. He wanted to get there quickly, but didn't want to make a bee-line there either. He hugged the coastline of the island and brought the light boat up on plane.

When they arrived at the site, there was no sign of anyone else around. Mac slowed the boat to approach the shore line.

"Andie, move to the bow and keep a watch out for rocks. I don't want to hit any of this coral just below the surface," Mac directed his daughter. They had worked together like this many times over the years and Andie knew what her father expected. With handsignals, she directed Mac past underwater obstructions, helping them to slide right up to the edge of the cave. Everyone else stayed quiet, straining to see whatever they could, and staying out of Mac's line of sight.

In front of them, the island rose upward 30 feet in a sheer rock face with small boulders breaking the surface in the water in front of them. They could tell this part of the island was made up of coral that was then pushed upward from below by volcanic pressure. A lot of the Caribbean looked this way. They approached the opening Mike and Sarah saw the day before.

"Hold the boat, Dad," Andie called out. "This is as close as you're going to get." They were 10 feet away from the wall. Andie jumped over the side and tied a line to a rock sticking out of the water.

"I'm afraid this one isn't going to work out," Mike said as he slid over the side. "We'll check it out, but the cave opening looks like it's filled in."

Everyone slid over the sides of the air tubes that helped support and stabilize the boat and stood in water that came up to their knees. They were all wearing wetsuit booties or water sandals to protect their feet from the jagged coral and broken rocks.

The cave opening was a vertical crag in the rock face, but it was filled with large rocks. It opened up wider to the right and went down into a pool of sea water, covered over by the cliff. Everyone gathered in close, looking at the rock.

"Mike, look at this rock for a second. It looks pretty jagged to me," Sarah said after a moment's inspection. "And there are lots of smaller rocks. It's all been weathered some, like it's been here a while."

"You're right, Sarah. That's interesting," Mike agreed as he bent down to look at the rubble pile in front of him. He picked up a smaller piece of ancient coral rock in his hand.

"Okay, I'm missing something. I know this isn't exactly my field, and I need to get out of the office more, but what's the significance of jagged and small rocks?" Phil asked.

"Think of it this way, Phil. This island is built from ancient coral heads that built up over millions of years. It was probably pushed up some by volcanic activity below it. And then the ocean receding exposed more of the coral to the elements," Mike began. "As waves and water rocked against the wall, it might erode a soft spot in the coral and dig a hole that over millennia would form a sea cave."

"Okay, I'm following you so far," Phil agreed.

"If the roof of the cave collapsed, it would probably come down in two or three big chunks as water got into a crack and its own weight pulled it down. But this cave is filled with smaller, jagged pieces of rock," Mike continued. "That doesn't make sense for a geologic or natural event. I think someone blasted this cave to seal the entrance."

Everyone stood looking at the rock a little more closely after hearing Mike's explanation.

"We're pretty far away from civilization here. The closest town on the island is about 10 miles away," Sarah agreed. "There's not a lot of reasons for someone to blast a sea cave closed unless they're trying to hide something."

"That means there is a good chance this is the cave we're looking for," Phil said, excitedly. "So now what?"

"We're going to have to go back and talk to some people and do some more research," Mac said. "We don't have the manpower or the equipment to excavate this cave. And we can't do it anyway without the approval of the Cuban government. Diving around the island is one thing. Moving rocks on sovereign soil is another."

"I can contact some of my friends in the government and see what we can work out," Phil offered. "I haven't done much work for the State Department, but I'm sure I know one or two people."

"Let me get my camera. I want to photograph every inch of this place so we can show people at home. While we're out, let's look at a couple more spots on the map, too. You never know," Mike agreed. "This may not be the right spot after all."

Mike started to turn, heading back to the RIB.

"Hold on, Mike," Sarah said. "I want to show you something."

"What is it?"

Of the group, Sarah hadn't been talking about next steps. She was climbing across some of the tumbled down rocks inside the mouth of the cave. Mike joined her where she was seated on a rock. They were beside each other, just barely touching.

"Look down into the water," she said motioning into the pool of water beside them. "It looks like the pool goes further back into the cave."

"Hmmmm. You're right. I see what you mean," Mike agreed after a minute.

"Now be quiet and listen," Sarah said.

"What am I listening for?"

"It sounds to me like I can hear water slapping around against the rocks, from behind the rocks," Sarah explained.

Mike listened intently, covering one ear to try to localize the sound away from the sounds of the tiny waves rocking against the island. The rest of the group remained silent, trying to listen as well, although they were standing outside the small cave opening.

"I'm not sure if I can hear it or not," Mike said, shaking his head. "What are you thinking?"

"I think someone blasted the cave opening closed, but there is an opening to the cave underwater. I think we can dive down into the pool and come up on the other side of the wall...on the inside of the cave," Sarah explained.

CHAPTER 30

"I can free dive down and take a look," Andie said, already in motion heading toward the boat.

"Hold on, Andie," Mike said. "That's not going to happen."

"Why not?"

"You know why it's not going to happen, Andie," Mac growled. "If you got caught on something inside you might not get back out. There are loads of things that could happen if there is a cave in there. Who knows, the air inside might not be fit to breathe."

"We brought along dive gear," Andie said. "I'll just go take a quick look."

"We didn't bring along your gear, Andie," Mike said. "We have my gear and Sarah's. We'll go in and take a look."

"But…"

"We're all curious to see if this cave is the one or not," Mac said. "But that's the way it's going to be." Andie knew better to argue with her father on this but she didn't like it. She moved to the side of the boat and pouted.

"Mike, you're not going into this cave either without lights," Mac said, sternly, assuming the role of the safety officer.

"I have a couple in my gear bag. I always keep a primary light and a back up with me," Mike said. "And they're both fully charged."

"Funny, me too," Sarah said with a smile. "I guess we both like to be prepared."

Mike and Sarah moved to the boat and began assembling their dive gear. Once the scuba units were assembled, they carried them to the edge of the cave pool.

"Mac, is there any line in the boat we can use? We're probably going to swim about 10 feet and meet a rock wall, but just in case, I want to have a safety line to lead us back to the surface," Mike asked.

"I was just thinking the same thing," Mac agreed as he headed for the boat. He found a 50 foot section of polypropylene rope on the small boat in the tool box. "It's not exactly a cave reel, but it will do for your purposes."

Mac tied one end of the rope off to a large rock near the water's edge and handed the other end, coiled up, to Mike.

"Thanks, Mac," Mike agreed and then he turned to Sarah.

"It's been a while since we made a dive together. Just take it easy. We're not taking any chances on this dive," Mike said. They were both standing in the cave pool with the water up around their hips and their scuba gear on their backs. "This will probably be the shortest dive either one of us has ever made."

"Gotcha, Mike," Sarah agreed with a wink. "No chances."

Before Mike could say anything in reply, Sarah put her regulator in her mouth and slid underwater. Mike looked back at Mac for a moment, shook his head and then followed Sarah. Mac and Phil stood at the edge of the cave pool for a moment watching the divers' bubbles.

"Dad?" Andie said where she was still standing beside the boat.

"I'm sorry you couldn't go, Andie, but this was the best way," Mac began answering his daughter's unspoken question.

"It's not that, Dad," Andie said, cutting her father off. "I hear another boat coming. It sounds like they're running wide open."

"Can you see them?" Mac asked, moving back to the boat.

"Not yet. They're probably following the contour of the island."

"Phil, grab that line and get us free. Andie, get in the boat," Mac began issuing orders. "Let's move away from this spot. I don't want anyone looking at us too closely."

"What about Mike and Sarah?" Phil asked while he untied the rope holding the boat in place.

"Since they didn't come back immediately, they must have gotten somewhere. They will probably be gone a few minutes. We'll just ease away a little bit," Mac said. "It's probably nothing, and we'll be right back. Besides, Mike gets himself in trouble all the time. He'll know what to do."

As soon as everyone was in the boat, Mac started the RIB's outboard motor and backed slowly away from the cave entrance. He moved the boat to the middle of the small cove and faced it the other direction, keeping the outboard idling. As soon as he did, the other boat appeared. It was moving fast as it rounded the opening to the cove. As soon the man driving the boat saw the threesome on the RIB, he pulled back on the throttles and stopped his boat about 100 yards away.

Mac realized there were two men on the newly arrived boat. He couldn't make out what they were doing, but he could see them talking and pointing his way. He kept his hand on the throttle, ready to react.

"You two keep down," Mac said to his daughter and Phil. "I don't know what's going on here, but I don't trust these guys."

"The upside to Mike and Sarah being underwater is from a distance we look just like you did yesterday. Three people on board," Phil reasoned. "Is that the same boat you saw yesterday?"

"I'm pretty sure it is," Mac said.

"Then they don't have any reason to suspect we have two people in the water," Phil said. "They wouldn't have any way of knowing that five of us left the Espial."

Suddenly, the sound of automatic rifle fire ripped into the air. One of the men on the boat opened up with a machine gun in their direction while the other threw the throttles forward and charged at the RIB.

"That also means they don't think the three of us will be missed!" Mac yelled as he twisted the handle on the RIB's outboard, the engine screamed to life and the small boat leapt forward. With the larger boat charging straight at them, they didn't have much time to react and less space to maneuver.

Mac accelerated as quickly as he could straight for the opposite side of the cove — away from Mike and Sarah. Andie was hanging over the bow watching out for shallow rocks, but trying to keep down. The RIB was more nimble on the water than the heavier boat chasing them. Andie raised a hand to warn her father that they were approaching a rock in the water and Mac dodged to the right.

The heavier boat was closing in on them. The second man on the boat cut loose with another strafing blast from the machine gun. They were trying to drive the RIB toward the back of the cove and run them into the rocks.

Again the machine gun cut loose with an ear-splitting blast as the boat got closer. The RIB lost power and began to slow.

"Dad, did they hit the engine?" Andie said as she looked around. She saw Mac slumping forward, losing grip on the throttle. "Dad!" Andie yelled as she jumped for the back of the boat. She grabbed her father and the throttle at the same time. Phil just as quickly realized what was going on.

"Take the throttle, I've got Mac," he said.

"But it's my dad!" Andie started to argue.

"And if we don't get out of here, they're going to kill us all," Phil shouted back. "Now move. You've got more experience with boats than I do."

Phil dragged the older man forward into the boat and began to check him out. Mac was still semi-conscious, but was bleeding from a bullet wound to the upper back. He had blood on his mouth. Andie sat numbly watching Phil examine her father.

"Andie, he's still alive. But we've got to get him help fast. It looks like the bullet hit his lung. He's bleeding internally and will drown in his own blood if we don't get out of here fast," Phil said. "Now move!"

That information and Phil's shout broke Andie from her stupor. She glanced over her shoulder and cranked the throttle on the RIB as hard as she could. The boat seemed to sense her rage at the men chasing them. It leaped into the air like a scared dog. The bow of the larger boat barely missed the RIB as it came barreling down at them. The men on board were trying to run them down.

Phil grabbed a towel and attempted to slow Mac's bleeding while Andie ran the boat wide open around the inside of the cove. The larger boat continued to chase them. Andie began to back off a bit and Phil looked around, trying to understand what was going on.

"What's wrong?" he shouted.

"Not a thing. I want them to get a little closer is all," Andie said.

"You have a plan?"

"I noticed some shallow rocks over that way when we first came in," Andie said. "I'm going to run them aground."

"Just keep us off of them in the process," Phil said.

As he said it, the RIB lurched to the side, scraping off of a submerged rock. The small boat didn't stop and no water came in. Andie paused for one more moment, and then dodged to the right, heading for deeper water in the middle of the cove.

The larger boat didn't have time to react. Its hull extended deeper in the water than the lightweight RIB. Where the RIB bounced off the rocks, the bigger boat slammed directly into them throwing the men on board forward.

Andie pulled the RIB toward the mouth of the cove about 200 yards away and then she slowed down. She didn't see any movement on board the other boat.

"Do you think they're dead?" Phil asked.

"I doubt it," Andie replied. "Probably just shaken up some."

"Mac is going to need medical attention. We've got to get him back to the ship," Phil said. Mac was still breathing, but he had lost consciousness.

"I can't just leave these killers here with Mike and Sarah underwater. What if they come out of the cave to find us gone?" Andie asked, torn between her father and her friends.

"Mac said Mike had been in worse spots than this. When he realizes our boat is gone, he'll know something happened. He'll be cautious. When he sees the wrecked boat, he'll hide until it's safe. We'll send someone back for him," Phil argued. "That's all we can do for now. But we've got to get Mac help or he is definitely going to die."

Andie stared at her father for a moment and then made up her mind. She gunned the throttle and headed toward the Espial as fast as she could.

CHAPTER 31

The water closed over Mike's head. He could see Sarah just ahead of him, but he paused for a moment to let his eyes adjust to the cave-created shadows. The warm Caribbean water felt like bathwater. He was only wearing shorts and a t-shirt, but he was more than comfortable. Sarah had on a one-piece swimsuit but she kept her shorts and t-shirt on as well. Her curly hair was tied back in a pony tail. They were both wearing dive booties with their adjustable fins and they both had dive lights in their hands.

As Mike became accustomed to the gloom, he panned his dive light across the rock wall in front of him. If nothing else, Sarah had been right that it opened up further into the cave than they could tell from the surface. He still wasn't sure if there was an opening inside the cave though. They would figure that out in a minute.

Mike caught up with Sarah and put his hand on her arm. She turned and looked at him. She was clearly smiling behind her mask and regulator. She motioned him forward as she picked her way along the rocks inside the cave. Mike kept a hand on the rope that led back to the surface. It was tied off on a rock just below the waterline outside the cave entrance. Even though he could still easily see the light shining into the water from the cave opening behind them he didn't want to lose the way back out.

As Mike got closer, Sarah pointed upward with her light. There was an opening in the rocks over their head. Mike could see Sarah's light reflecting on the surface of the water. The floating, quick-silver-like reflection meant there was an air space above the water. From where they were, there was no way of knowing if it led to anything or not, however. It might simply be a bubble just a few inches above the waterline.

Sarah pointed to herself and then toward the opening. Mike wasn't thrilled with her decision, but he grudgingly nodded okay. She was going to go up and take a look.

The opening through the rocks was going to be too small for her to fit through with her scuba gear in place. She was going to have to take it off and push it ahead of her through the hole. She would keep the regulator in her mouth and follow the gear into the hole.

As Sarah began unbuckling her scuba gear to push it through the opening, Mike heard the whine of a boat engine starting up. He realized his friends had started the RIB for some reason. He didn't know what was going on topside, but knew that would have to wait. For safety's sake, he needed to keep his attention focused on Sarah and their dive.

In their tight confines, Mike held Sarah around the waist to keep her steady while she prepared to push her scuba gear over her head into the opening. She wrapped her leg around his while she got everything into position. For a moment, Mike's mind wandered again, but this time he was thinking about something more immediate — the feel of her skin on his. Sarah must have sensed his thoughts because this time she looked him in the eyes again. She was still smiling, but this time there was a different expression on her face. She squeezed his arm tightly and nodded.

After a moment, she released her grip and began looking upward again. She pushed her gear ahead of her with one hand and her dive light in the other. Mike watched as Sarah's scuba cylinder and buoyancy jacket slipped through the hole, followed by her head and then her shoulders. In a moment, she was completely out of sight.

It must go up further than it looked, Mike thought to himself. He sat still, waiting and watching for what felt like 10 minutes, but was probably no more than a few seconds. Then, Sarah's head reappeared back down through the hole. She motioned for him to come up.

Mike repeated the steps Sarah had just gone through. He unbuckled the buoyancy jacket that kept the scuba gear and air cylinder in place and then bundled it all together in tight package. He kept the regulator in his mouth and turned the scuba unit upside down. To give him the most room to move around the top of the unit had to stay close to his face. He pushed the bottom end of the cylinder through the hole first and then began swimming up after it.

The hole had been a tight fit for Sarah. Mike knew it was going to be tougher for him to fit his broad shoulders through the space into the cave above. Mike just hoped it opened up quickly once he was through the hole. Keeping his arms above his head helped him narrow his profile slightly. He felt the rocks scrape against his arms and shoulders. Mike was afraid he was going to get stuck for a moment until he felt Sarah grab his arm and pull him through the sticking point. It was only in his imagination, but he almost thought he heard a pop when he cleared the narrow opening.

Mike quickly realized he was seated on a rock in three feet of water. His head had broken the water's surface. Sarah was standing up. She had taken her regulator out of her mouth and was taking off her fins.

"Are you nuts?" Mike shouted. "The air might not be safe to breathe!"

"You're breathing it now, too," Sarah replied, her eyes dancing.

"Only after I saw you doing it," Mike grumbled.

"I knew you were right behind me. If I passed out, you could get me out of here," Sarah reasoned. "One of us had to test it."

"Fine. But next time at least let me get through the hole first," Mike said.

"Sure. Next time you and I wiggle into an air-filled sea cave, I'll let you be the one to test the air," Sarah laughed.

"You better," Mike said smiling.

"If you're finished being grumpy, take a look around."

"Pffft." Mike snorted, but he did shine his light toward the ceiling of the cave. It was much higher than he expected, rising at least 15 feet over the water level. It was larger than he expected, too. Toward the back of the cave, he could see what looked like an opening into another room. The floor was mostly flat, almost worn smooth.

He turned to face the front of the cave, where it should have been open to the outside. What he saw confirmed that the once-open cave had definitely been closed off. He had no way of knowing if it was closed intentionally, or if it was a natural rock slide, but the opening was filled with rocks and other rubble.

Sarah pulled herself out of the water and laid her gear beside the opening to the pool. Mike pushed his dive gear toward her and she lifted it out too. Mike climbed out beside it. The air inside the cave was cool, but neither of them was uncomfortable even though they were dripping wet.

"Let's take a quick look around, but we can't stay in here too long. The guys outside will freak out," Mike said.

"Agreed," Sarah said, already in motion with her light pointed at the ceiling. "Look at this. Are these cave paintings?"

"I've read about pre-Columbian paintings in some caves in this area," Mike said. "They looked similar to these. The ones I read about were only discovered after the beginning of the 20th century, though."

"That could mean this cave was closed off before then. When did you say the Huron wrecked again?" Sarah asked.

"It went down in 1877. I know what you're thinking and it makes sense. If the cave was where the Huron was headed but never made it, maybe they closed it off," Mike agreed. "I wish I had brought my camera along."

"We didn't quite know we were going to go cave exploring today, after a quick dive and cave penetration," Sarah said with a smirk.

"It never occurred to me to grab my underwater housing for my camera gear," Mike agreed. "We'll have to come back later."

They looked around the small cave room but saw nothing else of significance. The walls looked like they had been eroded over time, making them nearly smooth. The roof of the cave was egg-shaped with the fat, rounder part of the egg ending in the water.

"Do you want to check out the next room?" Sarah asked, gesturing toward the small opening near the floor.

Mike shined his light at the opening for the first time. It was nearly three feet high and rounded. But Mike immediately realized there was a problem. The hole was blocked.

"We're not going through that way," he said.

"Why not? Oh. I couldn't see that before," Sarah said as she moved closer.

Two feet inside the opening there was a flat wall. Sarah kneeled down and touched it. It was cool to the touch. Iron. It was a man-made plate of some kind.

"Does it move?" Mike asked as he kneeled down beside Sarah.

She pushed with one hand, and then with two, but the iron plate didn't move at all.

"Let me try," Mike said. He dropped onto his stomach so he could get a better angle to push with both hands. Nothing. He turned around and pushed with his feet. Still nothing. Mike kicked it, but all they heard was a hollow ringing sound.

"Just like a man, always going for brute force," Sarah said with a chuckle.

"Checking to see if it's rusted shut. Who knows, maybe I can break it free," Mike said, but after Sarah's teasing, he didn't kick the plate again.

"Come here and look at this," Sarah said, shining her light at the cold metal. "It almost looks like a key slot on this side."

"You're right. Hmmm. Well I'm not carrying any old skeleton keys on me right now." Mike said, trying to think of what to do. He knew there was something he was missing, but he couldn't put his finger on it at the moment. "There is something here, though. Or at least there was at one time. We've got a cave that was intentionally blocked and then another cave off of that with a man-made, locked door built into it. Someone wanted to keep this place secure."

"I vote we go get some tools and get this door open," Sarah said.

"I'm right there with ya," Mike agreed. "But for the moment we need to get back topside. We need to tell the others what we've found," Mike agreed. "I'm sure they're waiting on us and getting angrier by the minute."

CHAPTER 32

Andie drove the small RIB as hard as she could toward the Espial. She needed to get help for her Dad! She couldn't look down. She just had to concentrate on the job in front of her. Getting back to the ship.

In the back of her mind she remembered Mike and Sarah in the sea cave. And she knew two armed men were close by them. If the divers surfaced in time for the men to recover their senses, there could be trouble. But she also knew she couldn't wait on them to resurface and there was no way to recall them back to the boat. She was sure Mike would have made the same decision.

"How is he doing?" Andie shouted over the roar of the outboard. The water was still calm with only small wavelets passing through. Andie was able to run the RIB engine wide open toward the ship. With only three people and without the dive gear, the boat was light and fast.

"I can't really tell, but he's still breathing and his heart is still beating. That's a good sign. The bleeding seems to have slowed down, but I don't know what's happening on the inside," Phil yelled back.

Andie watched Phil for a moment. His movements were sure and confident. He might be a cryptanalyst and a lab geek, but he knew what he was doing too.

"Where did you learn first aid?" Andie asked to distract herself.

"I love to hike and mountain climb," he replied. "I took a wilderness first aid course last year. Pretty intense stuff."

"I'm glad you're here now."

"How much longer until we get to the Espial? Hey, does this boat have a radio?" Phil asked.

"About five minutes. I just caught sight of the ship," Andie said. And then she glanced down and shook her head. "I never even thought about a radio. Yes, it does have one."

"Didn't think of it 'til just now myself," Phil replied. "Give me the mic. You keep driving."

Andie turned the radio on and handed the handset to Phil while she corrected her course slightly.

"Espial, Espial, Espial. This is Espial RIB boat," Phil shouted over the radio.

"Espial RIB, this is Espial. What do you need?"

"Espial, this is Dr. Phil Parrot. We have a medical emergency. Severe trauma with internal bleeding. We are approaching at full speed from the east. Please have the medical doctor meet us to bring injured party aboard."

"I read you, Dr. Parrot. I'm alerting the captain and the medical doctor right now. The expedition director Dr. Fallow left the Espial earlier today. I will try to reach him as well," the radio man replied. "We'll have a team ready to meet you. Can you give us details on the nature of the injury?"

"I'd rather not say over an open channel," Phil replied. "Patient seems stable for the moment, but there is some blood loss. ETA about three minutes."

"We'll be ready. Espial out."

"Why didn't you say dad was shot?" Andie asked, still trying to distract herself.

"It's an open channel. Anyone could be listening. The Cubans. The Coast Guard. The people who did the shooting. I'd rather not broadcast to the world that we were attacked and where we were headed," Phil said.

"That makes sense," Andie said, nodding her head. She reached up and pulled back on the throttle. She was still going to come in fast, but she didn't want to hit the Espial and hurt her father more. Having spent most of her life to this point on and around boats, she could handle them as well as anyone. She had enough time behind the wheel to sit for her Captain's License, but she hadn't done it. She had been more interested in school and her degree lately.

The Espial had a small doorway built directly through the hull, just above the waterline. They lowered the smaller boats into the water using winches, but passengers were able to step out onto a small platform and then into the boats. Andie saw a several crew members on the small platform with a stretcher to care for her father. She slid the boat right up beside the platform as one of the crewmen grabbed the bow of the RIB and began tying it off.

Everything happened quickly. The crew had an emergency response team for situations like this. Dr. Rae was standing there as well, but she let the crew members aboard the small RIB and lift Mac into the basket stretcher. They quickly strapped him in and lifted him out of the boat and onto the platform.

Phil moved out of the way while the crew did their jobs. He stepped onto the platform beside Dr. Rae.

"Doctor, our friend was shot. He has a gunshot wound in his ribs. He was coughing up blood, but that has stopped. He is breathing and his heart is steady, but it seems fast to me," Phil reported.

"Okay, thank you Dr. Parrot," Rae said. "I'm not going to ask right now how he was shot but there will be lots of questions to answer later. What can you tell me about his health?"

"I don't know the man that well. Hold on," Phil replied. "Andie. Andie. ANDIE!" he shouted to get her attention.

She hadn't moved since she brought the boat to the platform. She was rooted to the floor watching the men bundle her father up. At Phil's shout she came back to the world.

"What?"

"I need you to talk to Rae about your dad's health. Any medical conditions. That sort of thing," Phil explained.

"Oh, Okay. Sure. What do you want to know?" Andie was back to reality. She stepped from the boat to the platform just as Mac came on board as well.

"Follow me, we can talk as we get back to my office," Rae said, moving to Mac's side. She began her examination, cutting away Mac's shirt to get a better look at the wound. "Let's move guys. Fast!"

CHAPTER 33

Mike and Sarah quickly donned their dive gear to return to the surface. He wanted to let his friends know what they had found and then get back to the cave. He wanted to work on getting the iron door open and see what was hidden behind it. Mike tied the rope they had used as an emergency line inside the cave. That way when they came back, they could all just follow the rope and move quickly. There would be no guessing to find the hole in the opening. If Mike or Sarah wasn't the first one through on the next trip, anyone could do it. It would lead them from the rocks outside the cave entrance all the way to the first room.

When they were ready to swim back out, Mike pulled himself underwater and leveraged himself out through the tight-fitting gap using the rope. When he was through the hole, he turned around and shined the light on the hole behind him until Sarah wiggled through.

After being underground their eyes had adjusted to the dim glow of their dive lights. The sunlight that illuminated the exit in front of them was almost too bright to look at as they swam forward. Mike looked at his dive watch for the first time since they began the dive. It was still early morning, but he noted it had been more than a half an hour since they began their dive. Time flies, he thought.

The pair surfaced side-by-side outside the cave entrance, directly beside the rock where they tied the rope off. Together they realized everything was quiet. The RIB was gone.

"I forgot about it while we were in the cave, but just before we slipped up through the hole in the rocks, I heard the boat engine start up," Mike said. "I hope everything is all right."

At least they didn't leave us at sea," Sarah said. "Let's get out of our gear and take a look around. Maybe they left us a note or something."

The divers slipped out of their buoyancy jackets and set their scuba units on a rock just inside the cave entrance. They left their masks and fins with their gear and climbed outside of the cave entrance so they could see the cove.

"Does that count as a message?" Mike said, pointing to the wrecked boat on the rocks about 50 feet away from the sea cave.

"It sure tells me something. And it's not a message I like," Sarah said. "Should we check it out?"

"Yes, let's go see if anyone is hurt. But I think we need to be cautious about this. We've been gone a half an hour. In that time a strange boat has wrecked and ours is missing. That tells me something went really, really wrong here," Mike said.

"You have a gift for the understatement, you know that?" Sarah asked.

"It's one of my charms," Mike agreed. "Just be on the lookout for whoever wrecked this boat."

Mike and Sarah moved forward slowly, keeping low to the water and constantly looking around for any movement. They made it to the boat without seeing any signs of life. After listening for a moment, Mike stood up and looked over the side of the boat. He could see the interior of the boat. There was no one there. What he saw disturbed him more though.

Blood. Mike motioned to Sarah that it was all clear.

"Care to guess what happened here?" Sarah asked.

"I have no idea," Mike said. "From the way everything in this boat is thrown forward, it looks like it hit the rocks moving really fast. There is blood on the deck and up there on the dash. I'm guessing that's from the crash. Someone got hurt pretty badly."

"Mike, are those bullets?"

"Yes. Well, not bullets, but empty brass. Someone was shooting a rifle from inside this boat. And they were shooting a lot," Mike said as he noticed all of the empty shells that had been flung forward in the crash. "This isn't looking good at all."

"What do you want to do?"

"Not sure. I don't think it's safe for us to hang around here, though," Mike said. "Whoever was doing the shooting might come back. Since this doesn't look like a friendly boat, I don't think I want to meet them."

"What if our people come back looking for us?" Sarah asked as she scanned the land around the cove.

"I'm sure they will, if they can. But until then, we're on our own," Mike said, thinking for a second. "Let's see if there is anything on the boat we can use. And then let's move out."

Sarah stepped on a rock and climbed inside the boat. "Looks like they took about everything with them. The guns are gone. No portable radios," she said. She attempted to use the radio connected to the boat, but it didn't come on. The crash had shorted out the electrical system. She did find a couple bottles of water.

"It seems like there's a small village a few miles west of here. I remember seeing it on the map. Let's head that way. Maybe someone there will have a marine radio. Or a phone. If nothing else, that moves us back toward the Espial."

"Do you trust the ship?"

"This boat isn't from the Espial. At least we know that whoever was doing the shooting isn't from there. No clue if someone on board sent them, though," Mike agreed. "I just don't see that we have much of a choice at this point."

"You're right. We head out on foot toward the village and the Espial. Maybe we'll see a boat we can signal along the way," Sarah agreed as she slipped back over the side and into the water. She handed Mike one of the bottles of water.

"It looks like there is a way up the hill just over there. And then we head around the cove and back the way we came," Mike said pointing at a sandy area that would lead them out of the water. Before they left the water, Mike went back to his dive gear and pulled the smaller dive light off. He stuck it in the cargo pocket on the leg of his shorts and then submerged their dive gear just under the water. He didn't want it to float away and didn't want anyone else to see it, either.

They began their trek back to the ship. Both of them were quiet as they walked. They were concerned for their friends. And not sure about what was going on.

CHAPTER 34

For Andie, the next few minutes went by in a blur. All she could see was her father bleeding on the boat. She couldn't stand to lose him. After her mother died, he was everything for her. Mac was older, in his late 50s. He had married her mother later in life and had her a few years later. Still, he was a strong, robust man. He loved to be outdoors on the water. In Andie's world, her father would be there forever. She couldn't imagine anything else.

While Andie sat still, in shock, everyone else was in overdrive.

Dr. Rae Lesley was a former US Army doctor who specialized in battlefield medicine before leaving the service and working in various emergency departments around the country. She had burned out, finally, and opted to take what she believed would be a more comfortable position on board the Espial. She was just beginning to get a little bored when Mac arrived with a gunshot wound in the ribs. Adrenaline took over and she was back in battlefield mode.

"Let's get an x-ray on his chest. I need to see where the bullet is," Rae said with urgency for the situation, but without yelling. She was thoroughly in command in her medical suite. "It didn't come out. I need to figure out if

I need to remove it, or if we can stabilize him with it in his chest."

That was the last thing Andie and Phil heard as Dr. Rae moved Mac into the small operating room she had set up on the ship. She had two medics among the crew trained to help her.

Phil and Andie sat in chairs just outside the swinging doors to wait. They were both lost in their own thoughts for a few moments. Finally, reaching for Phil's hand, Andie broke the silence.

"Thanks, Phil."

"For what?"

"Taking care of Dad. You stopped the bleeding. I appreciate it," Andie said with a wan smile and a slight squeeze of the hand.

"I did what I could. I'm sure he's going to be just fine," Phil replied.

"I hope so," she said with a deep sigh. "But now, what are we going to do about Mike and Sarah? I'm worried. Did we do the right thing by leaving them behind? We've got to go get them. The men who shot at us might catch them or there might be others."

"You did what you had to do in the heat of the moment," Phil said trying to ease Andie's mind. "Yes, I think you did the right thing. I get the feeling Mike has been in worse scrapes than this. I mean, I don't know him as well as you do, but just from a few of the stories he has told me, he has seen some hairy situations. Being left to walk home along the sea with a beautiful woman doesn't even qualify. My guess is they're heading back this way. They're probably walking toward the town to call for help."

Andie looked up at Phil. She smiled. "If you only knew half of the stuff he has been through, you would laugh. This is a walk in the park."

"See. Don't worry about it. Mike and Sarah will be fine," Phil said. "They're probably working on their tans right now. I'll let the bridge know that we had an injury and had to come back to the boat. I'll ask them to get a boat back out to look for Mike and Sarah as soon as they can. Okay?"

CHAPTER 35

While Mike and Sarah were getting sun, neither one of them considered the walk they were taking time to work on their tans. Both divers were still wearing their dive booties to protect their feet and both of them had taken off their t-shirts and tied them around their heads to keep the sun out of their eyes. The salt-soaked shirts would only chafe once they dried out anyway. Sarah had on a one-piece swim suit and a pair of shorts. Mike was only wearing a pair of shorts.

Instead of thinking about themselves, they were doing the same thing that Phil and Andie were doing. They were worrying about their friends.

"They'll be all right, Mike," Sarah said as they trudged down a small dirt road they found not too far from the cove. "I'm sure they're back on the boat relaxing with a perfectly logical explanation for what happened."

"I hope you're right, Sarah," Mike said. "I hope you're right."

"People live on this island, right?" Sarah asked to change the subject. She was looking around and couldn't see anything that looked like a structure or anything man-made…except for the road itself.

"Yes, there are people on the island," Mike said with a laugh. "Quite a few, actually. We just happen to be in the mostly-uninhabited part. We are heading in the general direction of Punta del Este. I don't think we're too far from it, actually."

"So I shouldn't start worrying about rationing water in this heat or anything, huh?"

"I think we'll both survive long enough to get to the town and get some help. If you collapse, I'll send help back for you," Mike said.

"You'd just leave me?" Sarah asked, feigning offense.

"Hey, I said I would come back for you, didn't I?"

"Well, no. Actually you said you send help back for me," Sarah argued. "I get the feeling you would be sitting in air conditioning while I was dying out here."

"That's not fair!" Mike said, grinning as he turned to face her. "I doubt anyone in this town has air conditioning."

"Well, that certainly helps this issue," she said shaking her head. "And it looks like we'll get a chance to find out pretty soon." Sarah pointed to the west up the dirt road. A car was coming with a trail of dust billowing out behind it.

"Here's the question," Mike said when he looked at the car headed their way. "Is it friend or foe?"

"Aren't you a killjoy?" Sarah said, growing quiet. She had been too relieved to see the car coming that she hadn't thought that it might not be someone there to help them.

"I don't think we can afford to hide and let this car pass us by. We need to get back and check on our friends. They've probably sent someone out to find us," Mike reasoned.

"So, friend or foe, we really don't have a choice but to wait here and let them find us, do we?"

"Not really, no," Mike agreed.

It only took a few minutes for the car to reach them. It was a 1950

Studebaker, its distinctive bullet nose obvious in spite of the worn paint. Neither Mike nor Sarah moved from their spots as the car slowed down beside them. They didn't see any point in continuing to walk.

As the dust cleared, they were both relieved to see Dr. Fallow open the passenger door and step out of the car.

They were relieved that is, right up until they saw the gun in his hand.

CHAPTER 36

It was 20 long minutes before the doctor came back out to speak to Phil and Andie. Still holding hands, they released and stood up as she came into the hallway. Rae had a vague smile on her face, which immediately helped Andie breathe.

"We've got your dad stabilized," Dr. Rae began. "The bullet is still in his chest, but it won't cause any problems for now. I was able to close off the wound and get his lung re-inflated before it totally collapsed. A helicopter is on the way from Guantanamo Bay. The army base has a full surgical suite, so they can operate on him there."

The US army base on the island of Cuba was on the far eastern end, approximately 500 air miles from where the Espial was anchored. A US Army search and rescue helicopter, a Sikorsky HH-60 Pave Hawk, had been dispatched from the base. It was carrying extra fuel tanks to make the journey, but it would still take better than two hours to get there and would be low on fuel when it arrived. Politics kept it from flying the most direct path over land.

The research ship carried the fuel necessary to refuel the helicopter and get it back to the base. The Pave Hawk was just barely able to land on the Espial. The fuel would normally be used for the Espial's own smaller helicopter but that aircraft didn't have the range to make it to Guantanamo so they had to send the bigger aircraft.

To increase the helicopter's safety margin, the Espial's captain had recalled the research boats and was heading east. He hoped to save flying time and reduce the helicopter's distance.

"Can I go along?" Andie asked.

"I already told them you would be," Rae said.

"Doctor, we have another problem. When Mac was shot, we had to leave two of our people behind. They were underwater and we couldn't wait for them to resurface. We had to get help for Mac," Phil explained. "We've got to send a boat back for Mike and Sarah now."

"I need to know what happened. How did he get shot? Was this some sort of argument between your dad and someone?"

"We were attacked!" Andie said, her voice getting loud. "Men came out of nowhere and just started shooting at us. I have no idea why!"

"Strange men just started shooting at you?"

"Hold on, Andie. Let me explain what happened," Phil said, putting his hand on the girl's shoulder. He knew Andie was stretched to the limit and doubted she could recount the events of the morning. Phil quickly explained their trip to the cave and the strange attack by the men in the boat. He only left out what they were looking for.

"I see," Rae said. "With the boat underway to meet with the helicopter, we can't send a boat out to look for them. They are on their own until the helicopter arrives and leaves again with Mac on board. There is another problem, too."

"Oh no," Andie said, hanging her head down.

"What's the other problem, Rae," Phil asked.

"There's a storm coming. It's out of season, but there is a hurricane forming in the eastern Caribbean. It'll be here in a day or so," Rae explained. "It pretty much came up out of nowhere. If the storm moves faster than we expect, we might not be able to get a boat out to look for them at all."

"Phil, we abandoned them!" Andie said, her voice getting an edge of hysteria.

"Andie, listen to me!" Phil shouted, grabbing her by her shoulders. "You need to pull it together. You did what you had to do to save a man's life. To save your father's life. Don't give up now. I'm sure you did exactly what Mike would have told you to do if he had been there."

"Now it's my turn to tell you two a story," the doctor interrupted. "I feel like you're telling me the truth so now I have to trust you. I am a medical doctor, but I also work for a special branch of the US Department of State. We look out for people smuggling antiquities into the country. We learned about a group that was trying to use this research trip to recover items and bring them in without reporting them. Frankly, we thought it was you and your people."

"Why are you telling us this?" Phil asked.

"A couple reasons. First, I've had you all checked out very thoroughly. Between your security clearance and Mr. Scott's international reputation, I find it hard to believe you're smuggling antiquities. People in that business try to keep a low profile," Rae explained.

"Well, in truth, we were looking for something. It may be antiquities. We just don't know. But the main reason we were searching for whatever it is, was to help figure out why Dr. Peter DeSutton was kidnapped," Phil said. He went on to explain what had happened before the foursome came to the boat.

"This is a real mess, isn't it?" Rae said, shaking her head. "The other reason I don't suspect you now is that my partner and I were also keeping an eye on someone else on board. And that person has disappeared."

"Who else were you watching? Was it that crewman who came on board at Fort Jefferson? He made us all pretty nervous," Andie asked.

"Actually, no, that's my partner. He was delayed in leaving and just caught up with us at the fort. He's been checking out the ship though. That's probably why he made you nervous. As I said, we suspected you at first," Rae said.

"Who has gone missing, then?" Phil asked.

"It's Dr. Fallow, the head of the science team, if you can believe it. He disappeared this morning and we weren't able to reach him on the radio when we tried to recall the boats. He's just gone," Rae explained.

CHAPTER 37

"Somehow this doesn't shock me," Sarah said. She was the first to speak as she and Mike stared at the gun in Dr. Ian Fallow's hand.

"It just confirms why I didn't like him from the moment I met him," Mike agreed, speaking to Sarah, but looking Fallow in the eyes. "I thought he was creepy."

"I've had enough of both of you," Fallow said. "Just shut up. You're going to tell me what you found. Or I use this gun."

"Oh sure. I found this 20 foot tall golden statue. It's right here in my pocket. Wanna see it?" Sarah asked, her voice full of sarcasm.

"What makes you think we found anything?" Mike asked. "We're just out for a walk on the island. We wanted to get on dry land for a little while."

"Felix, I think I can use your assistance with these two," Fallow said over his shoulder.

The old car creaked with relief as a large man got out of the driver's side of the Studebaker. He was carrying a gun, but it was in a shoulder holster. Felix was imposing. At a full six and a half feet tall and pushing 300 pounds, he was menacing enough that he didn't need to draw the gun. But even more unsettling was the fact that while he was big, he wasn't fat. It was solid muscle.

"You know, that car is in great shape," Mike said to the driver. "Is it yours? You should be proud of it."

The large man simply glared at Mike.

"Sarah, do you remember that time in the Keys?" Mike said. "Something tells me we're going to have to do that again. Very soon."

"Really?" Sarah said, cooing. "I think I'd like that,"

When the pair originally met, they had run across land developers attempting to put a small marina out of business to get the waterfront land. That time, men had pointed guns at them, too. They had to fight the developers to get away.

"Me, too," Mike said, smiling at her. "When we do go again, why don't you take the car and go on ahead. I'll entertain our friends. I'll miss you, but that's the only way I think it will work. You go get some more people for the party. It'll be great."

"What are you talking about? I need to know what you found and where it is. Now!" Fallow barked at them.

As Fallow yelled, both Mike and Sarah jumped into motion. Mike dived at Felix, catching the larger man in the stomach with his shoulder. The two men fell together on the ground. Mike was on top, but Felix wrapped his arms around Mike and began to squeeze.

Sarah punched Fallow in the jaw. As he fell backward against the car from the force of the unexpected blow, she slammed the still-open door on his body and he fell to the ground in a heap.

Her only thought was of getting away. Mike had told her to run, when he talked about going to get other friends for the party in the Keys. And that he would entertain their friends. He meant he would keep Fallow and Felix busy long enough for her to escape and get help.

She slid across the bench front seat. Yes! Felix had left the keys in the ignition. The car had a manual transmission with a shifter on the column. She cranked the switch, but nothing happened. She tried again, with the same result. What was wrong? "Think, Sarah, think," she said to herself. "What is wrong with this thing?"

Then she saw it. A light switch had been installed on the aging dashboard. It was obviously not factory equipment. Suddenly she remembered that Cuban mechanics had to make do to keep these pre-revolution cars running. They often rigged equipment from other vehicles or whatever they could find. This time she flipped the switch on the dashboard. Still nothing.

"Arrrrgh," she screamed inside the car. "Okay, Sarah, one more try," she said, talking her way through it. "Is it both the ignition and the switch? If they had completely replaced the car's ignition with the light switch, there wouldn't be any reason for the keys. But that would make it too easy to steal. And something has to tell the starter to move into position against the flywheel. It must be both. The switch for the electrical system and the key for the starter."

This time she flipped the switch into the "On" position and twisted the key in the ignition. She heard the starter engage the tired, old engine just as she guessed. At the same time she pushed the clutch to the floor. The old car roared to life, just as she saw Fallow stand up. He was unsteady on his feet from her attack. She couldn't see Mike. He and Felix were still fighting on the ground.

She grabbed the shifter with her right hand and pulled it into reverse. She wanted to get clear of their attackers and then find help. She didn't think they would kill Mike if they knew there was someone out there who could identify them. She gunned the engine and threw dirt and gravel as she backed away in a cloud of dust.

Crack! She heard the unmistakable sound of a gunshot. Had they killed Mike? Did Fallow shoot him? Oh my God! Sarah hit the brakes about 50 feet away and stared at the scene through the windshield. It took a second for the dust to settle well enough for her to see.

Fallow was standing up with his gun pointed at Mike and Felix. Mike had Felix pinned to the ground with an arm raised back to deliver a final, knockout blow. He had frozen when Fallow fired the pistol. Fallow turned his eyes back to Sarah. He motioned for her to come back with his left hand while he kept his right hand, and the gun, pointed at the two men struggling on the ground. His intent was clear. He would shoot Mike in cold blood. From the look in his eyes, he didn't care if he hit Felix in the process.

Sarah deflated behind the wheel. Fallow had lost it. Whatever this was all about had pushed him beyond reason. She could see that he was capable of anything and wasn't worried about the future. Murder certainly wasn't out of the question.

Slowly, she restarted the car. It had stalled when she had slammed on the brakes. She put the car back in gear, forward this time and moved back toward the three men. For half a second, she thought about ramming Fallow, but she realized if she gunned the engine, he would know it and have time to fire before she reached him. Mike would still be dead. She eased the car forward and stopped a few feet away from where she started.

Felix flipped Mike onto his back on the ground. Both men were dirty and breathing heavily from the struggle. Felix didn't hesitate. He punched Mike in the cheek, knocking him unconscious.

"Get out of the car," Fallow growled at Sarah. "Your friend is still alive. I'll be happy to shoot you and beat him until he tells me what I want to know. Either way works just fine for me."

Sarah glared at Fallow, but did as he ordered. She didn't like where this was going, but with Mike unconscious, she didn't have much choice.

"Felix, get him and put him in trunk. I don't want to deal with any more escape attempts," Fallow ordered.

Felix grabbed Mike's arms and began dragging him toward the car. In spite of Felix's greater size, Mike had hurt the man. Felix was struggling. Sarah could see a bruised eye and bloody lip as well.

"Are you going to ride in the trunk with your friend? Or in the car with us?" Fallow asked.

"I'll take the trunk, thanks," Sarah sneered. "I think it sounds a lot better than having to look at you. What happened to you? You are a successful scientist? How could you become a murderer?"

"I haven't killed anyone yet," Fallow replied. "But don't think for a second that I won't."

"What is this all about? Money? Gold?" Sarah asked. "You're better than that."

"Really? You think you know me?" Fallow asked, pausing for a moment. "You have no idea what drives me. You have no idea what I've seen. Don't even talk to me. Now get in the car. Sit down and shut up."

"I won't shut up. I want to know what is so valuable that you would throw away your entire career," Sarah said.

"This was all supposed to be secret. I had no intention of throwing away my career, not that there was much of it left after those short-sighted fools stripped me of my tenure," Fallow said quietly.

"Sorry to mess things up for you," Sarah smiled sweetly.

"I've had enough of this. Felix?" Fallow said, turning to the other man.

Felix pulled his gun from his holster. In his fight with Mike, Felix's gun had been knocked away, but the man had recovered it after he had gotten Mike into the trunk. He approached Sarah. She stubbornly turned to face the giant of a man.

"What are you going to do?" Sarah asked the Cuban man. "Kill a woman in cold blood?"

He didn't say a word. He simply grabbed her arm and jerked her sideways. With his gun held flat, he hit her on the back of the head and neck. Sarah's knees buckled, but Felix bent forward and lifted her in the air over his shoulder. He holstered his gun and then dropped her in the trunk of the car beside Mike before he slammed the lid shut.

CHAPTER 38

The room swam into view for Mike. Everything was cloudy and dark, but he could make out rough shapes. He shook his head trying to clear the fog and immediately it felt as if his head was going to explode. He saw stars. The room didn't get any lighter, but once the pain receded it helped him focus on his surroundings.

He was tied to a chair with his arms behind the chair back. He couldn't move his feet either; they were tied to the front legs of the chair. He was numb from sitting in that position for too long.

"These boys aren't messing around," Mike said, talking to himself.

"It's about time you woke up," Sarah said softly.

"Where are you? I don't see you."

"We must be back to back. I could hear you breathing, but I can't see much of you either," Sarah said. "I knew you were here and alive, but didn't know if you were ever going to wake up."

"I've been knocked unconscious before. I don't know that it ever felt like this, though," Mike said. He was attempting to move his muscles and stretch as much as he could with his bindings. "My head is still really foggy. I think they may have drugged us with something."

"Lovely. How long do you think we've been out?" Sarah asked.

"No clue. It's dark, but I don't know if that's just the room or if it's dark outside," Mike said turning his head from side to side slowly trying to shake out the cobwebs without eliciting the shooting pain. "It's been a while, though. It would have taken them some time to get us wherever we are now, to get us out of the car and in here and tied up. Could be an hour. Or more. If they drugged us, it could be several hours."

"What are we going to do now?" Sarah asked, some worry slipping into her voice.

"Good question. Are you tied up the same way I am?" Mike replied.

"Well since I can't see you, I have no idea how you're tied up," Sarah chuckled.

"Good point. I'm tied to a chair with my arms behind me," Mike laughed. "Hurts pretty bad. Or it would if I could feel anything."

"That pretty well sums it up for me, too."

"Well, then I think we're going to have to wait for a while. Keep fidgeting and try to get the blood flowing again. See if you can loosen up any of the ropes. Barring that, we'll have to see what they have in store for us. Obviously they want something from us, or they would have just killed us," Mike reasoned.

"You're pretty matter-of-fact about this. Being tied up and all," Sarah said, her humor returning to her voice now that she was talking.

"I'm not terribly proud to admit it, but this isn't the first time I've woken up tied to a chair," Mike replied.

"Sounds like an interesting story," Sarah quipped. "Angry girlfriend?"

"Tell you what. When we get out of here, I'll give you all the gory details over a beer," Mike laughed. He knew it was helping Sarah to joke around. She had sounded nervous a few minutes before but she was already getting her spirit back. He also knew this situation would probably get worse before it got better…if it ever did.

They were in a foreign country, and one that wasn't exactly friendly to the United States. They had been taken captive by men using guns. And they knew one of them. Dr. Fallow had clearly determined he wasn't going to return to his former career so he had very little left to lose. This wasn't shaping up well.

As if on cue, the door to the small room opened letting light inside. For the first time, Mike was able to survey his surroundings. It was a small room, probably a bedroom, in an old house. The rough timber walls indicated it was probably a farm house. Cuba had long been covered with plantations for sugar cane and tobacco among other things. Since the communists took over, Mike wasn't sure how many of those farms existed. He guessed this one had been abandoned for quite some time.

The door was on Mike's left. He had reacted to the sound of the door opening and the flare of light from the doorway by turning his head and was rewarded with pain from the cheekbone where Felix had punched him to knock him unconscious. When his vision returned to normal, Fallow was standing in front of him with Felix.

"Turn them around," Fallow ordered. "I want to see their eyes and I want them to see each other."

Felix moved in front of Fallow and grabbed the chairs Mike and Sarah were pinned to. He twisted them around quickly and roughly, at the same time, jarring Mike's injuries. From the groan that escaped Sarah's lips, Mike realized she hadn't fared any better.

"What do you want?" Mike growled at Fallow, before his vision had fully cleared. He wanted to get the upper hand on the man by taking away the initiative.

"Quiet!" Fallow snapped. He paced around the room, trying to regain his composure.

"I need to know if you found the location," Fallow continued a moment later, more quietly, but both Mike and Sarah could tell he was seething. They didn't know why he was agitated at the moment but something had definitely set him off.

"Location for what?" Mike asked, innocently. "What are you talking about? It's a pretty big ocean." Mike paid for that tone and little bit of sarcasm with a back-handed blow across the mouth from Felix. Fortunately for Mike, the man struck him on the side of the face away from the one he had punched earlier. Mike was beginning to think his cheekbone was broken the way his head continued to hurt from that earlier blow. Still, the blow stung and made him dizzy for a moment. He could taste blood in his mouth.

"Did that make you feel better? I have no patience for this. And I definitely do not have the time to listen to your juvenile attitude," Fallow said, glaring at Mike. "I can have my friend here beat you to death if that is what it takes."

To prove his point, without warning Felix spun around and punched Mike in the ribs, lifting him up in the air and knocking him over in his chair. He landed hard on his arms and hands where they were bound behind him. The blow and the fall knocked the breath from Mike's lungs. He lay on his back gasping for air. Fortunately, Felix didn't continue the attack.

"Stop it!" Sarah yelled. "You animal, stop it!"

"You only need to tell me what I want to know and this will all stop and go away, my dear," Fallow said, looking at Sarah for the first time. "Who knows, I might even find a place for you where we go. I'm sure I would enjoy having a woman of your beauty along."

"That's not gonna happen, Fallow," Sarah snarled. "I'm not going anywhere with you."

"Ah, such beauty, but marred by such insolence. So be it," Fallow said. He turned to Felix. "Stand him back up. Maybe he's ready to talk, now."

Once Felix had righted Mike's chair, Fallow moved his own face within inches of Mike's. It took Mike a moment to focus on the other man. He was still dizzy from the pain and lack of oxygen from the blow to his ribs.

"I know you and your friends have been looking for the gold left here by the Spanish for the Cuban revolutionaries. I know you followed the secret message you found in the Huron's sea chest. I don't know how you decoded the message, but I think you have done it. If those fools hadn't shot your friends in the boat, I think we would have found out right then and there, but they screwed up and they will have to pay for that mistake," Fallow said, his voice tight. "Now, for the last time, stop playing games and tell me where the gold is."

Felix glanced at Fallow when he talked about the other men, but he didn't say anything. He looked troubled.

Mike simply glared back. His head hurt from the broken bone in his cheek and the bloody lip. He had been beaten up before while on assignment. All it ever served to do was make him more stubborn.

He didn't want to tell Fallow anything simply because he knew the man would steal what they found and sell it. There was no doubt in his mind that Fallow and his men had already killed or hurt others to find this secret. Mike didn't care for the money himself. That was the last thing on his mind. He had everything he needed. If anything, he thought, if he got a finder's fee for whatever they found, he would use the money to support a medical mission foundation he had set up years before after seeing life in the third world he so often covered.

As it happened, Mike hadn't actually seen anything. He and Sarah had found one empty cave and an iron door blocking the entrance to another one. He really didn't know what was behind that door. It might be an empty room that was built for the treasure long ago. It might all be gone. It might even hold something else entirely. They wouldn't know until they figured out how to open the door and looked inside.

Regardless, he wasn't going to tell Fallow anything. He didn't care about the money. But from sheer stubbornness, he didn't want to tell Fallow what they had seen. He knew the man was evil and would only use the money for his own greed. More troubling was what he had just said about his friends. Fallow said they had been shot. He had no way of knowing what had happened, but he didn't like the sound of it. If any of his friends were hurt, Fallow would pay.

Mike continued to glare at Fallow for a moment, until Sarah's voice broke the tension between the two men.

"Dr. Fallow," she said, trying to sound reasonable. "How could you give up your entire career for gold? Even if you wanted to find it, you could have done the research, and done all this above board. There was no reason people had to be kidnapped, hurt or killed for some gold."

Fallow straightened up for a moment, taking on an almost professorial air after he heard Sarah use his title.

"Several years ago, a group of treasure hunters spent a considerable fortune finding a lost shipwreck and bringing the gold to the surface," Fallow began lecturing. "After they had recovered millions of dollars worth of treasure, the Spanish sued them and claimed it all saying they had never surrendered the rights to that gold. The salvage company got nothing. I wasn't about to lose everything we worked for by doing this publicly. I want it all for myself. You talk about my career, but you know what that they did to me at the university. They stripped me of my tenure and put me on that god-forsaken boat. They put me out to pasture instead of giving me the respect and the recognition I deserved. This is my chance to live like I want to live. I've given my entire life to science and now it is time I get something back!"

Fallow ended his speech by shouting. His professorial air had degenerated.

"Now, tell me what I want to know. We are running out of time!" he screamed again, getting in Mike's face.

Just then, they all heard the sound of a car door shutting outside. The change on Fallow's face was remarkable. He went from crazy to cringing in the space of a moment. He looked at the door behind him. Over the silence, they could hear the sound of wind and rain beginning.

"It's too late now," he said, quietly. "You've waited too long."

The man straightened up and smoothed out his clothes. He took a moment to pull himself together and motioned for Felix. Without another word, he left the room.

Mike and Sarah were alone in the small room. They could hear others outside speaking, but they couldn't make out what was being said.

"Wow, he is a full-on nutcase," Sarah said first.

"I believe they call that a psychotic break," Mike agreed. "He has definitely lost it."

"What do you think he meant about the others getting shot?"

"I don't know. I'm hoping for the best. If they had simply been attacked and our friends killed, the other boat that did all the shooting wouldn't have been wrecked. So, something doesn't add up. Regardless, I don't like the sound of it," Mike said. "There's a lot of what he said that doesn't make sense to me. How does he know about any of it? How does he know about what we were looking for? The encrypted message? Any of it? The only thing that makes sense is if he kidnapped Dr. DeSutton and got that information from him. Fallow must have stolen the original message and kidnapped DeSutton to help him find the gold."

"So now what do we do?" Sarah asked. "I don't want to tell Fallow anything. I don't care about the gold, but I don't want to give him the satisfaction."

"I feel the exact same way," Mike agreed. "We have to figure out a way to escape."

"Any thoughts on how that is going to happen?" Sarah asked.

"Well, no, not at the moment, but I'm working on it. When Felix hit me and knocked me over, it loosened up the ropes on my hands. I'm not free yet, but I'm looser than I was," Mike explained.

"That'll help," Sarah agreed. "How are you doing? He's clipped you pretty hard a couple times. I'm not sure I could deal with that."

"I'm okay. It hurts, but I've seen worse," Mike said. "He doesn't seem to want to hurt you. That's a good thing."

"So, we try to make an escape whenever we get the chance, right?"

"That's the plan. And just like before, if you get a chance to escape without me, do it and send back help," Mike said.

"Would you leave me behind?" Sarah asked, knowing the answer. Mike's eyes met Sarah's and it took him a moment to reply.

"No, I wouldn't," Mike said, he said slowly shaking his head.

"So, why do you think I would leave you behind?" she asked. "Stop the chivalry stupidity. We're in this together."

"Sounds like a storm is coming up," Mike said, listening to sound outside the old farm house. "It sounds like a big one."

"Changing the subject on me?" Sarah asked.

"Well, yes and no. Yes, I'm changing the subject, but the cover of a storm might help us get out of here. If the power went out or something like that, you never know," Mike said.

As he said that, the door to the small room where they were held prisoner opened up. Fallow and Felix entered first. Right behind them was Dr. Peter DeSutton. He was well dressed and his hands were free. He hadn't been kidnapped at all.

CHAPTER 39

"Hello, Mike," DeSutton said.

"Well isn't this interesting," Mike said leaning his head toward Sarah. "I guess that explains how Fallow knew everything that was going on."

"Who is this guy?" Sarah asked, looking from the man who entered the room to Mike. "Do you know him?"

"Sarah, this is Dr. Peter DeSutton. This is the man we've been trying to rescue. But now I'm guessing that isn't important anymore. Is it, doctor?" Mike said.

"No, Mike, I appreciate your efforts, but I don't need rescuing," DeSutton said. "I assume you are now beginning to realize that I staged the entire kidnapping. I had hoped you would sit at home and wring your hands, wondering what had happened to me while I disappeared. I guess I misjudged you on that one."

"I apologize for that mistake. Don't worry, it'll never happen again," Mike said.

"That's funny, Mike. Honestly, at this point, you probably need someone to rescue you from me," DeSutton said casually.

"Well that doesn't sound good, Mike. If we don't need to rescue this guy any more, can we just go home?" Sarah asked.

"I think so, Sarah. Let's go," Mike said, feigning an attempt to stand.

"Very cute, both of you," DeSutton said. "But now it's time for you to tell me what I need to know. My associate, Dr. Fallow has indicated that you have been less than helpful so far. I think my methods will prove to be more encouraging for you."

"Sarah, I was wrong. Fallow isn't just in the middle of a psychotic break. His boss is a sociopath," Mike said, shaking his head.

"I see that," Sarah agreed. "I'm sorry, but I don't think you'll get anything more from us than your flunky did."

"I'm no one's flunky and he isn't my boss!" Fallow shouted as he lunged forward, but DeSutton stopped him with a raised hand. Fallow halted as quickly as he had started. He growled but turned around and sulked to the corner of the room to watch.

"I don't have time for these games right now," DeSutton said. "There's a storm coming and I have no intention of being caught out here when it arrives. Felix, I understand from Dr. Fallow that you worked on the man to get information. That's Dr. Fallow's weakness, but not a problem I have. I want you to concentrate your efforts on the woman. Either she will break and tell us what we want to know, or he will to make us stop. Either way, I'll learn the truth."

Felix grunted his assent, but remained silent.

"So, I'll give you one more chance to tell me what I want to know and everything will be okay. I won't have Felix hurt anyone," DeSutton said.

"How could you be like this?" Mike asked. "Andie trusted you. She spoke so highly of you."

"Ah, Andie. Yes, I'll miss her. Such a beautiful girl and so bright, too," DeSutton said. "She was so easy to convince to do just about anything I wanted."

"What do you mean by that?" Mike asked, growing wary and angry at the same time.

"Not what you're thinking if it makes you feel better," DeSutton said, shaking his head. "Although I thought about taking her to my bed and I'm sure I could have. I'm sure she would have been an 'A' student there, too. Frankly, she is a little too old for me. I like more girls younger and more pliable."

DeSutton was grinning in a way that made Mike's blood run cold. He now realized the man was truly evil and wanted to know what else he had been up to. He didn't have to ask, though, because DeSutton seemed to be in the mood to talk for a moment.

"No, I just convinced Andie to keep me up to date on some of the shipwrecks off the coast. The Huron was only one of several I asked her to keep an eye on although it was the one that I truly wanted to know about," DeSutton explained. "If you remember back to the day we first met, when you found the lock box from the wreck, I told you I had a family member on board. That is true. The lie was that my family member was lost at sea. He got away from the wreck and went on to continue his career for many more years. In fact, he set up a family business that I am still involved with today."

"He set you up in a murder, kidnapping and extortion business?" Sarah asked, sarcastically.

"That sums it up nicely, Sarah," DeSutton said, the same smile on his face. "How very intuitive of you. My dear ancestor, a Mr. Samuel Frame, worked for a group called the Consortium. They were industrialists, politicians and business leaders of the era. His job was to wreck the Huron and stop it from ever making it to Cuba. He did his job perfectly and got off the ship without a trace. He was, after all, the only person on board who realized how close they were to shore before the sun rose. He knew he could swim to shore easily."

"So your great ancestor killed more than 100 men that he served with and destroyed a ship from the navy he served in," Mike said. "I can see why you're proud of him. He was a mass murderer and a traitor."

DeSutton continued without acknowledging Mike's comment. "He knew the Huron's real mission and attempted to find the storehouse in Cuba, but he failed. Without the encoded message, it was hopeless. But, for his success, he was made a full member of the Consortium. And that membership was passed down through the years, in our family, and now I am a full member as well."

"This Consortium of yours tries to find sunken ship wrecks?" Sarah asked.

"Not at all, dear," DeSutton said, as he walked closer, moving his face within inches of Sarah's. "We start wars and fund revolutions to profit from them. I can use the gold and other valuables sent by the Spanish to aid the Cubans and multiply it several times over selling arms and other supplies. And all at no risk to me."

DeSutton turned to Felix. "I want to move this along. Let's exert some pressure on the woman."

Felix walked forward and grabbed Sarah's right arm with his left hand, just below the shoulder. Still tied solidly to her chair, she couldn't resist, but she screamed, spat and tried to bite his hand.

"Get your filthy hands off of me," Sarah yelled. "I'm not going to tell you anything!"

Without hesitation, Felix slapped her hard across the mouth. Sarah tasted her own blood.

"Stop it!" Mike shouted. He received a punch to the face from DeSutton for his trouble.

Mike recovered quickly from the blow. DeSutton hadn't hit him as hard as Felix had hit Sarah. He tried to stall to find some way out of this.

"How did you pull all this together," Mike asked. "I'm confused."

DeSutton's ego forced him to explain what had gone on. He had a truly captive audience and couldn't resist the temptation to show how brilliant he was.

"That doesn't surprise me, Mike," DeSutton agreed. "There is too much going on behind-the-scenes that you don't know about."

He went on to explain that the Consortium owned the Espial and Dr. Fallow. Fallow had been released from his university and needed a job. DeSutton gave it to him, but he controlled where the ship went, using science as a cover for more covert purposes. Most of the time, the Consortium didn't bother Fallow's operations and he pursued real science, but from time to time, they asked him to do certain things.

"And that was how you got on board," DeSutton said. "I heard about your interest in going to Cuba before I had gotten out of town. Your editor was calling research ships to see if anyone was heading in this direction. I knew you must have found some clue and realized what was going on. That was my only mistake. I should have waited and taken the cryptanalyst with me instead of staging my kidnapping before he got there."

DeSutton explained that when he realized where Mike and his friends wanted to go, he decided to help them out and then follow them.

"It was easy for me to let you do all the leg work on this one," DeSutton finished. "I called Dr. Fallow and told him to get you on board and to take you exactly where you wanted to go. He wasn't happy about my interference, but he really didn't have a choice."

By this time, Sarah had recovered from Felix's punch enough that her sarcasm came back in full force. "So what we have here are two 'doctors' of science and neither one of them has any spine or integrity," she said with a sneer.

"Sarah, this can end now. Felix doesn't care one way or the other," DeSutton said, turning his attention directly to her. "Just tell me what I want to know and I'll make it all end."

"What you mean is that you'll kill us," Sarah growled. "We didn't find any gold so there is nothing to tell you about anyway. But even if we had, I wouldn't tell you anything just because I think you're a slime ball."

"That's unfortunate, but what I expected you to say," DeSutton agreed. "But what I know about Mike here is that he won't let a woman suffer if he can do anything about it. So, really, I don't expect you to tell me anything. I expect to exert a little more pressure on you and Mike will tell me whatever I want to know to make it stop. This is something Dr. Fallow didn't understand, but I know all too well. You hurt a man like Mike and it will simply strengthen his resolve. But hurt an innocent woman and he can't stand to let it happen."

"You really are a sociopath," Mike said. "You have no regard for anyone but yourself."

"I don't know if that is the clinical diagnosis or not, Mike," DeSutton said. "But, I will concede that I have a different belief system than you do. I believe in whatever is best for me and won't hesitate to use whatever means are necessary to get to it."

DeSutton again raised his hand to signal Felix. The Cuban man stepped forward and punched Sarah in the jaw. While she was reeling from the blow, he untied her hands from behind the chair and retied one arm to the arm rest in front. He left one arm untied, but kept his hand on her wrist.

"DeSutton, stop this!" Mike yelled.

"Mike, don't! Don't let this son-of-a-bitch be right! I told you I wouldn't tell him anything and I don't want you to do it for me!" Sarah yelled back.

"Whatever is there, it's not worth getting hurt for it," Mike said.

"No, Mike. No!"

Felix began twisting her right arm behind her back, straining the muscles and bones around the joint in her shoulder.

"DeSutton stop this!"

"Mike, all you have to do is tell me what you found and where it is and this will all be over. Sarah won't hurt anymore," DeSutton said calmly.

"Aaaaah, Mike, don't tell him anything," Sarah screamed.

"Come on, Mike, you can stop this. You don't want to have your friend hurt like this," DeSutton said. "Make this all stop now."

"Tell him to stop it," Mike yelled back.

It seemed like everyone in the room was screaming. The tension continued to mount as Felix bent Sarah's arm further and further backward. Suddenly, it popped. Everyone was still for a second. There was a look of disbelief on Sarah's face as she looked at her shoulder. And then the pain flooded in. She moaned as she lost consciousness.

"Sarah, Sarah!" Mike yelled, but Sarah didn't respond. He could tell she was still breathing. He assumed she had passed out from the pain of her shoulder being dislocated.

"That wasn't very effective, now was it?" Mike growled, turning his attention back to DeSutton.

"Felix isn't an expert at these matters, unfortunately," DeSutton said with a clinical air, as if his experiment had just failed. "So, where do we go from here, Mike? Do I tell Felix to continue to hurt you? Or are you going to answer my question?"

Mike's answer was going to be to tell DeSutton where he could shove his question, but before he could open his mouth, the back wall of the old farm house slammed forward with a crash. The wind from the storm outside had been building all evening, but the hurricane had finally arrived with full force. It was a huge one, making landfall on the southeastern end of the Isle of Pines as a Category 3 storm.

The falling wall knocked Mike's chair over and completely covered Sarah with debris.

"Damnit!" DeSutton said as he jumped backward away from the falling wall. The storm outside was blowing harder and the rain was coming into the farm house sideways. In spite of the hurricane, DeSutton stood and looked at the situation for a moment before he made his decision. He was plainly afraid of the storm blowing outside. "Let's get out of here."

"What about them?" Fallow asked, speaking for the first time since DeSutton had dismissed him.

"Leave them. Let the storm take them. We'll leave Felix behind to keep an eye on them and we'll check on them after it's passed. If they're still alive, we'll get the information out of them. If not, we'll get to the others. You said two were still alive and on your ship?"

"That was the report I heard over the ship's radio," Fallow nodded.

We'll get to them there," DeSutton said. "I won't lose my chance to get this gold."

CHAPTER 40

It took Mike a moment to realize what had happened. His chair was knocked on its side and part of the building was across his legs. He could see DeSutton speaking to Fallow and then saw the two men leave. He saw them pause to speak to Felix and the big man shook his head, but Mike couldn't make out what they said over the roaring of the storm. It looked like the men argued for a moment and then they all left the room. Mike thought it was amusing that Felix closed the bedroom door behind him. It seemed silly since the rear of the house had collapsed.

As soon as they were gone, Mike started to squirm against his bindings. He had been loose before, but this second fall seemed to have loosened his ropes further. Mike was a big man at 6'2" and 220 pounds. Falling over twice in the old, rickety chair had severely weakened it. He pushed backward with his legs and arched his back at the same time. Nothing. He tried it again.

"Okay, maybe I'm pulling the wrong way," he breathed after a moment. The beating and his injuries made it difficult to exert himself for long.

When he collected his energy, he bent his body forward while kicking his legs out. He heard the chair crack. He reversed directions and arched backward. More cracks. With an effort, he threw everything into it one more time. He pushed forward with everything he had left. Crack!

The chair broke in half. The back came loose from the seat and the seat split in half as well. Mike lay still, panting from the strain for a moment. Breaking the chair allowed Mike to move around more and return blood flow to his body. Still, he had pieces of chair attached to his arms and legs and his arms were still bound behind his back. He was a long way from free. And the storm felt like it was getting worse. Mike was partially exposed to the rain and wind — the falling house hadn't completely covered him. And his exertions had moved him further out from under the farmhouse wreckage.

The wind and rain were harsh, but Mike rested for a moment, feeling the rain on his face. He opened his mouth to get some water. He wasn't sure how this one was going to end. He and Sarah were under a fallen house, in the middle of a hurricane. His friends were missing and presumably had been shot at, if not hit. Things were not going well.

"Was it all worth it, Mike?" he asked himself, out loud. "You take risks for stories all the time, but this time you brought your friends along. Was it fair to them?"

"You're not feeling sorry for yourself are you?" he heard Sarah say from behind him. In spite of the storm, Mike heard her voice clearly.

"Is that really you, or is it just my imagination?" Mike asked over his shoulder.

"My shoulder is on fire, there is an elephant lying on top of me and the rain and the wind are pouring down around me and my hair is a tangled mess. I think it's really me," Sarah replied with a smirk.

"I don't know, I have a pretty vivid imagination," Mike said.

"Are you going to keep this up, or are you going to help me get out from underneath this pile of house?" Sarah finally asked.

"I'm working on it. Still trying to figure out how to get some of these ropes off," Mike said. "I broke my chair, but my hands are behind me and they are still bound up."

"Slide backward some. I was able to push some of this junk off of me," Sarah explained. "When the big guy tied up my hand in front of me, he didn't do a very good job. I've gotten it loose," Sarah said. "Maybe I can untie your hands."

Mike began kicking his legs and worming his body, struggling to push himself and the broken chair backward.

"Okay, that's enough. I can reach your hands," Sarah said as she began picking at the bindings holding Mike's hands with her left hand. "Stay still. I'm right handed. This isn't going to be easy."

"I'm really sorry about your arm, Sarah," Mike said while she worked.

"You didn't do it to me, Mike," Sarah said.

"No, but I got you into the middle of this," Mike argued.

"First, I volunteered for this," Sarah replied. "And second I'm glad I'm here. I can't imagine working for Dr. Fallow any more. And it seems like my job was about to end anyway. This is a lot more interesting than what I was doing."

"But you didn't sign on to be a punching bag," Mike continued.

"Mike, listen. I know you're feeling guilty. DeSutton was right about one thing. You're the kind of guy who wants to protect everyone around you. I get that. But let it go," Sarah said while she worked. "You can't protect me from everything. Bad things happen. There are bad people in the world. You do amazing work shining a light on that. Let some of the other people around you help you from time to time."

"How is it coming back there?" Mike asked when he realized Sarah had stopped working at the ropes. He was afraid she might have lost consciousness again from the pain. "Are you all right?"

"Mike, that's exactly what I'm talking about. I'm fine and you're free. I got the ropes loose," Sarah said.

Mike pulled his arms in front of him for the first time in hours and began rubbing at his wrists to get the blood flowing again. "Thanks, Sarah." As quickly as he could, he bent forward and got the ropes off of his legs, kicking away the remains of the chair. Once he was clear, he rolled on to his hands and knees and crawled toward Sarah.

He stayed low to the ground while he worked to get her free.

"I don't know if there is anyone still around watching us or not," Mike said. "I saw them leave, but they might still be close by."

It took him just a few minutes to get the ropes off of Sarah's legs. He pulled her out from under the building debris that had been covering her. Together they slid toward the front wall of the farmhouse bedroom, near the door, to get out of the wind and rain as best they could. Sarah was cradling her arm against her body to protect it from the pain.

"How does that feel?" Mike asked.

"Like it's on fire, mostly. I think my tennis serve is shot," she said.

Mike noticed a piece of cloth on the floor beside him. It looked like an old towel left behind by the previous tenants. He picked it up and moved behind Sarah.

"I'm going to make you a sling. It should help relieve some of the pain a little. We're going to need to get out of here and I can't carry you," Mike explained.

"You mean we can't stay here forever? It's so nice. OW!" Sarah said, the last was when Mike moved her arm into place in the makeshift sling. Mike felt her lean back against him and close her eyes for a minute. She was fighting off the waves of pain coursing through her body. Her breathing was coming fast and he could feel her heart beating in her chest.

"You gonna be all right?" Mike asked.

"Yeah, just a minute. It's getting better," Sarah answered. "So, now what?"

"We slide out of here and get away. I'm going to take a look around and see if anyone is still watching this place," Mike said. "We need to get somewhere safe and then find a radio or a phone so we can get some help."

"Sounds like a plan to me. I've decided I don't really like this place anymore," Sarah agreed.

Mike began to move toward the bedroom door. He opened it slowly and peered through. The front room in the small farmhouse was empty. He motioned for Sarah to follow him. She crawled toward him. Once they were in the front room, they were at least out of the wind and rain.

Mike crawled toward a window on the front of the house and peered out. He saw a car about 50 yards away. It looked like someone was inside.

"Okay, they left someone here," Mike said. "Probably Felix. He can't be happy about being here."

"I'm sure he's not. So, what do we do?" Sarah asked. "He'll see us if we go out that way."

"Let's check out the house. Maybe there's a back door," Mike said. "If not, we can climb out through the hole in the wall in the room we just came out of. We're not in any shape to fight our way past Felix again. Even if we had surprise."

"You got that right," Sarah agreed.

Crawling along the floor to stay away from the windows, they quickly discovered a door that lead to a kitchen on the back of the small house.

"You ready to go back out into this mess?" Mike asked.

"It sounds like the storm is dying down some," Sarah answered.

"That's a good thing and a bad thing," Mike said after he stopped and listened to the storm for a second. "It'll help us make a run for it, but Felix out there will come and check on us when the storm lightens up."

"Sounds like it's time to go, then," Sarah agreed.

"I don't know anything about this storm. If it's a hurricane, this might just be the eye of the storm. We might have to ride out the back side of the storm here in a few hours," Mike said.

"We should probably get moving then," Sarah said, moving into a crouch and sliding through the back door. Mike followed her into the storm.

CHAPTER 41

Sarah was right; the storm had died down some. It was no longer blowing as furiously as when it knocked down the back wall of the farm house. But the wind was still blowing hard and it was still raining. They were soaked to the bone as soon as they stepped outside. Fortunately, though, their captors hadn't thought about disabling them. They still had their clothes and shoes. Sarah had her t-shirt back on over her swimsuit and Mike had his t-shirt on too. They were both wearing their wetsuit booties from their dive as shoes. The temperature was still in the upper 70s in spite of the storm so they were in no danger of freezing to death.

They stepped away from the dilapidated farm house, but didn't take off in a dead run. First, they didn't know where to go. Second they didn't want Felix to see them escaping. They did their best to move away from the house keeping the structure between them and the car. They moved from palm tree to palm tree looking for anything else that might give them cover. About 30 feet from the house, their cover started getting thin. No one had farmed the area for a while.

"Do you see anything?" Sarah shouted directly into Mike's ear as they did their best to share the shelter of an old palm tree. The wind made it hard to speak.

"Not much!" Mike answered the same way. "I think I see a drop-off over that way. It might be a stream bed. That would be good cover if we could reach it!" He gestured and used his hands as much as he spoke to communicate what he was saying.

"Let's go for it," Sarah said. She was cradling her shoulder and obviously feeling the pain.

"Let me go check it out first. I can move better than you right now," Mike said. "There's not a lot of cover between here and there. I don't want to risk both of us if it's nothing."

"Funny, I was going to suggest that you go, too," Sarah answered with a wry smile, her attitude still present through the pain.

"Then it's unanimous. If I get there and it's something good, I'll wave you over. Otherwise, I'll be back in a minute."

Mike got as low as he could, just above a belly crawl, and started to work his way forward. He kept looking over his shoulder, past the house straining to see the car where Felix was waiting. Nothing. The storm and a small rise helped to block his view. He knew, though, that Felix might be able to see him since the man was sitting higher up in a car. Mike hoped the storm conditions would be enough to obscure his view.

Mike made good progress. The sandy soil was soft enough that he was able to move along without catching on rocks or slipping in gravel. He spotted an area filled with tall, thick switchgrasses blowing in the wind. When he got close, he took four quick steps and dived in, landing with a roll. When he recovered his footing, he turned around and listened, but he didn't hear the sounds of anyone raising an alert. No shouts. No warnings and better still no gunshots.

Once inside the switchgrass, Mike could move easier and he made better time. He was only trying to get 30 yards from where he left Sarah, but it still took him several more minutes. Moving short distances while trying to remain hidden wasn't easy.

He finally found what he was looking for. It appeared to be an old irrigation culvert cut to move water around on the plantation. Mike couldn't tell what they had farmed there, but guessed it was sugar cane. That industry had seen better days.

The bottom of the culvert was about five feet below ground level and seemed to run on as far as he could see, in a straight line, toward the interior of the island. It was half-filled with water from the storm. "Even if it only goes 1000 yards, it will still take us away from Felix. That'll be all we need to get out of here," Mike said to himself. He knew they would have to run hunched over, but it would still be easier than on the open ground. Now, he just had to get back to Sarah and then he had to get her to the open ditch. After that, everything would be easy. He hoped.

Mike climbed back out of the culvert and then crawled on the ground through the tall grass. When it started to thin out, he looked around and got his bearings on where Sarah was hidden. He was relieved to see that she hadn't moved. Her eyes were open, but she was leaning back against the palm tree resting. Her shoulder injury was taking a lot out of her. Her eyes appeared glassy, like she wasn't focusing on anything.

Mike scuttled across the ground crab-like and reached Sarah in just a moment. It was easier moving toward her than away. He could look where he was going and keep a watch for trouble at the same time. Sarah realized Mike was coming when he was about 15 feet away.

"How are you feeling?" Mike asked Sarah as soon as he reached her.

"It hurts, but I'm functional," she answered. Mike began checking her sling to make sure it was tight and offering her the support she needed. "I'll make it, Mike. I'm not going to let that monster win."

"Okay, good. That's what I needed to hear," Mike said. He went on to describe the irrigation culvert. "I think it will be our best bet to get out of here. It'll be hard on you to get there, but it should make it easy going once we do. It'll keep us out of some of this wind, too."

"Let's do it, then. I'll make it," Sarah agreed.

"You go first. Keep low and just head straight for the switchgrass. I'll keep a watch out behind you. When you get there, you keep a watch out for me and I'll run. Okay?" Mike asked.

"Sounds like a plan to me," Sarah agreed. She moved into a squatting position and then took a minute to steel herself from the pain. When she was ready, she moved out. To protect her shoulder, she cradled one arm with the other, holding it in front of her. She kept as low as she could and simply took off running. Sarah made it to the switch grass without being seen, but she stumbled when she got there, rolling into the grass. It took her a moment to catch her breath and then she got up and faced Mike. She gave him an Okay signal with her hand and then motioned him to come on.

Mike took one last look behind him and then took off running for the safety of the switch grass. The wind continued to swirl around him and the rain was still falling.

The plan would have been perfect and Mike nearly made it to the switch grass without being seen, except for one thing. Felix, sitting in his car, had realized the storm was letting up. He decided to check on Mike and Sarah. He hoped they were dead so he could leave and go home.

Felix was at the front door of the farm house when he looked to the side, alerted by something moving in his peripheral vision. He realized it was Mike. His captives were escaping.

"Alto!" Felix yelled at the top of his lungs, but the wind took his voice away before it reached Mike. He yelled again but with no luck. Felix took out his gun and fired a shot at Mike. He was too far away and there was too much wind to have any real chance of hitting his target, but he hoped it would scare the man into stopping his run. Mike and Sarah heard the gun shot at the same time. She began frantically signaling for him to hit the dirt. Mike slid face first to the ground. They both looked around and saw where Felix was standing. In an instant, Mike was back on his feet running. He began gesturing wildly for Sarah to run, too.

"Come on! Run for the culvert!" he shouted. Mike was not about to be caught again. If he was going to face Felix again, he would do it on his own terms, not on the open ground near the farm house. Especially since the other man was armed. Rather than chasing them on foot, Felix turned around and ran back for his car. He wanted this to be over quickly.

Mike and Sarah slipped and fell into the culvert and then turned and continued running to their right. Neither spared the breath to speak. It wouldn't have made any difference. The storm was getting stronger.

Felix fired up the aging Studebaker and took off straight toward where he saw Mike disappear into the switchgrass. He was barely able to hit the brakes before he slid into the ditch. He tried to back up, but his tires dug into the sandy soil. He spun his tires, slinging dirt forward and over the car. The tires on the rear-wheel drive car were nearly bald.

Mike saw Felix slide to a stop at the lip of the culvert. He paused for a moment to see if the big man was going to get out of his car and chase them on foot. When he heard Felix attempt to back the stuck car out, he took off running again, straight up the channel. Sarah was just ahead of him. At this point, there was no point in trying to hide. They were running for their lives.

On a positive note, Felix wasn't paying any attention to Mike and Sarah at that point. He was too focused on his getting his car, his pride and joy, out of the ditch. He continued to shift from forward to reverse, rocking the old car backward and forward, trying to gain some traction.

"He's stuck, run!" Mike shouted. "Keep going!"

Sarah didn't bother to answer. She saved her breath and kept moving. But she was slowing down. The pain in her shoulder was sapping all of her energy, making it hard to breathe and move.

The culvert was soft, sandy and quickly filling with water. Disuse had allowed the switchgrass to fill in the slopes as well. They were protected from the wind above, but other than that, the culvert wasn't helping them much now that they had been seen.

Behind them, Mike heard the old car roar to life as Felix got it unstuck. He was moving toward them, again.

"We need to get out of this culvert and run," Mike shouted when he got close to Sarah. "It's slowing us down."

"There's a bridge up ahead," Sarah said, pointing as she stopped for a moment. "We can climb out there."

"And that means he can follow us as well," Mike said. "Doesn't matter. We're sitting ducks down here now. Let's go!"

They took off running again, making for the small wooden bridge. When they got there, Mike grabbed the pilings sunk into the ground and began climbing up the steep bank away from Felix. Halfway up, he turned and stuck out a hand for Sarah. She grabbed his arm with her one good hand and Mike dragged her up to the top of the grade. Mike climbed out after her and then they took off running. They heard Felix shouting something out of his window and then heard his gun fire again, but they didn't pay any attention to him. They just kept running.

Felix slid to a stop in front of the small bridge. He had to back up to get a good angle to cross it. He paused for a moment. The small structure was built for carts and wagons, not cars. He couldn't tell how old it was or how solid it was. All Felix could see was that Mike and Sarah were escaping on the other side. He made his mind up quickly and gunned the engine.

The bridge was about 20 feet across. The Studebaker hit it moving quickly. The bridge held up until Felix was halfway across, but then it started to collapse when the car was at the peak and the car's full weight was being supported by the bridge. The Studebaker was built in the era long before air bags, and even before seat belts were common. The bridge dropped out from under the car and Felix crashed into the earthen side of the ditch with a thump. He slammed into the steering wheel and then was thrown backward as the car settled into the culvert with a splash.

Mike and Sarah had stopped to look for a moment. But just a moment. They knew this was their opportunity and they took it, running as fast as they could. They knew they had a lead and they were going to take it. There was no reason to hide now.

And the storm was getting worse again. The brief reprieve must have only been the eye of the hurricane.

CHAPTER 42

Back on board the Espial, the storm was also causing things to move quickly. The hurricane developed faster than the meteorologists predicted. It came in right behind the helicopter, although slightly to the north. It was making a track to head straight up the main island of Cuba and make a beeline for Havana. That put the ship on the weaker side of the storm, but it still made things hectic. The only upside about this off-season storm was that it was moving to the west quickly.

Rather than attempting to fly back to Guantanamo, the helicopter had landed on the deck of the Espial, refueled and picked up Mac and then it headed due south for the airport and hospital in Georgetown, Grand Cayman. The distance there was less than 200 air miles. The Espial also turned south to get away from the track of the storm. The captain had pulled out all stops to move the research vessel, running at approximately 12 knots. While they were able to get away from the worst part of the storm, they were still getting bounced around pretty well by the wind and waves.

Andie flew with Mac to the hospital in the helicopter. That left Phil on board the ship. The worst part for him was the feeling that he had abandoned his friends. He hadn't known any of them very long, barely a week, but the excitement, adventure and sheer terror of what had happened had bonded him more closely to this group than anyone he had known since college.

After the helicopter took off and flew ahead of the ship, the crew secured everything on board that was loose or could fly away with the winds from the storm and then everyone huddled up inside to ride out the storm. Everyone except for Phil. He went in search of Dr. Rae Lesley, the ship's doctor, who also worked for the US

Department of State. He found her in the ship's radio room, just off the bridge.

"Hi Dr. Lesley, can I speak to you for a minute?" Phil began.

"Dr. Parrot, I told you and Mike before to call me Rae. There are too many doctors on board this boat already," Rae replied. "But, sure, I have a few minutes. I'm waiting on a radio connection and the storm is making things pretty difficult. What can I do for you?"

"Okay. I'll call you Rae if you'll call me Phil," Phil agreed. "I don't stand on a lot of formality either. I understand the need to move the ship away from the storm and all that. The needs of the many outweigh the needs of the few, of course. But I'm concerned about Mike and Sarah on the island. Someone attacked us. They shot Mac. I'm worried about my friends."

"I understand that. What do you want me to do?" Rae asked.

"Let's be straight with each other for a minute. You work for the State Department. I do a lot of contract work for the National Security Agency. I'm guessing between the two of us, we have some pull to get some help on this one. I don't want to cause an international incident or anything, but can we ask your people to alert the Cuban authorities and get them out looking for Mike and Sarah?" Phil asked as he paced back and forth in the tiny radio room. "If you want, I'll go to my contacts and ask them for help. We've just got to do something for them!"

"Phil, sit down and calm down for a moment," Rae said, using her physician, bed-side voice. "The radio connection I'm waiting on is a contact in the Cuban government. I just got off the phone with my superiors in Washington. I explained everything that is going on and they gave me permission to talk to the Cubans and ask for help. If it makes you feel any better, I dropped your name in relation to the NSA as well. I wanted to apply as much leverage as I could."

"So. You're already a step ahead of me?"

"I'd say I'm a couple steps ahead of you, to be honest, but that's why I work for State," Rae said with a wink. "Who knows, this whole mess might actually turn out to help international relations. If we can pull this off, we can actually help stop treasure hunters from stealing from the Cubans. That has got to put them in a good mood. And with things changing in Havana, who knows what we might accomplish."

"That's a pretty big 'if' in there," Phil said smiling. "I'll be happy to get everyone off the island safe and sound. But I like the way you think."

CHAPTER 43

Mike began his career as a photographer working as a photo pro on Grand Cayman. Since then, he had spent a lot of time in the Caribbean, both topside and underwater. He had seen more than his fair share of storms come raging up through the warm waters, hitting the small, unprotected islands. He had been on the islands during storms and covered the aftermath, seeing the damage they left behind.

But something about this storm seemed different. Almost familiar. Mike was having a déjà vu moment, but he couldn't seem to put his finger on it. He just wished he knew what was going to happen next.

Mike and Sarah were making an wide-open run past abandoned farm fields. They were looking for someplace safe to hide from the storm. Just a few minutes before they had watched Felix crash his Studebaker into the quickly flooding irrigation culvert when the bridge collapsed below him. They paused for a moment and talked about going back to check on him. Considering what had happened to them, they decided against it. If he were still alive and conscious, they assumed all they would get was a gun barrel for their trouble. That decision made, they quickly moved away from the area.

The hurricane winds had regained full force. The air was flying chaos. Sand, grass and palm leaves driven by the wind all flew past them sideways, sounding like a freight train flying past.

It was growing dark as the day was finally coming to an end and Mike wanted to get them to shelter. He knew Sarah's shoulder had to be killing her. Lightning struck through the clouds in the distance and there were flares of blue, electric light from the ground level. Mike guessed those were electric power transformers exploding in the storm. That was the good news. It meant they were getting closer to civilization. Where there was electricity, there must be houses.

As they ran, they came up a gentle rise and spotted a small farm house ahead of them.

"In there. I think we'll be safe!" Mike shouted, pointing at the house to Sarah. He had to grab her and pull her close so he could shout in her ear. The wind was pushing them around mercilessly.

"Anything has to be better than this," Sarah yelled back as she ran up onto the broken-down porch of the small bungalow. She grabbed the door handle and pulled the old door open in one motion. The wind nearly wrenched it from her hand as they jumped inside. Mike reached to help and with a combined effort, they got the door closed behind them.

Mike continued to feel like he had been here before. It all seemed familiar, but he couldn't remember why. It wasn't an exact memory, but it seemed so close.

Inside they surveyed their surroundings and realized the house had been abandoned for a long time. Mike shined the small dive flashlight around to see if there was anything they could use. The few remaining furnishings were toppled and lay strewn about. The windows were broken and rain leaked through holes in the roof. It was still better to be out of the wind and rain for a moment. They could at least talk without screaming.

"Do you think Felix is following us?" Sarah asked after she caught her breath, leaning against the wall.

"Don't know. Probably best if we don't wait to find out," Mike said.

"I'm not too thrilled about going back out into a hurricane right now," Sarah said, looking outside through the broken window as the remnants of an aging curtain flapped in the wind, her sodden clothes glued to her body. "My shoulder is killing me."

"I wish I could do something to help you with that. I know it must be pretty tough keeping it in a sling when you're running for your life," Mike said. "When we get out of this I'll find a way to make them pay for what they did."

"It's not your fault, Mike. It was easier to hurt me to get to you. With tough guys like you, that's always the way it goes," Sarah rationalized. "Hurts like hell, though. And you'll have to stand in line behind me to get some payback for it."

Mike explored the two-room shack. Something told him that there was a safe place through the kitchen, like he had been there before. It was hard to concentrate on keeping them safe from the storm when what he really wanted was to check on their friends and call for help. When the storm passed, they were still going to be on the run.

"Hold on, it looks like this house has a storm cellar. If it's solid, it'll keep us safer than up here," Mike said as he pulled on the small door built a few steps down from the kitchen. The angled door seemed to point straight into the ground.

"How does it look?" Sarah asked, as she stood and began to follow, but then hesitated at the top of the steps. Mike eased his way down the narrow steps. The room was built into the earth below the house with wooden walls to keep the sandy soil from collapsing. The ceiling was so low; Mike couldn't come close to standing up. The air was musty and stale, but dry.

"Looks dry and solid. I definitely think this is going to be safer than staying up there. We'll be out of the wind and away from prying eyes," Mike shouted back up the steps. "Come on down." He shined his light on the steps.

Sarah began climbing down, gingerly holding onto the wall with one hand while she cradled her injured arm against her body. Suddenly Mike knew what was going to happen next, but his shout came too late. Sarah was on the third step when her instincts told her it was time to move. She leaped forward into the small, dark room. A fierce wind from the storm slammed the angled storm cellar door shut behind her.

"Did I suggest diving in?" Mike asked with a laugh as he lay sprawled on the floor where Sarah had crashed into him.

"You made it sound so appealing, I just couldn't wait to join you. You know how I am," she said with a chuckle as she rolled away, and then hissed from the pain in her dislocated shoulder. She moved to sit up, but Mike held his arms around her for a minute.

"Do you really think this is the time and the place for that?" Sarah asked, looking at Mike through the dim light and dust.

"Probably not, but it felt pretty good," Mike said, relaxing his hold and letting her wiggle free. He watched Sarah move in the cellar's half-light for a minute. After a moment he half-stood up to examine their surroundings — his 6'2" frame filled up the room.

Sarah began moving around the cramped, musty cellar, looking through shelves and behind boxes with Mike's flashlight. Mike moved up the steps toward the door. He turned the knob but nothing happened. He pushed against it and then shoved upward with his shoulder, bracing on the steps below. Nothing.

"We're not getting out this way any time soon. Part of the house must have fallen against it," Mike said.

"Then we aren't getting out at all. That's the only way out. No back doors," Sarah said. "I did find some candles, though. Got any matches?"

"No such luck."

"It's going to be a dark, wet night until this storm passes," Sarah said. "Maybe we'll see another opening in the light of the day. I see lightning flashes through cracks in the ceiling from time to time. We'll find a way to get out when we can see something."

She slumped down to the floor with her back to a wooden wall. Mike moved toward her and placed his arm around her shoulders. She leaned into him and they sat still for a few minutes, listening to the wind and rain above them.

"Are we going to make it through this?" Sarah asked during a lull in the clamor.

"Of course we are," Mike said, doing his best to lighten the mood. "If we don't live through it, you can tell me I was wrong."

"Very funny."

"Who knows? Maybe Fallow and DeSutton will get killed by the storm," Mike said, trying to sound reasonable. "It could save us a lot of trouble."

"That would be nice, wouldn't it?" Sarah said, looking up with a sparkle coming back in her eye. "Although it would be a little disappointing – I wouldn't get my revenge."

They sat quietly for a moment, their muscles slowly began to relax while their breathing returned to normal. Mike couldn't believe everything that had gotten them to this point.

"I know this is going to sound funny," Mike began. "But I feel like I've been through part of this before. Like I dreamed about it or something."

"So, how does it end?" Sarah asked.

"Unfortunately, I don't remember that part of the dream."

"Isn't that always the way? I never remember my dreams," Sarah said, her voice getting low.

"I don't usually remember them either. This one is sort of weird, though," Mike agreed. "It seemed perfectly real until I woke up. I mean too real. And then the day flooded in and it was over."

Mike surveyed the room from his spot on the floor. His light was beginning to grow dim so he switched it off. He felt Sarah relax into his side and he smiled. They always did fit together nicely.

"What we talked about yesterday, about giving it a shot again if we get the chance. You still think it's a good idea?" Mike asked.

After a moment, when Sarah didn't respond, he glanced down at the woman leaning against him. She had fallen asleep. The exhaustion had taken over.

"Probably the smartest thing to do," Mike said to himself. "We're not out of this yet."

CHAPTER 44

A bright light shined in Mike's eyes. Considering everything that had happened in the last day, Mike couldn't figure out if he was being interrogated or what. He just knew he was groggy and he couldn't see. The light was too bright. His left arm was numb as well. He dodged his head to the side and the light wasn't as bright. He could see a little, but it didn't help solve the mystery of what had happened. Had Felix found them? Was he tied up again?

He glanced to his left to see what was wrong with his arm. Sarah was there, leaning against him. Her arm was in a sling. Oh, yeah, that's right. We must have fallen asleep, Mike thought. But the light?

Sunlight was shining above and a sliver pierced the gloom of the storm cellar through a crack between the boards. It was shining directly in Mike's face. He felt Sarah begin to stir against him.

"How are you feeling?" Mike asked.

"Hungry," Sarah said after a moment. "And sore. Where are we?"

"In a storm cellar," Mike answered. "It looks like the storm has passed."

"At least that's good news," Sarah said, rubbing her face with her one good hand. "I guess I crashed."

"Exhaustion will do that to you," Mike agreed. "I was right behind you."

"Now what?"

"We get out of here and we find some help," Mike said as he slowly moved his arm away from Sarah and began to stand up. He couldn't stand up straight because of the low ceiling, but he did his best to stretch out his sore, tired muscles. It had been a rough day and he was feeling worse for wear.

Mike moved around the small room while Sarah watched his progress. They could see around the room now as compared to when they fell into the cellar.

"Try the door again," Sarah offered. "Maybe it's not blocked anymore."

"Can't hurt to try," Mike agreed. He placed his shoulder against the angled door and shoved, but no luck. "Still solid. Not getting out that way."

He continued moving around the walls, looking for weak spots or back doors they couldn't see in the dark the night before.

"So, you've been dreaming about me?" Sarah asked, still seated on the floor.

"What?"

"You said last night when we found this place that you remembered it all in some sort of dream," Sarah said. "I assume I was in that dream, too."

"Oh that. Ummm, yeah. You were in the dream. If it was a dream. Everything seemed exactly like it was last night," Mike agreed while he worked his fingers through a crack in the boards that made up the walls to the cellar.

"I never forgot about you, either, Mike," Sarah said softly.

"That's nice to hear," Mike said, turning to face her. "I always wondered what would have happened if we had been able to work out our schedules or find some happy medium with our careers. I guess you're 'the one that got away' in my mind."

"I'll tell you what, Mike," Sarah said. "I'm willing to try it again if you are. Maybe we can figure it out this time."

"That's a deal," he said quietly, but smiling. "But first...we need to get our butts out of this hole." Mike returned his attention to the cracks in the ceiling and walls. He wasn't sure if Sarah was serious or not. Stressful situations often made people say things they couldn't support later. Emotions came out that they might not feel when things were back to normal. But that was for later. They had work to do. He also knew nothing had changed on the outside. They both had their careers and he knew at some point he would be jetting off on some new story.

Mike continued prodding at boards in the walls. There was a low gap between the floor of the house above them and the ground. It had been a crawl space at one time before the owners had dug out the cellar and then boarded up the openings. He found a board that looked loose and pushed on it. It gave about half an inch. He got his fingers inside a crack and then pulled backward on the board. It moved the same amount. He began pushing and pulling, feeling it give a little bit more with each pull.

"What did you find, Mike?" Sarah asked, finally standing and moving beside him. He could see the pain on her face.

"This board is loose," Mike said. "If I can pull it out, we might be able to wiggle out through this opening and get out of here." As he finished the sentence, the board creaked and gave way on one end. Mike almost fell the board broke free so suddenly.

"Ask and ye shall receive," Sarah said laughing.

"No doubt about that," Mike agreed. He pulled the board free and looked at the boards surrounding it. The opening would be too small for Mike to fit through. None of the other boards seemed to budge when he pulled on them. They both stared out at the sun through the window Mike had just opened. They were close, but not close enough.

"Mike, I think I can wiggle through that if you hoist me up," Sarah said. "And then maybe I can kick the other boards loose."

"What about your shoulder?"

"I didn't say it was going to be fun, but I think I can do it. You'll basically have to shove me through the hole," Sarah agreed.

"Let's give it a shot. The sooner we get out of here, the better off we'll be," Mike agreed. "Whenever you're ready."

Sarah took a minute to concentrate and relax. She knew sliding on the ground and wiggling through the small opening was going to aggravate her injury, but she didn't see that she had any choice. She had to do it for both of them.

When she was ready, Mike knelt down and wrapped his arms around her legs and hips. He stood slowly. Sarah extended her good arm in front of her and began working her way through the small opening. The fit was tight and the boards scraped her skin, but she kept going. Once her head and shoulders were through, she could move a little better. She was fit, but had she curves and her hips were the next challenge.

"Mike, you'll have to push me the rest of the way through," Sarah said over her shoulder. "I can't get any traction."

"It's going to be tight," Mike said looking at her lower half sticking out of the hole.

"Just do it and stop looking at my butt, Mike," she said.

Mike gave her posterior a quick pat and then put his hands on her feet and shoved her forward. She popped through the hole and wiggled out. A moment later, Mike saw that she had turned over and was in position to kick on the boards. In just a minute, she had pounded a second board loose with her feet, giving Mike enough room to slide through the crack and join her outside.

When he made it through, Mike rolled over on his back and stared at the sky. It was clear and blue, the way it can only look after a storm has come through and scrubbed everything away. There wasn't a cloud in the sky. The sun was still low on the horizon. He judged it was still early in the morning.

Once he caught his breath, Mike stood up and helped Sarah to her feet.

"Do you remember the way to civilization from your dream?" Sarah asked.

"Unfortunately, we're on our own, now," Mike said. "My dream ended in the cellar. But, I do remember flashes of light coming from that direction that looked like they were coming from the ground, not lightning. That tells me there is electricity that direction."

"That way it is, then," Sarah agreed. "Any direction is as good as any other. Except back the way we came."

They didn't talk much as they made their way toward what they hoped was a town. All they needed was a small town with a radio or a phone. More importantly, though, they needed water. Other than a few rain drops caught the night before, the last water they had was the water bottles taken from the wrecked boat in the cove the day before. They were both suffering. But they kept moving. They didn't have any choice.

CHAPTER 45

The sun was inching higher into the sky as Mike and Sarah moved toward what they hoped was a town. They still hadn't seen anyone else, but they had stumbled across a road and it was looking more and more solid the further they went. That gave them hope they were moving in the right direction. Still, the heat and the trauma of the past day were taking their toll on both of them. They were walking slower and slower.

As they crossed a small rise, Mike was the first to spot what they were looking for. He saw a building.

"Sarah, look," he said, pointing.

"Is it really there or is it a mirage?" she asked, half seriously.

"I don't think we'll see mirages until it gets a lot hotter," Mike said with a laugh. "Come on. You can make it. I bet there's an ice cold beer in there for us."

"I'd be thrilled with some lukewarm water right now," Sarah said. Still, the sight of the building helped her find energy that she didn't think she had any more. She stood up straighter and began moving faster. They both found renewed hope and energy.

It took them about 15 minutes to reach the structure. Mike realized it was a small gas station as they approached.

"Probably one of those 'last fuel till the end of the island' sort-of places," he said. Then he saw the first thing they really needed. On the back corner of the building there was a rain barrel full of water fresh from the storm.

"Look over there. I think that will help both of us," Mike said. They rushed to the water. Mike let Sarah plunge her face in the water. She drank deeply before she said anything.

"Oh my God that tastes good," she said, water dripping down her front.

"Well, move over and let me have some," Mike said. He took a deep drink of water and then splashed more on his face and head.

Sarah began drinking again, but Mike cautioned her to drink slowly.

"Our stomachs are pretty empty right now," Mike said. "I'd hate for you to throw it all right back up. Take it slow and easy."

After a couple drinks for both of them, Mike walked to the front of the gas station to see if there was anything they could use to call for help. The building was locked up tight, but he could tell it was still a functioning business. He tried the doors, but they were locked.

"Whoever runs the place probably locked it up and went into town to take shelter from the storm," Mike said when Sarah joined him at the front.

"We'll pay the owner back when we get out of here, but let's break in and find a phone," Sarah said.

Mike picked up a rock and broke a small window in the side door of the business. He had the door open in a second.

"Looks like you've done this sort of thing before," Sarah commented.

"I read about it in a book somewhere," Mike said grinning while he gestured with a sweep of his hand and a bow. "After you."

The interior of the gas station was nearly bare. There were a few old, tired posters on the walls, showing Fidel Castro and his brother Raoul in their uniforms. A few others showed sandy beaches and beautiful women.

There wasn't much else to the shop; a small counter, a couple chairs and some basic auto parts. Sarah found a small display with candy bars and handed one to Mike. He moved around behind the counter and looked for a phone.

"Nothing back here," Mike said.

"Check that door over there," Sarah pointed. "It may be an office of some sort."

She was right and there was a phone on the desk. Mike picked up the receiver, but got nothing. No static. No signal.

"It's dead," he said.

"Do you think the storm knocked the phones out?" Sarah asked.

"Probably. Let's rest up and then we'll keep moving. At least we've had some water now. And something to eat. It'll help us keep moving," Mike said.

As the last word came out of his mouth, a car slid to a stop in front of the gas station.

"Do you think they have a security system?" Sarah asked.

"I seriously doubt it, but maybe someone saw us come in here," Mike said. "Regardless, we can ask for help."

Except it was exactly who Mike and Sarah didn't want to see. It was Fallow, DeSutton and a bruised and battered Felix, along with a couple other men Mike had not seen before.

"Lovely," Mike said.

"What is it?" Sarah agreed when she came to stand beside Mike. "Oh. You're right. Lovely."

"You thought you had escaped us, didn't you?" DeSutton said as he got out of the car, the pompous tone in his voice apparent.

"I had certainly hoped so," Mike said as he and Sarah stepped back outside of the small structure to great their adversaries.

"Please don't try to run, Mike," DeSutton said. "We'll just shoot you this time. We're through playing nice."

"You're right. If your idea of nice is leaving us tied up and trapped under a fallen house in a hurricane, I don't want to see your version of mean," Mike said, mockingly. "But at this point, I think this is over, don't you?"

"No, Mike, I don't think this is over at all," DeSutton said, shaking his head. "And neither does Felix, here. He is very angry that you destroyed his car."

While they were talking, the two Cuban men Mike had never seen before moved around behind Mike and Sarah, blocking any possible escape. Both men had guns drawn. They were both banged up and bruised from where they crashed the boat the day before, shooting at Mac, Andie and Phil, but Mike didn't know that part.

"My car belonged to Father. He worked on it every day," Felix said in broken English.

"Felix, I think that is the first time I've heard you speak," Sarah said. "We're very sorry about your car, but I don't recall us telling you to chase us and drive it over that bridge."

"You will pay for breaking my car!" he yelled.

"These people are just not listening to reason, are they?" Sarah said to Mike.

"No, I don't think we're getting through to them at all," Mike smiled. He loved the fact that Sarah's preferred mode of dealing with adversity was sarcasm.

Without warning, Felix charged at Mike, swinging a fist straight at Mike's head. Mike ducked, but barely in time.

"Whoa there, Felix," Mike said as he dodged out of the way. "We can talk about this, can't we? I know people who would love to restore that old

Studebaker."

"I'm sorry to tell you, Mike, but we've promised Felix that he can kill you. He prefers to do it with his bare hands, by the way," DeSutton said. "Once you're dead, we'll get what we want from the girl."

"Sarah, run!" Mike shouted over his shoulder while he dodged another punch from Felix. The swings were slow, but Mike knew they were deadly.

Sarah turned and bolted away from the gas station, but she only made it four steps before one of the men behind them pistol-whipped her to the ground. Mike saw her fall out of the corner of his eye, but he didn't have time to worry about it. Felix attempted to close on him again.

Mike was 6'2" and weighed a fit 220 pounds, but Felix made him look small. The Cuban killer stood at least 6 inches taller and 80 pounds heavier. Mike could tell he had led a hard life, too. The calluses and scars on his ham-sized hands told the story of a man who worked hard for a living.

Mike dodged an overhand left, but he wasn't quick enough to react to what Felix had in store for him. Mike dodged down and to his left, but Felix threw a second punch with his right. Mike moved right into the large hand, catching it in his ribs. The blow knocked the wind out of him and spun him around.

Felix smiled at Mike for the first time. He was clearly enjoying this. Mike needed to think for a minute. He wasn't fighting for escape, just his life at this point. Even if he beat Felix, he clearly wasn't going to escape. He was outnumbered and surrounded. And they had guns. He was also exhausted. He was running on fumes at this point and couldn't keep this up for long before Felix hit him with a punch and he would be done for. One problem at a time.

"Come on, Felix," Mike said, spitting out his words as he attempted to draw a breath. He kept moving from side to side, trying to stay out of the bigger man's reach. "What have these gringos ever done for you? I bet

DeSutton treats you like an animal. He's too full of himself to be nice to you."

Felix hesitated for a second and then he lunged forward, landing a punch to Mike's shoulder.

OK, I guess I'm going to have to fight this guy, but that seemed to work a little, Mike thought to himself. Do it again and give him a little bit back.

"Do you always do the dirty work for men like DeSutton over there? Don't you get tired of doing what arrogant men want you to do?" Mike asked. This time Felix glanced over his shoulder at DeSutton. Mike took that opening and landed a punch to Felix's jaw as the bigger man turned his head back to Mike. He hit Felix with every ounce of energy he had left in his body, but it wasn't much. Just what he had gained from a few drinks of water and a stale candy bar.

Felix stepped back. His eyes glazed for a moment. Then he shook his head and charged forward, trying to tackle Mike. Mike feinted to his left and then jumped to his right. He clipped Felix behind the ear as the big man charged past.

"Come on, Felix. We really don't have to do this. I'm sorry about your car. Really. If we end this now, I'll help you fix it up. I can get parts for it in the United States. We can fix whatever is broken," Mike said.

Mike had landed two solid shots on Felix and the big man was a little dazed. He wasn't used to being hit. And Mike's words were having an effect as well. He really didn't like DeSutton and wasn't happy about fighting for him.

"Felix, kill him and get it over with, or I'll kill you," DeSutton yelled. "I've had enough of this!"

Without warning, Felix jumped forward. He grabbed Mike by both shoulders and threw him to one side. Mike wasn't expecting that move and was totally caught off-guard. Mike landed at DeSutton's feet.

"Finish him now!" DeSutton yelled. "Kill him, you mindless brute!"

Mike tried to stand in time to face his attacker, but Felix closed in quickly. Mike was even less prepared for what the giant did next. He punched DeSutton in the jaw with his right hand. With his left, he grabbed Fallow's arm and lifted the scientist off his feet, then threw him on top of DeSutton.

"If you want someone killed, you do it yourself. I don't work for you no more," Felix shouted at DeSutton.

"Help fix my car," Felix said, pointing at Mike where he was still lying on the ground.

"Sure, Felix. I'll do whatever I can," Mike said. "Help me up. I need to check on Sarah."

"Take care of girl. Sorry my brother hurt her," Felix replied. "Sorry I hurt her before."

"Your brother?"

"Both my brothers. They not stop you," Felix said, pointing to the two men.

Mike got up and ran to Sarah. She was coming around. There was a small trickle of blood on her scalp where Felix's brother had hit her in the head with the gun. She was in pain, but at least she was alive.

While Mike was checking on Sarah he forgot about DeSutton and Fallow. He was startled to hear a gun shot. He covered Sarah with his body and then looked behind him. He saw DeSutton standing behind Felix with a gun out, pointed straight at the big man. Felix had dropped to one knee and there was blood on his shoulder.

"You do as I say or I will kill you!" DeSutton screamed. He was clearly coming unhinged. Everyone was in shock for a moment at what happened. And then Felix's brothers took action. They still had their guns out, although they were holding them at their side. Simultaneously, they fired.

The bullets from the old revolvers they carried struck DeSutton in the chest. He was dead before his body hit the ground.

Fallow realized everything was exploding around him and he took off running. He didn't want Felix's brothers to shoot him next. He only made it 25 feet before three cars came flying down the road and slid to a stop in front of him.

The cavalry arrived in the form of the Policía Nacional Revolucionaria — the Cuban Federal Police. Two officers jumped out of each car. Behind them, Mike saw Phil and Dr. Rae Lesley. He relaxed. He knew everything was over.

CHAPTER 46

It took a while to get everything sorted out after the Cuban police arrived. They weren't happy to have a dead body, another man shot and a woman badly beaten in their country, but eventually everything calmed down.

An ambulance arrived and the medics took care of Sarah and Felix, binding their wounds. Rae helped out as well. After they had finished providing care for the living, two more ambulance drivers began to bundle up DeSutton's body to take it to the city morgue. Mike had been staring off into space just trying to come to grips with everything that had happened. Phil had given him an update on Mac and Andie so he could stop worrying about them. He knew all of his friends were safe, if in bad shape. Phil was the only one who had escaped injury on this trip.

"I guess that was the key to everything," Phil was saying. "This Consortium was behind it all from the beginning all the way back to the wreck of the Huron. Probably even before that. Who knows, maybe they started the civil war."

"Wait, what did you say?" Mike asked, tuning in for the first time in several minutes.

"I said for all I know, the Consortium may have started the Civil War,"

Phil said, mildly confused.

"No, before that," Mike said.

"I said I guess they were the key to everything," Phil repeated, looking at his friend and wondering if Mike's injuries were more serious than he thought.

"That's what I was missing. When we opened the message tube that we found on the wreck there was a key in the tube. But it disappeared when DeSutton went missing and I haven't thought about it since. We spent all of our time worrying about the message, but never even talked about the key after that," Mike said, running through things in his mind.

"OK, so there was a key in the tube. What does it go to? You look like you've figured it all out," Phil said, "but I'm still missing something here."

"That's because I haven't had a chance to tell you everything yet. When Sarah and I got inside the cave, we found an outer room with cave paintings on the walls, and then the passage to another cave was blocked with an iron plate of some sort," Mike explained.

"The iron plate would definitely have come from someone later than the cave paintings," Phil agreed.

"Well, yeah, but that's not my point. We tried to force the plate open, but it wouldn't move. Sarah saw what looked like a key hole on the plate. At the time, I didn't even think about the key from the Huron," Mike explained. "And then when we came outside, you guys were gone and things got pretty hairy for a while."

"So, you think this key that you found on the wreck might actually open the plate to the treasure room?" Phil asked. "Where is it now?"

"It disappeared with DeSutton. Or I guess I should say that DeSutton took it when he disappeared and faked his kidnapping. I wonder," Mike said as he got up walked over to where the medics were loading DeSutton's body onto a stretcher. The police had photographed the scene and were ready to take him away. His body would be returned to the United States.

"Hold on, let me see something," Mike said as he walked toward the men. At first the men ignored him.

"Alto, alto," Mike said waving his arms as he sped up. "I need to check that man's body."

"What is it, Mike," Rae asked. She had been speaking to the police captain.

"I think DeSutton might have something we need here," Mike said. He briefly explained what might be on the body, although he was a little leery of saying too much. He wasn't really in the mood to trust anyone around him at the moment.

Rae spoke to the police captain who waived his men aside and then gestured for Mike to check. Mike could tell, though, that the man wasn't going to tolerate this for long. DeSutton had been wearing a jacket when he arrived. Mike reached pulled back on the lapel and reached inside. He did his best to ignore the bullet hole in DeSutton's chest just inches away from where he was searching. It was empty.

He patted DeSutton's chest on the outside and could feel something inside that pocket. As he opened up the lapel, everyone else, including the ambulance men, stepped forward to see what Mike had found. Inside DeSutton's inner jacket pocket, Mike found the key from the Huron. DeSutton had been keeping it with him so he could use it soon as Mike or Sarah told him where to go.

Mike held the key up in the air to look at it in the sunshine. A lot of men had died to get that key to this island. And Mike knew what it was for and where it needed to go.

CHAPTER 47

It took a couple days and some wrangling to get everything arranged, but Mike was determined to be there when the key got fitted into the lock. Mike got his magazine involved, and Phil and Rae used their government contacts to make things happen.

In the meantime, Felix and Sarah were both taken to a hospital in Havana and then Sarah was flown back to the United States. Her shoulder was reset and she began physical rehab. Fallow was thrown into prison for his crimes in Cuba, including kidnapping and attempted murder. The Cubans weren't sure if they were going to deport him to the United States or not. They were definitely not happy with what he and DeSutton had tried to do on their soil. And since DeSutton wasn't around to punish, it was all coming down on Fallow's head.

On the other hand, the Cubans were very happy about the possibility of finding gold and treasure on the Isle of Pines. They mobilized conservators and divers to reclaim whatever was in the cave. Word quickly spread and the Spanish government immediately initiated a legal fight in international courts to get their treasures back. This was before anyone actually knew if there was anything inside the cave. It promised to be a long, drawn-out discussion.

Mike laughed to himself when he remembered that had been exactly what Fallow said he had been trying to avoid. That fight was none of Mike's concern, however. As the finder of the gold storehouse, along with Sarah, and the rest of his friends, he was able to exert some pressure and be included in the recovery efforts. Phil didn't want to be left out and since Mike didn't have any other dive buddies, Phil stayed around to help.

And that is how they found themselves back in the small cove near Punta del Este on the Isle of Pines, or Isla del Juventud, in dive gear making ready to go into the cave.

The Espial had moved as close as it could safely get, just outside of the cove. No one was sure about the research ship's status as Mike had also revealed the Consortium connection to the authorities. For the moment, though, the US Coast Guard had seized the ship, but allowed it to stay there and help out. None of the crew or the other employees seemed to be connected to the conspiracy and since DeSutton was dead and Fallow was in custody, everything was returning to normal on board. Most of the science teams had flown home, though. They quickly realized they weren't going to be able to get their work done.

"Phil, are you ready to see what's in the cave?" Mike asked as they donned their dive gear.

"You bet, I can't wait to get inside there. How did you convince them to let us be the first people back inside?" Phil asked.

"Oh, I pulled some strings. My magazine loves this kind of stuff. We're going to get three different stories out of it, all exclusive to us. It'll be all over the news for weeks. Who knows, I might even get your picture in there holding up something valuable. When my editor called, and the State Department called, the Cubans agreed to it pretty easily," Mike explained.

While they were going to be the first into the cave, they weren't going in alone. There were four more divers prepared to enter right behind them. They were bringing in lights and other equipment. Mike was confident the key would unlock the door to the inner cave, but he didn't know if the iron door would actually move after being exposed to salt air for more than 130 years. They had crow bars and hammers to apply some force just in case.

Mike was carrying his camera in its underwater housing this time. He hadn't photographed anything inside on his first trip inside since they hadn't really expected to find anything and he hadn't brought it along. He wanted to photograph the cave paintings in the outside cave and document the process of the opening of the iron door.

"Let's just hope this isn't like opening Al Capone's vault," Mike said, referring to the famous television debacle where a news reporter did a live event to open the famous gangster's vault, only to find it was empty.

"What's that?" Phil asked.

"You know, Al Capone," Mike said.

"I know who Al Capone was, but I'm missing the reference to opening his vault. What happened?"

"Never mind. I keep forgetting how young you are," Mike said shaking his head. "Let's get in there and see what we can find," Mike said as he pulled his mask into place.

He put his regulator in his mouth, turned on his dive light and slid beneath the warm water. The rope was still in place from where he had tied it off before so he grabbed it in one hand and pulled himself toward the opening in the rock. The first dive with Sarah had been cautious and slow. They hadn't known what to expect. This time, Mike moved quickly forward, directly to the cave entrance.

He had briefed Phil on the best way to enter the cave. When they reached the narrow opening, Mike went first. He took off his dive gear and pushed it ahead of him through the hole. Once he was out of the way, Phil did the same thing. It was the first time Phil had ever done anything like that, so he was a little slower about it than Mike, but the anticipation of seeing what was on the inside of the cave overrode his trepidation at what he needed to do. He was right behind Mike as they pulled themselves inside the cave and climbed out of the water. They were alone for a moment in the outer chamber.

"The iron door is over there, but I'm not sure if I am more excited about the cave paintings on the ceiling or what's in the next room," Mike said, stopping to look at the drawings. "Men and women used this cave before Columbus ever visited this part of the world more than 500 years ago. Some hermit probably lived out here by the water, fishing and living off the land. Maybe he was a shaman or something."

"They were probably from the Taino peoples. They lived all over the Caribbean," Phil agreed, staring up at the ceiling and shining his light on the drawings. "This is pretty phenomenal stuff. These drawings are in perfect shape. I guess that's what happens when they are locked away from the weather and vandals."

Mike moved around the small room photographing the drawings. He planned to come back later with more elaborate photographic equipment and lights to capture the details, but he wanted to be able to share what they had found with the Cubans and with his editor. One of the three stories he planned to file was on the discovery of these cave paintings. The other two were on whatever they found behind the iron door, and then the whole saga of the Huron and the Consortium. The magazine staff in New York was already working on that last one. They were following the money trail from the Espial to the parent corporations. It promised to be a big story with lots of powerful people exposed before it was all said and done.

The drawings over Mike and Phil's head were made with what appeared to be white and red chalk, probably from ground up shells. They combined images of animals and fish that made up the daily life of the Taino, with sea birds and men in small canoes. Other images were more abstract, at least to Mike and Phil. They were swirling images with lines and spots. Both men were quiet as they studied the images in front of them. They tried to imagine the lives of the people who made the drawings.

"Look at this one," Phil said, motioning Mike over. "It looks like a sailing ship."

"You're probably looking at a drawing representing the first contact between the indigenous people that lived here and the Spanish when they came here and "discovered" the islands," Mike said, his voice quiet. "Unfortunately for those people, the world was never the same afterward. They were enslaved or they died from the diseases those explorers brought with them."

"Not the stuff we learn in the history books," Phil agreed.

Behind them, the water began to glow. The Cuban divers were working their way up through the hole in the floor and the lights they carried signaled their arrival.

"I guess that's all the time we get in here by ourselves," Mike said. "Come on. Let's take a look at the iron door. I want to see if this key fits."

Both men kneeled down to study the blocked entry way to the Spanish gold — or at least that's what they assumed was there. As Mike saw the first time he visited with Sarah, the iron door was inset about two feet into the opening. Now that he had time to think about it, he realized the door was probably built on the inside of the next cave. That way, no one could attempt to remove the door from the opening by cutting the bolts off the door frame. They would have to use the key.

Mike looked all around the door and especially into the lock. There were signs of rust, but the door didn't appear to be in terrible shape, considering it was exposed to salt air and had been for more than 130 years. Mike guessed the act of sealing the cave had protected it somewhat. It wasn't exposed to fresh air or sunshine, or wind and rain.

Still, knowing that the lock might be rusted shut, Mike brought along spray-on cutting oil to ease the process. He stuck the nozzle into the key hole and pumped the opening full of WD-40. He waited a few minutes and did it again. While Mike and Phil laid on their stomachs looking at the door, the Cuban divers set up lights and other equipment in the antechamber. Two of them returned to the water to bring in more equipment. They were working under the assumption that they were going to be successful. On the other hand, Mike saw that they had brought a cutting torch along as well just in case the door couldn't be opened. They had no plans of going home empty-handed.

The door itself was black and had a slightly bubbled surface where the cast iron had corroded over the years. They couldn't see any hinges, supporting the theory that all of the door's hardware must be on the inside.

"Do you think it's been long enough?" Phil asked after a minute. He was getting excited and wanted to see what was on the other side of the door.

"We can give it a try. There's no way to know how long this will take," Mike agreed. He pulled the key from the side pocket on his leg and dried it off. Shining a small pen light into the key hole, he decided which way was the best to insert it and stuck the key into the mechanism.

"Here goes nothing," Mike said as he attempted to turn the ancient key. And he was right. Nothing. It didn't budge. "Maybe that was a little too fast. Give me the spray oil again."

Once again, Mike filled the key hole up with the cutting oil. He knew it would take time for the oil to seep into the rusted lock mechanism and allow it to turn. While he waited, Mike rolled over on his back for a moment to rest. He noticed one of the Cuban divers bringing in the cutting torch and a smaller hand torch. That gave him an idea.

"Phil, sometimes when I work on my old Jeep at home, it takes a little extra motivation to get the old bolts loose. They're made from better metal than this, but they take a lot more abuse, too," Mike began explaining while he grinned. "I don't want to cut the door out. I'd love to preserve it for its own sake, but I think a little heat might just help this situation."

Mike jumped up to talk to the Cuban divers. Using hand signals, a little English and some broken Spanish he got his point across. One of the divers, named Emilio, came over with a small torch and began applying heat to the key hole and the lock mechanism. He warmed the front of the door where they assumed the lock tumbler would sit and then directed the flame inside the hole. The WD-40 immediately caught fire, but it quickly burnt off. After just a couple minutes, Mike waved to Emilio and the man shut the torch off.

"Let's see if that helped any," Mike said to himself. He got back on his hands and knees and stuck the key in the slot. He turned. At first, nothing happened. He applied more pressure and when he stopped pushing he realized the key was now at a 45 degree angle from when he had inserted it. It was working. He turned it straight up and down and then back to the side again. He moved the key back and forth several more times until finally the key was at a 90 degree angle. They heard an audible 'thump' from the other side of the door.

"Sounds like that did it!" Mike yelled. He turned around to realize that Phil and the four Cubans were watching him intently. They all cheered.

"Now, let's see if this door moves," Mike said as he began pushing. Surprisingly, it moved easily. The rust on the cast iron door had sealed it against the door frame almost totally. The cave behind was sealed shut so no salt air, light or water got inside. The hinges were essentially rust free.

Mike grabbed his dive light from the floor beside him and started to crawl into the next cave until Emilio stopped him by grabbing him around the waist and pulling him backward.

"What are you doing?" Mike asked, growing angry. "Do you want to be the first one in? Is that it?"

Emilio took a step back, a little confused at Mike's reaction.

"Hey man, take it easy," Phil said. "He's just trying to help you. They want to blow some fresh air in their from a scuba tank. No one knows how long that room has been sealed up."

Mike looked from Phil to Emilio to the other divers. He hung his head for a moment. And then he started laughing.

"Mis disculpas," Mike said. "My apologies. It's been a long week and I thought you were just trying to stop me. I'm sorry. Lo seinto." Mike reached out his hand and Emilio helped him stand up. One of the other divers slid a scuba tank through the doorway and opened up the tank valve. Air came rushing out in a loud hiss.

"We wait for tank to empty," Emilio said.

"Makes perfect sense to me," Mike agreed.

"But no reason we cannot put lights inside to take a look," Emilio said with a grin.

One of the divers handed Mike a light connected to a battery pack on the floor and motioned for him to place it inside and to take a look. Mike bowed his head in thanks and took the light. As soon as he stuck his head through the opening, he knew they were right. He couldn't see anything specific, but he could see crates. Stacks and stacks of crates.

CHAPTER 48

It took about 15 minutes for the air tank to flow its 80 cubic feet of purified air into the cave. They planned to empty a couple more tanks inside to improve the air quality. The divers also brought fans with them to circulate the air as well. Mike and Phil agreed that someone had thought ahead when they planned to open the cave up.

"You can go in now, but if you feel dizzy, come back out," Emilio said to Mike.

"Gracias, Emilio," Mike said. "Thank you."

"It is only right. You found this place and you and your friends bled for it."

Phil handed Mike his camera and then Mike got back down on his hands and knees and crawled inside. As soon as he was through the opening, Mike stood up to look around. Phil was right behind him and he carried a light with him. As soon as they moved out of the way, the Cubans began crawling through the opening, bringing more lights with them.

Phil whistled when he stood up. He was impressed by how big the room appeared to be and by how much stuff was actually there. "This is going to take a while to sort out," he said. The cave was at least 50 feet deep and shaped like an upside down bowl. It was filled with crates.

"Looking in from out there, I was guessing there were 50 or so crates in here," Mike said as he walked to the first stack of boxes in front of him. As he did, he realized there was another stack behind it. "But now I'm thinking there may be twice that many."

Mike raised his camera to his eye and began taking photographs of the scene as they first found it. He was using a second camera that the divers had brought through in a waterproof case. He attached an external strobe light to the camera with a wide angle lens and lit up the room. He photographed the entire room from several different angles and then moved closer to look at an individual crate.

Each one appeared to be two feet wide by two feet tall and about three feet long. There were two crates in each stack. Each crate appeared to be made the same way, from rough timber. There were no markings on them, at least none that had survived in the cave for more than a century.

Mike sat his camera down for a moment and tried to lift the top crate. It was full. Whatever they were filled with was heavy.

"This place is amazing," Mike said, looking around. "And there are more cave paintings in here, too."

"I'm not sure which one I'm more excited about," Phil agreed. "But, for the moment, let's focus on the boxes."

Phil was carrying a small crowbar with him. He picked a box in front of him and began working it into the gap in the lid. Mike photographed Phil while he worked. The Cuban men stopped what they were doing to watch. They wanted to know what was inside the boxes as much as everyone else. With a low creak, the crate lid came loose. Phil pulled it up and away, and set it down on top of the next stack.

The inside of the rough hewn box was filled with straw. It had matted down over the years. Phil started pealing it back in layers while shining his light into the box with the other. Neither Mike nor Phil breathed as they waited with anticipation. They were quickly rewarded when they saw what appeared to be a gold bar. And then several more below that.

Phil moved to a couple more boxes, opening them at random. He found more gold bars and some jewels. He also found a box that appeared to be filled with antique dishes and silver.

"I'm guessing some of this stuff was looted from royalist homes. Spain was in the middle of its own civil war. So, if you were on the losing side of a battle, the soldiers probably came through and took what they wanted," Phil said.

"No doubt you're right. Should make this even more fun to straighten out," Mike agreed. "Some of those families will probably try to reclaim specific items in here too. So, you'll have governments fighting over it and rich families as well. They may never get this straightened out."

"At least we get to say we found it!" Phil said, laughing. "Care to guess how much all of this is worth?"

"No way of knowing until we know what's in all of the boxes and that could take months to catalog it all. Probably in the 100s of millions of dollars judging by what we saw in just the first few we opened," Mike said. "If there is anything really amazing like a painting from one of the old masters, it could go up ever higher."

"Wow, I hadn't thought of that. There could be an old DaVinci in here, couldn't there?"

"Anything is possible at this point. Probably not likely, but we'll just have to wait and see," Mike agreed.

CHAPTER 49

Mike ended up staying in Cuba for another week, but Phil flew home the day after they opened the treasure room on the Isle of Pines. He had to get back to work and explain to the National Security Agency how he ended up in Cuba. That promised to be loads of fun for him.

Mike spent a couple days in Havana debriefing with the Cuban authorities. They were surprised to discover this storehouse on the island and wanted his back story. While Mike never felt threatened, he knew that they were at least a little suspicious as to his role in the entire episode. Eventually, they came to believe that he didn't have anything to do with it.

The day he was leaving, as he was getting his things together in his Havana hotel, he was surprised by a knock at the door. He glanced at his watch. "The driver is early," he said to himself as he crossed the room. When he opened the door, he was surprised to see the men from the Policía Nacional Revolucionaria he had been talking to all week.

"What's up guys?" Mike asked. "I'm heading to the airport here in a few minutes. I have a flight to catch."

"We will see that you get to the airport on time. If necessary, we will hold your flight. We have one stop to make," the police captain said. Mike noticed then that the men were in their best dress uniforms. They looked spit-shined and neatly pressed. During their interviews, the men's uniforms had been soft and wrinkly — casual.

"Is everything all right?" Mike asked, growing a little leery of the situation.

"Si, everything is Okay. El Jefe wants to meet you," the captain replied.

"And that's how I got to meet the Castros," Mike said to his friends as he sipped a beer on the deck of his beach house.

"That's awesome!" Andie shouted. "How was it?"

"Fidel and Raoul were both there and they were very gracious. It only lasted a minute or two, but they thanked me for my involvement. They also told me to thank each one of you as well. They seemed like they had been well-briefed on everything that happened while we were there. I could tell they had read the full reports," Mike said. "I've met a couple heads of state before, just in passing, but this was really cool. I can't think of anyone I've ever met that has been the center of so much history."

Mike handed out gifts to everyone there, direct from the brothers Castro. Cigars from the Castro's private supply.

"The state department had some questions for me when I got home, of course, but it was definitely worth it," Mike said. "And we are all now national heroes in Cuba."

Using that special status on the island nation, Mike was fulfilling his promise and shipping replacement Studebaker parts to Felix, courtesy of the Cuban government. The Cuban government regarded Felix as a hero for stopping DeSutton, rather than as a criminal for his part in the conspiracy in the first place. It was an easier story to promote inside the country. It was a communist regime after all and they could manufacture the news to suit their needs. They needed a local hero from the story and Felix was it.

Mac and Andie got home from Grand Cayman the day before Mike landed in North Carolina. Mac was quickly recovering from his gunshot wound although he was still moving slowly.

In all, it was a busy couple weeks. They solved a kidnapping, solved the mystery of a 135 year old shipwreck, discovered a cache of gold and broke up a plot to steal the valuables and sell them on the black market. Not to mention helping restore a 1950 Studebaker back to running condition.

Mike sat back in a chair on the deck of his beach house on Roanoke Island and put his feet up. Another adventure in the books. He looked over at Mac and realized the older man was dozing off.

"It's good to be home, Mike," Andie said as she returned to the deck and faced the sun. She handed Mike a beer and kept one for herself.

"You didn't bring one for your dad?" Mike asked.

"Doctor's orders," Andie said, shaking her head. "With all the meds he's on right now, he can't drink alcohol yet."

"I'm sure that makes him happy," Mike replied, laughing.

"Not at all," Andie agreed with a grin.

"Have you heard from Phil?" Mike asked.

Andie blushed before replying. "He's coming down from DC for a visit this weekend," she said. The two had gotten close and were giving a relationship a shot.

"That's cool. He's a good guy. I like him," Mike said.

"What about you? Have you heard from Sarah?" Andie asked.

"Not really. I got a note from her after we got home that she was applying for a job, but she didn't say where," Mike said. "We had talked about giving it another shot, but our careers are just too different. No time for it, I guess. Just the way it goes. I'm sure she'll turn up somewhere when I least expect it."

"I'm sorry Mike. I liked her," Andie said, looking out over the water.

"Me too. Just the way it goes," Mike repeated.

They heard the ground level door open and someone began climbing the steps to the upper deck.

"It's probably Red," Andie said when Mike looked at her. "He's still angry about everything he missed."

They heard the sounds of someone walking into the kitchen and opening a beer.

"Yep, that's Red," Mike agreed.

"Hey guys, glad everyone is here," Red said as he stepped onto the deck.

"Hey Red, good to see you," Mike said.

"You guys ready for something to do?"

"Are you kidding? I just got home," Mike said. "I plan to put my feet up and rest for a few days."

"Are you sure about that?" Red asked.

"What's going on?" Andie asked, growing curious.

"While you guys were gone, I did some more digging into the Consortium that sent the secret message," Red explained.

"Yeah, we know about them. DeSutton was part of the modern day version of it," Mike answered.

"Well, it turns out, they are suspected of being connected to another ship that wrecked not far from here," Red explained. "This time it was a cargo ship carrying their gold that went down in a storm. It's never been found."

"What does that have to do with us?" Mike asked. "You know how many lost shipwrecks there are off this coast."

"I did some digging in the records and found something that gave me a clue about where it is. I think we can find it," Red explained.

"You know the location of a Consortium shipwreck?" Andie asked.

"What are we waiting for?" Mac said, waking up with a smile on his face. "Let's go!"

ABOUT THE USS HURON

The USS Huron is a real shipwreck located just a few hundred yards off shore in Nags Head, North Carolina. The "mystery" around the sinking of the ship portrayed in this story is total fiction and helmsman Frame did not exist. Neither did the special orders in the Captain's sea chest.

The rest of the story, including the names of the Commander and Crew of the ship are real. Generally the quotes and accounts of the sinking are taken from the accounts men who survived the wreck recorded in the PROCEEDINGS OF COURT OF INQUIRY ON THE LOSS OF THE HURON held by the NAVY DEPARTMENT, Washington DC, Wednesday, December 5, 1877. If you want to read more about this shipwreck, I encourage you to read it as well:

http://freepages.history.rootsweb.ancestry.com/~familyinformation/transcripts/huron.html

I want to be perfectly clear that these men died in service to their country and there has never been any suspicion of wrongdoing connected with the wreck. The conspiracy and the Consortium are pure fiction from my imagination. It was, however, a tragic loss of life. I mentioned it in the story, but this wreck and one a few months later persuaded Congress to fund the US Lifesaving Service year-round. At the time of the wreck the rescue boats and other equipment were locked up tight for the winter. That group eventually became the US Coast Guard.

The USS Huron was headed for Cuba when it sank, with a mission to perform environmental surveys. Cuba was in the midst of the first Cuban Revolution against Spain. The 10 Years War ended in 1878, the year following the wreck of the Huron. This revolution helped bring about an end to slavery on the island eight years later. Cuba did not gain independence for Spain until the end of the Spanish American War in 1898.

ABOUT THE AUTHOR

Whether he is creating a photoessay or writing a novel, a reference book or a children's story, life is an adventure for Eric Douglas.

Eric received a degree in Journalism from Marshall University. After working in local newspapers, and following a stint as a freelance journalist in the former Soviet Union, he became a dive instructor. The ocean and diving have factored into all of his published works since then.

Visit his website at: www.booksbyeric.com

OTHER MIKE SCOTT ADVENTURES
CAYMAN COWBOYS
FLOODING HOLLYWOOD
GUARDIAN'S KEEP

CHILDREN'S BOOKS
THE SEA TURTLE RESCUE
SWIMMING WITH SHARKS

SHORT STORIES
PEARL HARBOR CHRISTMAS
GOING DOWN WITH THE SHIP
BAIT AND SWITCH
PUT IT BACK
FROG HEAD KEY
QUEEN CONCH
SEA MONSTER

REFERENCE
SCUBA DIVING SAFETY

Made in the USA
San Bernardino, CA
04 January 2020